BOUND

A brutal home invasion shocks the nation. A man is murdered, his wife bound, gagged and left to watch. But when Detective Sam Shephard scratches the surface, the victim, a successful businessman, is not all he seems to be. And when the evidence points to two of Dunedin's most hated criminals, the case seems cut and dried . . . until the body count starts to rise.

VANDA SYMON

BOUND

Complete and Unabridged

AURORA
Leicester

First published in New Zealand in 2011 by
Penguin Books (NZ)
and in the UK in 2021 by
Orenda Books

First Aurora Edition
published 2021
by arrangement with
Orenda Books

A catalogue record for this book is available
from the British Library.

ISBN 978–1–78782–354–9

Published by
Ulverscroft Limited
Anstey, Leicestershire

Set by Words & Graphics Ltd.
Anstey, Leicestershire
Printed and bound in Great Britain by
TJ Books Ltd., Padstow, Cornwall

This book is printed on acid-free paper

For Smooch

For Smooch

Prologue

The image of the clock's hands burned into her retinas as she stared, willing her eyes to stay focused, there, on that spot. Above the sound of the blood pulsing through her ears, she could just make out the sharp click of its ticks, as the second hand flicked around the circumference of the dial.

Don't look, she thought. *For Christ's sake, you can't look.*

Her eyes stayed fixed on the clock.

He'll be home soon, please let him be home soon, she thought. *Don't be late. Not tonight.*

But what her eyes could avoid, her nose could smell; the wet, hot, metallic scent of blood, overpowering the sharp chemical tang of the adhesive on the tape stretched across her mouth. She closed her eyes, the photographic negative of the clock dancing in the darkness, but it was as pointless as resisting gravity.

They opened, their focus drawn to the inevitable.

She took in the ruined shell that had been John, the mangled mess that had been his face, now just dripping meat. She felt the spasm clench her stomach at the sight, the smell, and she started repeating the mantra in her head, *You vomit, you die, you vomit, you die.* She tried to take deep, even breaths.

Think of Declan, he's already lost one parent

1

tonight, don't let it be two.

She slammed her eyes shut, concentrated on breathing, on forcing away the nausea. But while she could fight that, she couldn't fight the tears, and as the sobs wracked her body, she began to realise that deep breathing was becoming more difficult. She strained against the ropes that bound her arms and feet to the chair, but nothing could stop the wave of panic that hit as she realised her nose was getting stuffier, and the more she panicked, the more she cried and the more she cried, the less she could breathe, until she couldn't pull in any air and she felt a band of steel tightening around her chest.

She pulled against her bonds, but nothing. She twisted. She pushed. Her body fought for air and with desperation she shoved against the floor with her feet. As the chair tipped backwards, the last thing her eyes found was the clock, its second hand ticking away her life, before a white-hot flare of pain, and then darkness.

2

1

Jesus, this place was creepy. I'd been called out at eleven-thirty at night to the scene of a home invasion, and from all accounts a nasty one. A man was dead, his wife in a seriously bad way and the poor son who found them in a state of disbelief. By dint of me being a woman, it had been decided by The Boss that I was the perfect candidate for Officer in Charge of the Victims. It was a given that he'd taken a perverse pleasure in sending me to a crime scene in the middle of nowhere in the dead of the night. He was good like that.

Seacliff, they'd said. Russell Road. The main route out there, off State Highway One from Dunedin, was bumpy and twisty enough by day let alone at night. I lost count of the number of times the car juddered across the railway lines, which seemed to play a cat and mouse game with the road. I drove between the macrocarpa and hawthorn hedges, looking for the turn-off, and realised I was going to be passing the site of the old Seacliff Mental Hospital. Despite the heater blaring, my body gave an involuntary shudder. Part of it was now the aptly named Asylum Lodge, though who the hell would want to stay there I didn't know. You'd have to be a slightly demented kind of tourist. The Seacliff Mental Hospital was notorious for all the wrong reasons. Back in the 1940s a fire in a women's ward resulted in the deaths of thirty-seven patients. Thirty-seven poor souls locked in their rooms, unable to escape the flames. I'd once gone out to the site for a day trip with my flatmate Maggie, who tinkered with photography — one of her many talents. We'd wandered around what was now the Truby King Recreational Reserve on a misty and clagged-in day and it was one of the most uncomfortable experiences I'd ever had. Despite the fact most of the old buildings had gone, their sorry foundations the only hint of their once grand scale, I swear I could feel the ghosts of inmates past, and I've never been one for spooky rubbish. In its heyday they'd incarcerated many a poor soul there, including Janet Frame, our world-famous writer, who was forced there due to the fact she was creative and different. Nowadays they gave you fellowships for that, not lobotomies. The day Maggs and I went it felt like some of those poor souls who had fried and died had never left. There was even a wood called The Enchanted Forest, and what with the mood and the mist there had been no way in hell we were going in there.

If I admitted to being wimpy, the effect it all had on Maggie was even more interesting. For a while, she kept up the pretence of enjoying herself, taking photographs of the old foundations and derelict walls, before admitting defeat, turning and pretty much hightailing it out of there. When we were looking through her images later, I half expected to see ghostly forms rising from the earth or faces in the trees. Instead all she had taken were some innocuous — looking pictures of a fairly bland, mist-shrouded and depressing landscape.

The headlights of my car illuminated the tree-lined avenue, but the fingers of light that reached in between their trunks didn't seem to penetrate the darkness. The sealed road turned to gravel, and I trundled along, getting a momentary scare when the ghostly eyes of a partly obscured horse reflected eerily in the lights, giving the effect of some disembodied ghoul staring back at me. It was with relief that I rounded a bend and glimpsed the strobing flashes of red and blue in the distance. Since when had I turned into such a sook?

I pulled up alongside the police officer stationed on point duty outside the property, his fluorescent vest lit up in my headlights with a radioactive glow.

'Drive on up, Detective Shephard,' he said, recognising me.

'There's plenty of room up there.' I still got a kick out of being called 'Detective'. I had only recently lost the baby 'Detective Constable' title. It had been a long time coming.

'Thanks, Chris.'

The house was situated at the end of a hundred-and-fifty-metre driveway and was partially surrounded by strategically placed trees. They hid it from the road, not that privacy would be an issue way out here. There was an impressive set of gates that probably cost more than my flat. I'd driven past another driveway on my way up here, about a couple of hundred metres before, also with flash gates, but it was too dark to see how close the next neighbour was on the far side. It looked pretty isolated though. Apart from the bevy of houses at Seacliff township, most of the properties around here were farming or lifestyle. I'd guess this one was lifestyle — farmers wouldn't bother with gates like that. Farmers also wouldn't bother to asphalt one-hundred-and-fifty metres of driveway, especially when you'd travelled on a gravel road to get there — they had more sense. It wasn't too hard a stretch of the imagination to think that the home-invaders had recognised the trappings of wealth.

I pulled up and parked behind a vehicle I recognised; he'd been called out too — how strange. Go figure. There were four squad cars, a dog unit, two mufti-cars and an ambulance in attendance, as well as a few strays. Even with that many vehicles there was still plenty of room to spare on the paved forecourt. There would be no hope of seeing tyre treads on this surface, and even less now with vehicles all over it, but everyone would have seen that as a lost cause.

I hopped out of the car, my body hunching inwards, reacting to the night chill after the blare of the heater. The first face I came across was adorned with a rather sheepish smile. That might have been because I had been busy shagging his brains out a couple of hours before.

'Paul, fancy seeing you here.'

'Yes, fancy. You got the call too?' he asked.

'Probably The Boss trying to catch us out. He's worse than my mother.'

Paul Frost was my colleague and my lover, so,

in the eyes of many, we were committing a cardinal sin. In all honesty, I was definitely in the 'don't screw the crew' camp until recently. Amazing how your standards could slip from black and white to an elegant shade of grey given enough provocation. Still, it wouldn't have surprised me if the powers that be made an intervention sometime soon and we found ourselves in different squads.

'So what's happening here?'

'It's pretty ugly, I'm afraid. The couple are Jill and John Henderson; their son is Declan. The boy came home at ten-thirty to find the father dead, shotgun to the head, made a hell of a mess, and his mother bound to a chair, semi-conscious. She's in the ambulance now. I think they're about ready to take her in. You'll need to go too. She's conscious now, but not very coherent. She said there were two masked intruders, and that's about all we could get out of her.'

'Did the dogs pick up on anything?'

'No, which most likely means they were in a vehicle rather than on foot.'

I could see the arc of torchlight in the paddocks around the house as officers did a preliminary sweep of the area. You couldn't make assumptions. I could also see the ambulance crew looking like they were ready to move off.

'I'll let you know of any further information I get from her during the night,' I said. It was going to be a long one. 'You've been into the house?'

'Yes, we had to get her out, but it's sealed off now. I'm just waiting for the scene-of-crime

7

officers to get here, and the photographer. There's nothing we can do for John Henderson, he's well beyond help. We did have to quarantine the cat, though. Let's just say Kitty got hungry and found a ready food source.'

I felt my stomach lurch at the thought. 'That's revolting. I hope you didn't tell the boy.'

'No, I'm not that stupid. Last thing he needs. Speaking of the boy, he's over there ready to go in the ambulance with the mother. You'd better go and work your magic.' I turned to see the figure of a young man hunched over, arms wrapped around himself, rocking. 'Just watch him too.'

'What do you mean?' I asked.

'Having talked with him, I don't believe it for a second, but until we corroborate his story, we have to look at him as a potential suspect.'

'Gee, thanks,' I said.

2

There was something about the unrelenting glare of hospital rooms that made me want to shrink away from the light like some vampire. That and the smell. That unpleasant fug of disinfectant overlaced with a chemical aftertaste. The last time I'd been in a hospital I'd been on the receiving end of the staff's attentions. This time I was the support mechanism. Jill Henderson's shoulder had been manoeuvred back into the correct position. It was a severe dislocation, so they weren't optimistic it would stay there, and it was a good bet she'd need surgery. For now, though, she'd been cleaned up, sedated and was benefiting from the respite of oblivion. Despite being asleep, however, her brow was furrowed with a frown that no amount of pain relief would erase.

The ambulance trip had been hard. She'd cried the whole way, and it was impossible to get any further information from her. I imagined I'd have been like that too, in her situation. How could anyone cope with seeing their husband's face shot off? And on top of everything else, it must have been awful for Declan to see her like that, bereft and in pain, but he had held her good hand the whole way in.

'How are you going there, Declan?' I asked the pale, subdued seventeen-year-old. 'Can I get you something to drink?'

'No, thank you,' he said. Even in the face of tragedy he was impeccably polite.

Everything I'd seen of this boy in the previous two hours had impressed me. He was clearly shocked and burst into tears frequently, but he'd remained calm, given the circumstances, and was really stepping up to the plate. He'd been asking the hospital staff about the care of his mother, questioning what they were doing, but always politely. It was as if he'd assumed the role of head of the family, which was a lot to ask of any adult who'd lost a father so recently and in such a violent fashion, let alone a teenager. I thought back to Paul's comment about him being a suspect and there was no way I could imagine this boy being responsible for the night's hideous crimes. There was no doubt in my mind that he was an innocent party here.

'Do you think you're ready to tell me what happened?' We were seated out in the corridor, out of earshot of his mum. Even though she was sedated I didn't want to risk her subconscious picking up any of our conversation.

He looked at me with his red-rimmed, pale-blue eyes and nodded. 'Actually, I think I'd better get some water. Would you like one?'

I thanked him when he handed over the flimsy, ribbed, white plastic cup. He took a gulp, then a large breath and started talking.

'I'd been at band practice at my mate Stuey's house in Dunedin. I play bass guitar. We were practising for the school rock challenge, which is in a month. Our band's called Munted. We're at Logan Park High School.'

10

Logan Park? With his parents being so well-to-do, I would have thought they'd have sent him to one of the flash, private boys' schools. They must have thought Logan Park filled his needs best, or perhaps they actually gave him a choice in the matter. Mind you, he had that muso look about him, with the shoulder-length blond hair swept to one side, Huffer T-shirt and skinny, drop-crotch black jeans. He also had that gangly look kids get when they've just grown half a metre and their bodies and neurones hadn't caught up with the fact.

'I came home from practice, opened the front door and, and . . .' he took a pause and a sip of water before continuing' . . . there they were. Dad was near the door, he'd been shot, his face was gone, I could see his bones and his brains.' Tears started to overflow and trickle from the corners of his eyes. He leaned back against the wall and looked up at the ceiling. 'The only way I knew for sure it was him was from his clothes, it was that bad. I ran to find Mum, and she was on the floor. I thought at first they'd killed her too, because she had blood coming out of her head, but then she moaned. They'd tied her to a chair but it was on its back so I suppose she must have accidentally tipped it over. When I ripped the tape off her mouth she gasped like she could finally breathe properly, like they had just about suffocated her. What if she'd died too?' He paused before asking me, in a quiet and tremulous voice, 'I didn't do that to her shoulder when I was trying to free her, did I? I tried to get her from the chair but it seemed to take forever

11

and I had to tip it on the side to undo her.' His face was crumpled with anguish.

'No, you don't need to worry about that. It most likely happened when the chair tipped back.' He didn't look that relieved. 'Did you ring the police straight away?' I asked.

'No, I rang the ambulance, as soon as I realised Mum was alive. I guess they sent the police.'

'And when you were driving home from practice in town, you came back via State Highway One and turned off at Warrington?' He nodded. 'Did you notice any other vehicles travelling on the back road?'

'There probably were some, I couldn't say.'

I could see he was exhausted. There was no point in pressing him further tonight. He'd had enough to deal with.

'In the morning I'll need to go over everything with you again in order to make a statement, but for now, we need to find you somewhere to stay tonight and to contact your relatives. Who will be the best person to get in touch with first?'

'Grandad. He lives in Dunedin.'

'Is that your mum's or your dad's dad?'

'Mum's. Dad's parents died when I was a little kid.'

I felt a twitch of relief. I wouldn't be informing a man of his son's death, but it would still be one of those phone calls we all dreaded.

'Do you have his number?' The question seemed to flick a switch on his face, and he looked at me first with a hint of excitement, then almost horror. 'What is it?' I asked.

12

He reached into the back pocket of his jeans and pulled out his cellphone. It looked very high end and probably cost more than my car. He handed it over to me like it was tainted with some disease.

'I, um, when I got home and saw what happened, I put it on video, in case it could help the police.' I looked at the boy in amazement, that he could be composed enough to think of it, but then his was the cellphone generation; they were born with them practically grafted to their hands. I could also understand his distaste at the burden the phone carried, a cinematographic record of the destruction of his family.

'Thank you, Declan, that was very clever thinking. I'll need to hold on to it for a while, if you don't mind. We'll get the numbers of your relatives off this too. I'll go and ring your grandad now.'

I went to stand, but he pulled my arm, making me sit back down. He leaned his head back against the wall, and when he turned back towards me, I could see the tears tracking down his cheeks again and the pain etched in his face.

'I was late,' he said, his voice hoarse and laden.

'What do you mean?'

'My curfew was ten, I was supposed to be home by ten, but we lost track of the time and I didn't get in until half past. If I hadn't been late, I might have been able to stop it, or save him, or something. It's all my fault.'

I looked at his young, tortured face, and my heart ached for the undeserved burden he would carry, regardless of anything I said to try and persuade him otherwise. Jesus, poor kid. I reached out and held his hand.

'It's all my fault,' he sobbed.

3

It was 3.00 a.m. before I'd finally got home and back to bed. I'd managed to get Declan organised and off to his grandad's house. The boy was reluctant to leave his mum, and it had taken a fair amount of reassurance that she'd be okay before he conceded that between the exhaustion and grief it was best he try and get some sleep. Although I didn't fancy his chances. A guard had been posted at Jill Henderson's door, just in case, though I didn't think it would be necessary. Whoever had done this had their chance to kill her and had chosen not to. They wouldn't come to a very public hospital to finish the job. My mind had been travelling at a hundred kilometres an hour and sleep did not come easily. Naturally, I finally drifted off just in time for my alarm to go at 6.00 a.m. so I could get down to the hospital early and talk to Jill before the morning meeting at the station. The powers that be were expecting a full briefing. And to top it all off, I had to walk to work as my car was still out at Seacliff.

I carried a cup of tea in to Jill and sat down by her bed. She looked at me with puffy, red-rimmed eyes and quietly thanked me for the drink.

'Declan is with your father. He's going to keep him home from school and he'll bring him in later to see you.'

She nodded quietly. Jill Henderson was the

kind of woman who could make even those butt-ugly hospital gowns look good. Even slightly spaced out, with messed-up hair and a row of stitches and bruising across her forehead, she radiated a natural beauty and grace. She also radiated profound grief and shock.

'He's a great boy, you know, the way he's been handling this. You should be very proud.'

'I know,' she said as she wiped her eyes. 'I just feel so bad that he had to see all that, that he was the one who found us. It's not fair. None of it is fair.' Murder never was.

'Are you able to talk about what happened last night?' I shifted the chair around to a better position as I could see it hurt her to turn her head. 'Any information you can give me now will help us get hot on the track of whoever did this to you. We need to work quickly before that trail goes cold.' I always hated having to press people for information when they would clearly rather be left alone.

'I don't know that it will be much help,' she said, and then took a long sip of her tea to steady herself. She must have been right — handed, because trying to drink it left-handed she looked as awkward as a cow with a musket. The shaking didn't help, either. 'We were watching *Criminal Intent* on TV and there was an ad break, so I went out to the kitchen to make a cup of tea. I guess it would have been around quarter past nine or so. The doorbell rang, which was odd, because it was late and we weren't expecting anyone. John got up and answered it.'

'Had you heard any cars come up the driveway?' I asked.

She thought about it for a moment. 'No, I don't think so, but the TV was quite loud.'

'Do you have a dog?' They were always useful advanced — warning systems.

She shook her head, and winced from the pain the action produced. 'No, we had to put our old boy down last year. He was fourteen. Rufus had a good innings.' She smiled with the memory. It was nice to see her face light up, however briefly. 'We haven't got a new dog yet, we couldn't decide on a breed. We've only got the cat now.' She looked concerned. 'Is someone feeding her? No one's at home; she'll have to go into a cattery.' My mind flashed a mental image of the cat's self-service activities and I had to work hard to suppress the shudder. What did you do with a cat after that? Would you put it down? Would you be able to live with a cat in the knowledge it had quite enjoyed its human snack? Would you feel safe at night? This might need to be a snippet of information none of them ever found out about.

'Don't you worry about that. I'll make sure she's being looked after. So what happened when your husband opened the door?'

'I heard him yell out. He sounded scared, so I rushed in and saw him backing into the room, followed by two men. And then, *bang*, one of them shot him, just like that, right in the face.' Her face crumpled and I passed the tissue box over as she broke down.

'Do you want me to come back? We can continue later if it's too much.'

She shook her head, and held her hand up, gesturing for me to wait.

'No, I'll do this now. It isn't going to be any easier later.' She exhaled a long breath and continued. 'The other man turned his head and saw me, so I spun round and ran back through the kitchen, thinking I might be able to escape out the back door. But he got to me so quickly, I couldn't get away. He threw me against the kitchen bench.' Her hand drifted up to the reminder stitched into her head. 'They were so quick and so strong, there was nothing I could do . . . nothing. I felt so powerless. They tied me to the chair. I tried to struggle but they just hit me again, it was hopeless. I kept looking at John, and I . . . ' She trailed off, quietly sobbing, and I reached out and rubbed her arm. 'Sorry,' she said, 'I was just so scared and it was so awful.' She didn't need to apologise to me. My imagination could work out just how awful it had been.

'Did you recognise them at all? What did they look like?'

'I couldn't see their faces. They were wearing blue boiler suits with hoods, and they had these hideous masks over their faces, plastic clown masks. I can't remember their eyes, other than that they looked angry. Their hands were covered — they had gloves on too.' It sounded like they were prepared to make a mess and had taken steps to ensure they didn't leave any evidence. This was no opportunistic or spur-of-the-moment crime. It was clearly a well-planned operation.

'Can you remember what they had on their feet?'

She shook her head slightly. 'No, I can't, sorry.'

'What about their builds then? Tall? Short? Skinny? Large?'

'One of them was quite large, overweight, and I suppose over six feet tall. He was the one who shot John. The other one was a bit shorter and medium build, I guess. Medium to thin.'

'No distinctive limps, mannerisms or anything like that?'

She shook her head.

'So what did they take?'

'Nothing. That was the thing — they didn't even go into the rest of the house, they just came in, killed John,' her voice started cracking again, 'and then did this to me.'

'Did they threaten you at all? What did they say exactly?'

She looked up at me, and I noticed how hollow her eyes looked and the dark purple rings under them. 'That was the strange thing. They didn't say a word. Nothing. Their silence was just awful.'

At this point Jill Henderson broke down completely. It was time for me to make an exit.

My mind went over all the things she had said, but it was her last statement that stuck in my head. Why would they have been silent? The only reasons I could think of were that they either knew the victims and were concerned that their voices would be recognised, or they had a distinctive accent that could narrow a field of suspects in an investigation. But then, when you've just callously slain a person by shooting them in the face, wouldn't you avoid leaving behind loose ends such as witnesses? Most of the bastards capable of something like this would have killed her, or, if it was sport they were after, raped her. But no, they'd spared the woman and, inadvertently, the son. To me this wasn't a home invasion, it was starting to look suspiciously like an execution.

What the hell had John Henderson been involved in?

4

After interviewing Jill, a bad case of the not-enough-sleep spins had forced me to take a detour on the way back to the office via The Fix to pick up a large flat white to accompany my morning paper. I was prepared to replace the spins with the caffeine-overload twitches. Last night's events had hit the media and were all over the radio and television news. The *Otago Daily Times* was running the headline 'Killer Home Invasion', along with plenty of long-distance shots of the Hendersons' home and the conglomeration of police vehicles around it. It was all the talk in the coffee queue, and I couldn't help but note the underlying tones of disgust and fear. Every man's home was his castle and the general public was shocked and appalled by this event. Hell, I was shocked and appalled. The headlines put a less-than-subtle pressure on the police to solve the case and find the perpetrators as soon as possible. With helpful copy like 'the killers are still at large' designed to strike fear into the masses, we were getting it from all sides. The police publicity officer was having a very busy morning, with all the radio and television networks picking up the story, and the mayor had even dropped by.

Returning from a meeting with a scientist about another case, I walked into the squadroom and almost turned heel and walked out when I saw who was there. It was too late though, I'd been spotted.

'Detective Shephard.'

DI Johns was my boss and the resident arsehole. We frequently grated, although unfortunately I was the only one who seemed to end up shredded. For whatever reason, he had it in for me, and nothing was going to change that. With him were Detective Malcolm Smith, or Smithy as he was affectionately known, who had been my mentor and babysitter when I was a complete underling, and Detective Paul Frost, my lover, for want of a better word. My head couldn't bring itself to call Paul my partner, but he was well beyond the boyfriend or shag-buddy stage. Smithy was not a fully paid-up member of the Paul Frost Fan Club, and didn't bother to hide it. The combination of testosterone and temper didn't make for a pleasant atmosphere.

'Sir?'

'You need to go back and try to get more information out of the woman.'

The woman, he called her. Jill Henderson had a name, and as far as I could judge, wasn't going to cough up anything new and useful.

'From what she has told me it was all very quick and, as mentioned in the briefing this morning, had the hallmark of an execution rather than a random act of violence.'

'Go and see her again.' It wasn't a request. He didn't do bedside manner.

'I need to get a ride back out to Seacliff to collect my — '

'Sort that out later. She should have had a

chance to rest, remember a few more things. Off you go. Now.' It was like being dismissed from the principal's office. He may as well have shooed me out.

I looked at the row of faces: DI Johns with his usual don't-you-dare-question-me expression, and Smithy and Paul sporting a mix of sympathy and efforts not to cringe. I turned on my heel and tried to avoid giving The Boss the gratification of seeing how pissed off I was.

The hospital room had improved somewhat in the few hours I'd been away. The Teleflora people must have done their rounds, as there were five huge bunches of flowers fighting for space on the bedside cabinet and the ledge above the bed. I hoped Mrs H didn't suffer from hay fever.

Declan was visiting his mother, along with his grandad. The boy was perched on the side of the bed, the old man in the chair. Both of them looked drawn and pale. I was guessing not a lot of sleep was had in that household last night. One of the best pieces of news I'd received that morning, via Paul, was that Declan's story had checked out — vouched for by his bandmates and their parents. He had been practising up a storm with his mates in a converted garage in Dunedin. Not that I believed for a moment he could have been responsible for this, but then, history was littered with the bodies of fathers who had oppressed their sons once too often. You never could tell.

'Morning Declan, good morning, Mr Thomas. Your flowers are lovely, Jill.'

'I guess they are, but I can't stand to look at them,' she said. 'It's all a bit too much. And people want to see me. I mean, I know they're sorry and concerned, but I don't know if I can handle more people today. The newspaper reporters want to speak to me too, and I can't . . . I can't do it.' Declan reached across and grabbed her hand.

I could add to her list the fact that my boss wanted me to grill her for more information.

'I can have a word to the nursing staff to screen your visitors, if you like. And don't worry about the media. For now the police will be briefing them, and that will be enough. You can fend them off for a while.'

'Thank you,' she said, wiping her eyes. 'And I can't even think about starting to organise a funeral.'

At the mention of the word 'funeral' I heard Declan draw a sharp breath. His face was battling to hold in his grief in front of his mum, but a few errant tears gave it away. Funerals made death very real. It would be a few days before John's body was released to the family. He had to undergo a post-mortem, although the cause of death was patently obvious. And not even the most talented of undertakers was going to be able to make him presentable; it would be a closed-coffin affair.

'I know you're tired, and probably don't want to think about it, but my superiors have urged me to come down and see you again, in case there is anything else you can recall about last night. I also need you to think back a bit further

24

than that, about the last few weeks. Did you notice any unusual vehicles, any that came and went repeatedly?'

'No, nothing. We can't really see the road from the house, and we don't hear much car noise because the house is double-glazed and quite well soundproofed. I can't think of anything that was out of the ordinary. I know that's not much help.'

'What about you, Declan? Have you seen or heard anything that seemed odd or out of place?'

He shook his head. 'Nothing, although there's a house further up the road for sale, so there have been a few more cars up this way than usual.'

I had to be careful how I broached the next subject.

'I'm sure you've thought about it yourself, given what's happened, but we do have to think that these people actually targeted John, because they didn't take anything from the house, and they didn't kill you too, Jill.' I looked at her, and she nodded slowly.

'I know,' she said. 'It's all I can think about. And it's the only way this makes any sense, because . . . ' she paused, looked over at Declan, and then spoke almost in a whisper; ' . . . they could have done far worse to me if they wanted to.' We both knew exactly what she meant, and judging by the looks on their faces, so did Declan and her dad.

'So we have to ask ourselves, if John was targeted, why, and by whom? Can you think of anyone who would do this, or who may have made it happen?'

I heard a cough from Mr Thomas. Jill looked over at him and I could see the unspoken communication that passed between them. 'Dad, would you mind taking Declan out to get a drink or something?' When Declan made a noise of protest, she reached out and squeezed his hand. 'I need to speak to the detective alone for a bit, okay?' He did his very best impression of a reluctant teenager as he left the room.

'He's trying to look after me,' she said, a bitter smile across her face. 'This is forcing him to grow up too soon.'

'He's a great kid, Jill.' Most of the youth we had to deal with were receiving the attention of the law for all the wrong reasons. I wished more were like him. 'I take it you have some idea as to who may have done this?'

'Well, not exactly who, but perhaps why.' She looked more than a little uncomfortable with the turn in conversation. 'You see, my husband was a good man, and a great husband and father, but he was involved in some things I didn't agree with.'

'What kind of things?' I asked.

'Some of his business activities were . . . ' I could see she was searching for the right word; ' . . . not always above board.'

'You mean illegal?'

'I don't know about illegal, but they were questionable.'

That was a very fine distinction to make. 'So what did he do?'

She looked uneasy. 'I don't know exactly.' She must have seen the sceptical look on my face. 'I

26

know how pathetic that sounds considering he was my husband, and as you can see, we do well for ourselves, but there were some things I didn't want to know, so I didn't ask and just turned a blind eye. I know this makes me just as bad as he was, in a way, but sometimes, when a loved one does something you find morally difficult, you look away. You have to, otherwise it can tear you apart. So please don't judge me, but I preferred to be kept in the dark.'

How could I fail to see her point when it was delivered with such obvious distress? At least she was honest and upfront about it.

'So what can you tell me?'

'John's office is in Dowling Street, Eros Global. His main business is selling and distributing vitamin-type supplements and, well, sexual enhancers, that kind of thing.' My eyebrows shot up to my hairline. I could see why she preferred to turn a blind eye. It wasn't the sort of thing you dropped into casual conversation at the dinner table, and I bet Declan never took him along to school for 'what my dad does' day, along with the firemen and farmer dads.

'How many staff did he have?'

'A few employees in town, including a PA and a business manager. He also had a manufacturing and distribution arm, but that's up in Auckland. They might distribute some things from here, I'm not sure. The Dunedin staff may be able to help you more about the finer details of the business. Although, I guess they won't be at work today.' A shock realisation jumped across her face. 'Would they have been told what has happened? God, someone has to let them know.' It was as if this one little detail had pushed her over the edge into panic land.

I reached over and patted her good shoulder. 'Hey, you needn't worry about things like that, we'll take care of it.' Considering his conspicuous absence, and the fact it had been all over the news this morning, John's employees may have guessed what had happened. The media hadn't been given leave to mention names until all the family had been contacted, but we all knew these things had a way of getting around quickly. Social media meant a rumour or a titillating piece of information could travel faster than the speed of light.

She relaxed back against her pillow. 'Their numbers and all his contacts should be in his phone. I suppose you have that?' No one had mentioned locating it at the crime scene. I'd have to check if it was still on him and was now inventoried at the morgue. 'Astrid Allen is his secretary, or personal assistant. She's a very capable person, so should be able to help you more than I can.'

Did I detect a hint of an undertone there? I looked at her closely, but there was no corresponding trace of anything — such as jealousy, perhaps — on her face.

'His main worker, or representative, I suppose you'd call him, is Blair Harvey-Boyd. He should be able to help with the core business.' This time there was no mistaking her inflection — the way she said his name was loaded with implication.

'I'll ensure that we talk with them both. Do

you think Eros was a front company — that he had other business ventures on the side?' If that was the case it was one hell of a ballsy front.

'I'm certain of it.'

'And did John do much work from home?'

'That was the beauty of living out at Seacliff. It was far enough away from town that he — we — were able to pretty much keep the business life separate from the home life. If John had lots of work on he just stayed later at the office, and people didn't come out to us, other than occasional dinner parties with his colleagues sometimes, the ones he knew I liked. He did a little bit of work in his home office. Please look through everything there. If there's anything you can use to find who did this, please, use it. But generally, his business dealings stayed in town, which suited me fine. John knew how I felt about some of his enterprises, so he kept them out of the house and in return I didn't ask questions.'

'So he respected your misgivings?'

'Like I said earlier, sometimes it's easier to pretend something isn't happening, for every-one's sake.'

5

'Sam? Is that you?'

Sheryl was the last person I expected to bump into in the foyer of Dunedin Hospital. Saint Sheryl was my sister-in-law. I tried not to automatically add the title to her name, but, try as I might, it always slipped in there. Probably something to do with the fact my mother always took great delight in extolling her virtues as the perfect daughter-in-law. Sheryl was a nurse — the perfect profession as far as the old girl was concerned — and she was the perfect wife and mother to her two perfect grandchildren. Of course we all knew what the unspoken subtext was.

'Sheryl, hi.'

I stopped and gave her a hug. Despite my mother's irritating jibes, I did actually like my sister-in-law. Sheryl was beautiful in the Irish princess kind of a way, with warm, auburn hair and a smattering of freckles to match. She was half a foot taller than me, which didn't qualify her as being a giant — it was more an indication that I was far from it. I barely scraped in at five foot, so had the disadvantage of looking up to Sheryl, literally and figuratively.

'What are you doing in Dunedin? Is everyone all right?'

I knew at once from the look on her face that no, everyone wasn't all right.

30

'What's happened? Are the kids okay?'

'Yeah, they're fine. Sam, I'm sorry. It's your dad, he's had a turn.'

I suddenly felt a little wobbly on my pins. 'Is it bad?'

'I don't know, but to be honest, I think it might be getting close to the end.'

I felt the sudden well of tears in my eyes and a constriction in my throat. This wasn't entirely unexpected. I'd lived with the knowledge of Dad's cancer for some time, but that didn't in any way prepare me for the grim reality that he might someday actually die. People with cancer could go on forever, couldn't they? This turn of events felt so sudden.

'But he seemed fine the other day when I rang. I talked to him — he didn't seem that bad. Mum didn't say anything about him being this ill.' Why hadn't they told me it was getting this serious? Surely they should have told me?

Sheryl's face softened, as if she could see my hurt. 'It was sudden. It seems to be neurological — they're talking about brain secondaries. No one expected it to happen like this.'

It took me a few moments to absorb that information. Brain secondaries? I felt an eddy of anxiety swirling in my chest. Anything involving the brain seemed so very final. I was dog-tired and emotional, and could feel myself starting to unhinge. If I didn't change the line of the conversation I knew I'd lose it completely.

'Is Mum here too?' I asked.

Sheryl reached out and touched my shoulder. Her loving concern almost tipped me over the edge. I took a shuddery breath.

'Yes, she's up in the ward with him.'

'What about the kids? Who's looking after them for you?'

'Steve's still on the farm. We couldn't find anyone to run things at such short notice, so he's home holding the fort until he can get some help in. I know he wishes he could be here.' I could see the upset in her eyes. 'You should come up and see them.' In a perfect world I would have, but as this little encounter had reinforced, the world was far from perfect.

'I can't right now. I want to but we've just started a big murder investigation — you probably read about it this morning — and I have to get back to the station with some information for a meeting that's in twenty minutes. But as soon as that's over, when I'm done, I'll come back. Tell them I'll be there as soon as possible.'

Sheryl hesitated, and I knew exactly what she was thinking. Mum would make a federal case out of the fact I didn't drop everything then and there and come running. But then, the thought dawned on me, why hadn't they rung me? They'd travelled from the sticks out the back of Southland all the way to Dunedin and no one had given me a call. The lump in my throat shifted to the pit of my stomach. For whatever reason, I was excluded again.

'We would have rung you, Sam, but it all happened rather quickly, and they decided to transfer him straight to Dunedin. We barely got to pack our bags.' You could add mindreading to the list of Saint Sheryl's attributes.

32

'Still, it would have been nice if someone had.'

She looked uncomfortable. We both knew we were on dangerous territory.

'Perhaps it would be better if I didn't mention we ran into each other to Mum.' Another reason why my mother adored my sister-in-law, she called her 'Mum'. 'Then I could ring you at work in half an hour, say, and make it all look kosher and then there will be no need for your mum to feel put out about you not coming now.'

I appreciated the thought, and I knew she meant well, but considering I'd been left off the invitation list for this little party, which happened to involve my favourite man in the whole wide world, it was a bit late for them to be concerned about people's feelings. I took a deep breath and decided not to shoot the messenger.

'Yeah, thanks Sheryl,' I said, and gave her another quick hug, 'that would be great.'

6

The metallic doors were just about to close when a big hand slid between them, forcing them to draw back apart. I raised my eyebrows when I saw who had made the last-minute dive for the work lift. The doors started their slide back together and the second they connected he pounced. I felt myself lifted into the corner, a warm hand nestle itself into the crook of my neck and a pair of urgent lips meld with mine. A thrill of electricity coursed through me and I wasted no time in kissing him back just as hard. In the scant five seconds before the lift found its destination and the doors began to open, I marvelled at how my body could become so warm and tingly in all sorts of interesting places. He exited the lift without a word and it took me a few moments to regain my composure before I could follow suit.

Working with your lover had distinct advantages.

* * *

'Well, Jill Henderson's story backs up what the SOCOs have found, which is not a hell of a lot.'

Paul was in the middle of the room filling us in on the reports that had come through so far. DI Johns was posturing for physical dominance against one corner of the desk he was perching on, while Smithy was doing the brooding male thing on the other. Otto was standing well back, out of the war zone — sensible man — as was Detective Constable Sonia Richardson, the designated newbie. I was busy trying to get rid of the ick feeling in my stomach after having had a look at the scene photos. I wasn't sure what had been worse, seeing John Henderson minus the top of his head, or seeing where the splattered remains of it had ended up. I wasn't normally prone to squeamishness, and I knew a shotgun blast could do a bit of damage at close range, but this was something else.

'There hasn't been much in the way of trace evidence from the intruders at the scene. The witness said they were dressed in full protective clothing, including gloves and masks, and were making very sure they left nothing of themselves behind. It seems very professional — or the CSI effect strikes again.' Bloody television had a lot to answer for; suddenly everyone was a forensics expert. 'We have one discernible set of boot prints in the kitchen that equates to Mrs Henderson being assaulted there, as does blood evidence from her on the cabinetry. There are no finger-prints, as you'd expect from their level of preparedness. The SOCOs are still examining the scene for fibres and other trace evidence.'

Although Paul was known to be a bit of a jokester, when he got down to business he was the epitome of professional and direct, which was yet another thing that got up Smithy's nose. Smithy tended to the organic method of detecting.

'The rope and tape used to gag and bind Mrs Henderson have been sent off to ESR. Both appear to have been brought to the scene by the perpetrators, as we haven't found any source of them in the house. They were prepared; this was a well-planned operation.'

Unlike on the telly, we didn't do our own forensic examination of evidence in ultra-flash, super-duper, in-house high-tech laboratories, wearing our coiffed hair and full makeup and best nightclubbing outfits. It was all outsourced to Environmental Science and Research in Christchurch for them to do in their fairly average laboratories, clad in the latest in comfy, androgynous, non-shedding, disposable sterile wear. Reality was far less fashion-conscious than fiction.

'Searches of the wider area haven't brought to light any sign of the protective clothing worn by them. It doesn't appear to have been dumped anywhere nearby, but extensive ground searches are continuing. I believe we're sending a boat out to search the bottom of the cliffs in the area in case items were disposed of into the sea. The spent shotgun cartridge hasn't been found at the scene, so it appears they took it away, and the murder weapon hasn't been located either.'

'So we're all thinking this was a targeted attack on John Henderson?' The Boss said.

'Highly probable. Nothing was taken, and they didn't kill Mrs Henderson, or the boy, who happened to be out. Considering the level of care taken with this killing, it appears they had done their research, checked the place out and factored the boy's absence into the equation.'

'If that was the case, wouldn't they have brought more people along to do the job, three instead of two?' Smithy's voice sounded a little sarky. It had sounded that way pretty much permanently since our friend and colleague Detective David Reihana had been killed in action and Paul had been chucked in as his replacement. Smithy himself had been shot and assaulted pretty badly in the same incident. His bitterness that the scumbuckets responsible for Reihana's death and his own war wounds had not been brought to justice, combined with his apparent intense dislike for Paul, made scorn and sarcasm his regular demeanour these days. The only time they failed to make a showing was when he was doing sullen instead. I missed the plain, old, grumpy Smithy. Paul, thank heavens, never rose to the bait and ignored Smithy's tone.

'Perhaps they were confident they could handle a woman and a teenager. From the eyewitness account they were pretty much all business,' Paul said.

DI Johns waved his hand and moved the conversation on. His patience for Smithy's moods had diminished along with everyone else's. 'What about the rest of the house?' he asked.

'All computers in the house have been removed and taken down to the Dunedin North Station for the electronic-crime lab, and a thorough search of Mr Henderson's home office is under way,' Paul continued. 'He was reported to have had an iPhone, but that hasn't been located as yet. Mrs Henderson said he carried it with him all the time, so its absence may mean it was removed by

37

the killers. If it was, it's the only thing they took. There is also a combination safe in the bottom of an office cupboard that is yet to be opened. Shephard, could you please ask Mrs Henderson if she knows the combination when you next visit?'

Although he directed his comment to me, my mind was distracted by the sound of the phone on my desk ringing. I wondered if it was Sheryl.

'Sorry, what was that?' I said as I moved towards the offending object.

'If you were paying attention you would have heard Detective Frost ask you to get the safe combination from the victim's wife when you go back to see her, and ask her if she saw them take his iPhone.' DI Johns had a tone that could cut through concrete when he wanted it to, which was frequently when it came to me. Paul threw me an apologetic kind of a look.

'Yes, Sir,' I mumbled in the general direction of the floor. He got one more shot as I noted Sheryl's caller ID and muted the call straight to messages.

'In fact, you can go there on the way to Henderson's office. Take Detective Smith with you. Maybe he can ask the right questions, seeing as you don't seem able to get anything useful out of our only witness.'

Bastard.

7

Our trip to the hospital involved two stop-offs, neither of which was very successful. Jill Henderson had no idea what the combination to her husband's safe was — yet another of those little secrets she was happy to overlook in the interest of maintaining domestic bliss. It was going to have to be opened the hard way by one of the local locksmiths we called in for these little inconveniences. She also had no recollection of the invaders removing her husband's iPhone, but she said it could have happened while she was in the kitchen having the crap beaten out of her by one of them. The timing was fortunate for us in one respect: we managed to catch her as she was about to be prepped for surgery — that shoulder wasn't going to get any better without outside intervention. The downside was that she was sore and fraught and not a happy camper.

The other visit left me with a bilious hollow in my stomach and feeling slumped over with the sheer burden of guilt lavished upon me by my mother. Dad was off having an MRI scan and out of earshot and so Mum was at her six-gun-packing best. After I found out the state of play with Dad, which was not sounding that flash, I'd had to carefully excuse myself in the name of duty. Naturally this gave my mother occasion for another lecture on the dereliction of my daughterly duties. Mounting a defence was futile. I didn't bother to mention that if my family had needed me so very badly, why hadn't they bothered to ring? Why was I the last to know? I tried to shrug off my coating of guilt as I exited the hospital doors, but it refused to budge and stuck like an oil slick over my mood.

'Sorry about everything that's happening with your dad,' Smithy said as he drove us down George Street towards Dowling Street and the registered office of Eros Global. He had to swerve for a couple of kamikaze pedestrians and a dumb-nut skateboarder with a death wish. 'You should put in for leave or use up some of your sick pay and go be with them.'

I'd entertained that idea for about three seconds before common sense stepped in.

'Thanks for the thought, but you don't quite understand. It's better for everyone if I keep out of it. Mum's a little . . . ' I groped for the right word, ' . . . tense right now and I just seem to set her off. So if you don't mind, I'd prefer to keep working. It helps me take my mind off it all.'

'Fair enough.'

8

As we entered the reception area of Eros Global the first thing to hit me was the smell of overheated electrical equipment and hot paper. The second was a telltale grinding noise.

'That's a bloody paper shredder,' Smithy said as he followed his nose through a wooden office door embellished with the name 'Blair Harvey-Boyd' in black glass lettering.

'And it's been working overtime,' I said as I followed him in.

Bent over the shredder, halfway through a wad of documents, was a thin man in his forties, dressed in what even I recognised as an extremely expensive pinstriped suit and looking for all the world like the kid with his hand caught in the cookie jar. The hand concerned was adorned with an impressive rectangular emerald ring set in gold, which coordinated with his elegant cufflinks and vibrant green cravat. With his perfectly coiffed hair and eyebrows, which looked like they'd been combed and set into position, he was a symphony of perfect and well-considered taste.

'Hey, you. Stop that immediately,' Smithy said, and strode across the room ready to intervene.

Suit Guy didn't look as if he was about to stop anytime soon. It was only when he realised the enormous detective bearing down on him meant business that he stopped feeding in the paper. Even then he stood there, puffed up, in a defiant, 'you don't intimidate me, I've done nothing wrong' kind of way.

'What do you think you're doing? Destroying evidence is what it looks like. We ought to arrest you right here for obstruction of justice. You'd better explain yourself.'

'No, no. No, I wasn't doing that,' the man said. The moment the words came out of his mouth I realised this man was gloriously camp. 'I was just clearing some of my personal correspondence, nothing to do with Mr Henderson. I'm perfectly entitled to tidy up my own business in my own office, aren't I?'

He was clearly lying his arse off, but I think his saving grace for now was the fact that even Smithy was trying not to smile. The man was a walking stereotype. It was like he'd researched every effeminate male who had ever existed and then cherry-picked the best bits to form the perfect gay package. Still, it was a package that was acting very dodgily and was caught shredding the crap out of a forest's worth of paper. The end result was that, despite his elegance, he hadn't made a good first impression on either of us. And we all knew first impressions tended to last.

'And you would be?'

'Blair,' he said, and looked at us with undisguised suspicion. 'Blair Harvey-Boyd. And you would be?'

I thought it was fairly obvious who we were, but undertook the formalities. 'Detective Shephard, and this is Detective Smith. I believe you were expecting us?' The fact he'd been destroying stuff told us he was expecting someone.

'Oh, yes, they said a detective would be coming when they rang about John.'

'Well, Mr Blair Harvey-Boyd, if you've finished with your wanton destruction of documents, perhaps you could answer a few questions for us about your employer.'

The man's face crumpled first into a frown, and then to a version of grief-stricken. 'Oh, I know. It's just awful. That someone could do that to him — to both of them — and in their own home. It almost makes me ill to think of it. But I suppose you are hardened to this kind of thing; it wouldn't affect you like it does the rest of us. For us it's just hideous.'

It was apparent he'd also studied at the Dame Edna school of melodrama. It had been amusing for about the first thirty seconds, but with the whole 'them and us' thing he was starting to annoy me. Smithy too, judging by the look of irritation on his face.

'Cut the theatrics. I'd like to have a sensible conversation, thank you.'

That was a bit harsh, even for Smithy, although I could understand the frustration. With his over-the-top mannerisms and bravado scattered with lapses into sorrowful expression, Mr Blair Harvey-Boyd was proving to be very difficult to read.

'It has become apparent that Mr Henderson was . . . executed, shall we say,' Smithy explained, 'and Mrs Henderson has alluded to the fact that some of his business practices were questionable, which your skill with the paper shredder tends to reinforce. Naturally, we have to consider all possibilities in our investigation, which also includes you, so your cooperation would be recommended.'

'Me, a suspect?' Suit Guy said, aghast. 'But I could never do something like that, and anyway, why would I? John was a good friend and a great employer.' I looked at the expensive suit, silk cravat and blingy cufflinks. He certainly must have been a generous employer.

'You had better help us figure out who would have, then. You can start by telling us exactly what Eros Global does and what it deals in.'

'Certainly. Why don't you take a seat?' He indicated a pair of expensive-looking mid-century-design leather chairs. They weren't as comfortable as they looked.

'We're an import-export business for nutraceuticals.'

'Nutraceuticals?' I asked.

'For those that don't know, they're pharmaceuticals really, but we can't call them that because in order to make any therapeutic claims for something you have to have it licensed by the Ministry of Health as a pharmaceutical, which costs a fortune and takes forever. You know what bureaucrats are like — you're civil servants. So if we have them lodged as nutritional supplements, it's a lot more straightforward.'

Well, that sounded dodgy for a start. The civil servants quip had left Smithy bristling. Suit Guy had a special gift for condescension.

'What sort of products?'

'Our main line is sexual-performance enhancers.' One of Smithy's eyebrows cocked upwards.

'Although we have others.'

'And these are imported, or do you manufacture here?'

'A bit of both.'

'And your manufacturing is done in Dunedin?'

'Auckland, actually, that's where it's all happening. Dunedin's too much of a backwater to bother with manufacturing, but we distribute from here. For some unfathomable reason, John liked this place.'

If Suit Guy was so fond of Auckland, why didn't he do everyone a favour and go back there? My fingers twitched and I had to try very hard to keep my voice level.

'And how do you market these so-called nutraceuticals?'

He blithely went on, oblivious to the chill in the air. 'We have stockists around the country, but we also have an online business, which is the part that I run — in fact, it's the area of fastest growth. That's where the future lies; shopping from the comfort and discretion of your own home. We're getting more and more business through the online store. In fact we are one of New Zealand's largest suppliers of Viagra and Cialis; our prices and service can't be beaten. I've captured that corner of the market.' He was clearly proud of this achievement. But even my limited understanding of medicine made that statement ring little alarm bells.

'I thought you said you didn't do pharmaceuticals. And I thought drugs like that could only be supplied on prescription, and then they could only be dispensed at a pharmacy.' Otherwise, surely, they'd be on sale everywhere from the local sex shop to the corner dairy.

'Oh yes, you're quite right there, but you see, I'm registered as a pharmacist and licensed to dispense, so we cover all the legal requirements. That's the beauty of the computer age: prescriptions can be sent by email, it's all paid for electronically with their credit card and then, *voilà*, we send it out. Easy.'

I was sure it was a hell of a lot less simple than that and my bull-shit-o-meter questioned the legality of it all, but that was something that could be looked into later. It would be interesting to talk to the fraud folk on the matter as well as whoever did the registration of medicines and pharmacies in New Zealand. Was this what Jill Henderson meant when she said she had moral issues with her husband's business dealings? Surely not. It must have been about something dodgier than old men popping a pill to get a leg over.

'So Eros Global is essentially a company that imports stuff to help sad bastards who can't get it up by themselves?' Smithy hadn't fallen for Harvey-Boyd's evangelical spiel either.

'Why? Do you need some assistance, Detective?'

Mr Harvey-Boyd stood there looking pleased with himself. His cockiness was severely misplaced. Smithy's face changed from a look of distaste to dangerously impassive. As of recently he didn't have to worry about enjoying a physical relationship with anyone as his wife, Veronica, had taken the kids and left. And, as much as I liked and respected Smithy, I had to side with Veronica on this one. Since the shooting, well, actually, since a significant issue before then, he'd been a different Smithy to the one we knew and loved. The new Smithy was moody and judgemental, and pretty bloody difficult too. I think we'd all hoped he'd get better. Veronica was the first one to admit that wasn't about to happen and the man she had fallen in love with wasn't coming back, so she had bailed. Naturally, that hadn't improved matters. It was a raw nerve that Mr Harvey-Boyd had severely jangled. Smithy looked like he was going to detonate. I stood up and stepped between them, for everyone's welfare, and started talking, fast.

'Mr Harvey-Boyd, can we clear one thing up straight away, please? What were you doing last night?' Jill Henderson's description of the offenders was of a very large man and a man of medium height and thin build. Mr Harvey-Boyd was short and slight, so I was pretty certain he didn't actually do the deed.

'Oh, that's easy,' he said and looked very relieved at the question. It had finally dawned on him how close he was flirting with disaster. 'I was out at our film-society night. The International Film Festival is on at the moment, so we went to the eight-fifteen session and then we all went to Nova for a drink. We left at about eleven, I suppose.'

'We?'

'Gregory, my partner, and I. He can vouch for my whereabouts, as can most of the society members.'

'We'll need to speak to Greg to confirm that,' I said. Although, even if his alibi did stack up, that didn't necessarily mean he was innocent. I was sure he was perfectly capable of paying someone else to do the hit. A little investigating into his financial affairs would be in order, to ensure there hadn't been any very large outgoing payments recently.

'If you must. But he likes to be called Gregory, Gregory Chingford-Owen.' Gosh, they were the Harvey-Boyd-Chingford-Owens.

'John Henderson had an iPhone, is that right?'

'Yes, he was never without it. It was like his lifeline. He kept everything in there.'

'Well it wasn't on him last night, and we've been unable to locate it at his house. Is there any chance he would have left it here?'

'Oh no. Like I said, he always carried it. We can look next door in his office, but you'll be wasting your time. I'm absolutely certain he would have had it on him. Come this way.'

We exited Harvey-Boyd's office (the paper shredder seemed to have recovered its composure by now), and moved through to what must have been John Henderson's PA's room. I checked my watch; she'd been asked to meet us here in about quarter of an hour's time. The room was precisely what you'd expect of a PA's office, with numerous filing cabinets, shelves of document boxes and ring binders. Dual computer monitors, keyboard and wireless mouse on a very tidy desk. The desk and shelving were all in a warm, brown mahogany-type finish, which complemented the brown textured carpet. The view of the waterfront out of the window was quite lovely. A healthy-looking large-leafed pot plant occupied one corner, and the earthy theme was completed with a spectacular canvas-printed photograph of Mitre Peak. I certainly wouldn't have minded this office.

Where Astrid Allen's office was elegant, John Henderson's office was all style. The shelves displayed carefully arranged product — boxes of Viagra, Cialis and what I guessed were prescription medicines, along with what were clearly the nutraceuticals. I'd never come across a medicine called 'Cock-up' before, but the name certainly gave away the purpose. As did 'Man-power', 'Thrust' and what I guessed must have been the female equivalents, with names like 'Vixen', 'Purr' and my personal favourite, 'Defrost'. He must have been very proud of his product lines, because I'd have been embarrassed to have them on display, let alone be seen by potential business clients.

Henderson had a large, almost sculptural glass desk, the transparent top supported by satin-finished steel disks sitting on the drawer units. His chair was dark-brown designer leather, as were the visitors' seats. A fifty-five inch LCD screen was attached to the wall, and my mind could not help but wonder if it was to play 'promotional DVDs'. Despite some of the product lines involved, the overall impression of the room was one of class, not kitsch. It was designed to impress and you could tell where the money had been spent.

'Well, this is nice,' Smithy said. He stood for a moment to admire the LCD screen.

'Where's his computer?' I asked. 'Did he use a laptop?'

'No, John didn't like the clutter of a computer on his desk, so it's over here.' Blair pointed to a vacant space on top of the waist-height cupboards to the left of the desk. Was I missing something here? There wasn't any computer. Harvey-Boyd looked like he was enjoying his joke, before he reached over and pressed a switch. I heard a whirring noise before, hey presto, like magic, panels slid open and the latest iMac emerged up like a rabbit out of a hat.

'Okay, that was cool,' I said. The keyboard even slid out on a little platform so you could sit at it without having to amputate your legs. Smithy was salivating. It was boy-toy heaven.

'If his iPhone had been here, it would have been on his desk, or charging over there by the computer.' Both spaces were conspicuously empty.

'Do you have the passwords to get on to this computer?' I asked.

'No, I'm afraid not, but Astrid may have.' If she didn't have it, the techie boys and girls would have fun cracking it. That would give them something to do for a few minutes.

I heard the front door of the premises open. It had to be Astrid. I didn't want Suit Guy here while we were talking to her, and I didn't trust him to wait quietly in his office without having another crack at destroying the evidence.

'Mr Harvey-Boyd, we are going to need to talk to you again. In fact, if you could be down at the station at four o'clock, we can take a proper statement then. In the meantime, I'm afraid you won't be allowed back onto these premises, so can we have your keys, please?' I put my hand out, expectantly.

He looked at it, horrified. 'But why? I've got so much work to do. We'll have to let all of our clients know what has happened. There's still the business to run.'

'Business is closed for the day,' Smithy said. 'And then there's the little matter of what you were doing with the paper shredder — which was a complete waste of time, I'm afraid to tell you, because our people will be able to piece that all back together, no problem. So be good, hand over the keys and run along.'

Blair Harvey-Boyd gave a theatrical humph, reached his hand into his trouser pocket, pulled out the keys and deftly removed the office ones from his substantial and flashy keyring. He then dropped them into my hand, turned on his well-shod heel and strode out of the room.

9

The moment Astrid Allen entered the office I understood why Jill Henderson had sounded wary when she spoke of her. Ms Allen was a bombshell in the traditional blonde sense of the word. Although dressed very conservatively in jeans, boots and a high-necked sweater, and with her hair swept back in an easy ponytail, there was absolutely no doubt as to her curvaceousness. I could see that, given the right attire, she'd completely erase any customer's need for chemical enhancement.

I whispered to Smithy, 'Wipe your chin.' He closed his mouth.

'Hi Astrid. I'm Detective Shephard and this is Detective Smith,' I said as I reached out to shake her hand.

Her grasp was firm and she looked both me and Smithy directly in the eye as she greeted us in turn. I could see the smudge of dark circles under her eyes; she hadn't tried to hide them with makeup. I guessed she was about twenty-five — the perfect blonde trophy PA, nicely complementing John Henderson's gorgeous brunette trophy wife. Still, I could understand that the trophy wife might feel a little threatened by the help. John Henderson liked to surround himself with the best.

'Thank you for coming in today,' I said. 'I realise this must be difficult for you.'

'Yes, it's truly awful. I still can't believe it. Poor Jill and Declan, they'll be devastated. And I can't imagine what it must have been like for Jill, to see John being killed like that.' Astrid had a quiet intensity about her. She was clearly upset, but not in the histrionic way that my prejudices would have expected from a young blonde thing. Her voice was low and rich, which, coupled with her sober demeanour, created an impression of a mature and capable young woman. 'You have to catch whoever did this; they are sick, sick people. I'll help in any way I can.' And I believed she would.

'What exactly did your job entail here, working for Mr Henderson?' I asked.

The corners of her lips curled up in a hint of a smile. 'We had a strictly professional relationship,' she said, picking up on my subtext, and without any sign of offence. 'John ran an international company and had a lot of overseas contacts, clients and suppliers to juggle. I acted as the intermediary, communicating across different time zones, organising times for teleconferencing as well as his travel. I also did a lot of traditional secretarial work. He did basic emailing, but his typing was lousy, so he preferred to dictate larger communications, which I'd type up for him. I also did the day-to-day financials and record-keeping. As for the business and web-development side of things, that was John and Blair's domain.'

'Did they have a good relationship? Was there any tension there?'

She looked around to make sure Harvey-Boyd was out of earshot. 'To be honest, Blair can get pretty irritating.' That wasn't hard to believe. 'And he'd occasionally get under John's skin, but they seemed to be a good combination when it came to business. I guess you could say Blair is the flashy ideas man and go-getter, whereas John was the more considered, quieter person who made things work. I think they respected each other.' She paused for a moment. 'If you're asking if I think Blair would have killed John, no, he wouldn't be the type to get his hands dirty. And if you're asking if he could have paid someone else to do it, then no also. He would have too much to lose.' She laughed then, low and throaty. 'Blair Harvey-Boyd is a high-maintenance man with expensive tastes and . . . ' again the pause, ' . . . habits.' Was she alluding to a chemical enhancement to keep him bouncing around like that? It wasn't a great stretch of the imagination. 'He is paid very, very well. I don't think he'd be the type to risk upsetting the gravy train.'

'And you are well paid too, I take it?' Smithy asked.

She shifted her gaze to him, and I tried not to smile as he straightened himself up to look taller. Not that it would do any good. I was guessing she wasn't the kind of girl to go for middle-aged men with well-lived-in faces.

She laughed. 'Yes, I get paid very well, and no, I wouldn't bite the hand that fed me either. I realise full well I am doing very nicely for someone of my age, and to be honest, I really enjoy the work. John was giving me plenty of opportunities for career development, paying for

54

me to do papers at the university to improve my skills, so as far as I'm concerned he was an ideal employer.'

'So, in your capacity as PA you would have been familiar with all of his business associates. Did he have good relationships with these people, and was there anyone who seemed to have a problem with him or bear him any ill will?' I asked.

A hint of a cloud passed across her face. 'By and large most of his associates were great. There were one or two of his, I suppose, business colleagues who made me feel uncomfortable.'

'In the personal sense, or in the wider sense?' I asked.

'Both.' Her eyes flicked over to Smithy as she spoke. 'I suppose in any innovative business you'll have your detractors, but I found a few of them quite intimidating.'

'And did any of them intimidate John Henderson?'

'No, he wasn't the type to be intimidated by anyone.'

10

'You practically salivated all over her.'

'Did not.'

'Did so.' I thought back to the look she had given Smithy. I'd never thought of him as being a bit leery before. Maybe it was something new that went with his recently acquired single status. 'We might not have been able to solve the password problem for the computer, but at least Astrid showed us how to get round the issue of the iPhone. She's a clever young woman, you realise,' I said.

'What makes you think that?'

I looked at him, incredulous. 'Duh, couldn't you tell. Oh no, that's right, you were too busy staring at her tits.' He couldn't deny it. 'We should have realised a lot of the information on John Henderson's iPhone would be duplicated on his computer — they're all integrated nowadays. It's all there, we've just got to be able to get into it.'

Astrid could update his schedule from her computer, but he hadn't given her access to his other files. That little fact made me wonder what else he was up to that he kept from his PA. Why didn't he trust her? Or did he just not trust anyone?

'It doesn't get around the fact the iPhone's missing, though.'

'No, but it means that if it was actually taken

56

by the perpetrators then any information on it that may be useful for the investigation is still available to us. If they took it because they thought it might contain information that could lead to them, they are out of luck, because it's all sitting in his computer. It also means someone might have it in their possession, which would mean they'd have a bit of explaining to do if we caught them with it. When the tech folk get into his computer they'll be able to activate the 'find my phone' app, provided the phone's battery hasn't died. Both Jill Henderson and Harvey-Boyd said he was basically married to the thing and couldn't do without it. It could hold the keys to his universe.'

'Or not. Cellphones are overrated.'

11

One of the gut-wrenching things about video is the inescapable sense of being there. Declan Henderson had been brave and forward-thinking to record his movements in the house when he came home and discovered the carnage, but the results were damn hard to watch. I think it was the soundtrack that tipped it over the edge into being intolerable: the sound of his sobbing, punctuated with the mantra of 'no, no, no'. He had briefly scanned the scene of devastation that was his father, before rushing to the aid of his mother. He'd propped up the phone on some piece of furniture so it still recorded as he frantically ripped the tape from Jill's mouth, all the while calling out to her, desperation and grief tearing at his voice. I could hear the raking gasps of air Jill took once freed of her gag, and imagined how very close she must have come to dying too. I got to see adrenaline in motion when Declan seemed to effortlessly flip the chair over onto its side and claw at the bonds that held his mother's hands. My stomach lurched as I could see her right arm at a very unnatural angle to her body. It was the uppermost arm so there was no way Declan was responsible for it — one piece of information I could give to ease his mind just a little. The last image I got to see was a glimpse of Declan's grief-stricken face before his hand eclipsed the phone, reaching out to call the ambulance. I had to turn the sound off before I could watch it again.

The scene photos were also difficult to detach myself from. It was the incongruity of such a normal domestic scene overlaid with such an act of violence. The sight of two mugs of tea still brewing, teabag corners bobbing above the liquid, the two-litre bottle of light-blue milk waiting to be poured, next to a smear of blood on the edge of the counter and a partial bloodied handprint on the floor. Jill must have reached up to the cut on her head and then put her hand back down while she tried to get away from her tormenter. I wondered if any of her blood had found its way onto the intruder.

Then there were the shots of the lounge. A modern, funky chandelier, dripping. A huge black-and-white photograph of the rib-like poles of the derelict St Clair groyne, embellished with a splash of colour that didn't belong there. The once-cream sofa and designer cushions misted with red. I took a more careful look at one of the close-ups of the sofa arm. There was a telltale pale rectangular patch. That solved the case of the missing iPhone. We knew where it had been when John Henderson had been murdered. Lastly I looked at the photos of John. I flipped these over quickly; the story was obvious. The clear demarcation between his lightly stubbled chin and then pretty much nothing told where the killer had pointed the shotgun, and that he'd been damn close.

I walked away from the office feeling an

overwhelming urge for a hot shower, to try and quell the deep-seated distaste and chill in my bones.

12

After another tense trip to the hospital to see Dad and tiptoe around Mum I was feeling dog-tired and close to emotional overload. All I wanted was to get home. Thank God Mum had declined my half-hearted offer to stay at my place. It was uttered out of duty, but I didn't know what I'd have done if they'd said yes, other than panic wildly. Their opting for a motel was a wise move for all concerned. I unlocked the door to my place of refuge and was relieved to wander into the lounge and see my flatmate Maggie sitting on the sofa, alone.

'You look like you've had a shit of a day.'

I loved the way she could read me with a one-millisecond sideward glance. It was a skill she'd developed over years of practice, helped by the fact I was not in possession of a poker face. For a friendship that had started from a flatmate-wanted ad in a backwater-town local rag many years and houses ago, it had endured despite the odds and mishaps. Maggs had become one of the rocks in my life.

'You don't know the half of it,' I said. 'I might even tell you about it but I'll have to work up the courage first.'

She screwed up her nose in sympathy. 'That bad?'

'Nope, worse.' I dumped my bag on the floor and listened for any hint of movement from elsewhere in the house. All was quiet. 'Rudy not here tonight?' Her lusty Frenchman was a frequent over-stayer, as was mine — not that Paul was French, just lusty.

'No, he's got some faculty thing on late, so he's at his own place. What about Paul, is he coming over?'

'No, too much happening with work.'

A slow smile started its way across both our faces.

'Girls' night!' we yelled simultaneously.

'I'll get the Milo and ToffeePops,' I said as I headed towards the kitchen. We'd start with the gentle stuff, but I had a strange feeling it would escalate into something a little more potent. Well, I hoped so anyway. God knew I could use some anaesthetic.

'I'll choose the DVD,' Maggs said, and headed towards the bookshelves.

Heaven.

13

The morning's squad meeting was charged with a frisson of anticipation. Officers were whispering among themselves, the low, questioning murmur of rumour and speculation. We were assembled in the large downstairs meeting room, with pretty much all duty staff called in. That fact alone added to the general level of excitement.

'What's up?' I asked Paul as I sidled in next to him. It was standing room only and he was holding up the wall towards the back. Although we kept it very professional at work and made believe we were just colleagues — well, when people were looking, anyway — he still managed to steal a surreptitious grope of my butt.

'I don't know for sure, but apparently there's been a bit of a breakthrough.' He looked down at me hard until I was forced to make eye contact. His blue crystalline eyes had a way of boring right through me, and he knew it. Combine it with the fact he made Ben Affleck look a bit on the plain side, and it was no wonder my autonomic nervous system always cranked it up in his presence. 'How are you going? You sleep okay?' he asked quietly. If people actually knew how caring Paul was it would completely blow his reputation of typical, inconsiderate, blokey guy. He was quite careful to hide the fact.

'Not really. Couldn't get things out of my head.' Those things had refused to budge, and consequently I'd given in, got out of bed and spent half the night up, watching crap American sitcoms and infomercials on TV. Now wasn't the time or place to elaborate on it, though. 'What do you think has happened?'

'Don't know. The Boss is keeping tight-lipped about it.'

No doubt. DI Johns had a theatrical bent, so if he was in possession of some substantial piece of news he was sure to use it to maximum dramatic effect. People like him just craved attention. As if to confirm my suspicions, I heard the procession coming down the hallway. The DI strode to centre front of the room and swung around to face us all. When he was quite certain everyone had noticed and appreciated his entrance, he spoke.

'Right people, can I have some attention please.' He also liked to treat us like schoolkids. 'We've got a lot to get through.' Everyone made sure they were turned to the front, sitting up straight, both feet on the floor and arms folded. Those leaning against the walls stood to attention. The principal had arrived.

He paused, waiting until there was absolute silence. 'I've had an interesting piece of information through this morning. Yesterday afternoon officers recovered the protective clothing used by the offenders. It had been discarded in a residential wheelie bin awaiting collection at Seacliff.' A buzz washed around the room. Some of us had heard that little piece of news first thing, so the reaction was from those who hadn't caught up with the fact. 'The owners of the house were questioned last night, but they're an elderly couple with a sound alibi. They didn't hear any vehicles or the sound of someone tampering with their bin, but it was quite a way from the house. Other neighbours were also oblivious. It would appear to be an opportunist disposal. The waste-truck operator noticed bloodstained clothing and called it in. There were two disposable cover-all suits, novelty clown masks, footwear booties and four pairs of rubber disposable gloves. These people were very organised and careful not to leave a trace; they even double-gloved.' He paused again, looking jubilant. 'They weren't careful enough, though. We got it all off to ESR pronto and they worked overtime last night to examine them. There were a few hairs caught in the hoods of the boiler suits that they may be able to get DNA off, but that will take some time. However, they processed the rubber gloves with ninhydrin in case they could recover a fingerprint.' A sharkish smile curled across his face. 'We have hit pay dirt, people.' He reached into the folder and pulled out two A3-sized photographs, looked at each as if admiring them, and then with the flourish of a game-show host, he attached them to the board and stepped away.

A collective gasp gripped the room.

My eyes quickly tracked down Smithy to where he stood against the wall opposite. I watched as his body stiffened and a wave of red washed up his face.

'I'm sure I don't need to introduce these gentlemen to you, but for those who have been living in a vacuum lately, let me present Gideon

Powell, aka Mr Big, and his associate Jacob Sandhurst, also known as The Cockroach.'

'Jesus,' I whispered to Paul. A wave of murmuring broke out across the room as everyone made similar comments.

'Back to attention, people,' the DI said. 'I clearly don't have to remind you of our unproven suspicions about the involvement of Mr Powell in the death of Detective David Reihana last year.' He didn't mention one of the other unpleasant results of that incident, which was the shooting and grievous injury of Detective Malcolm Smith. My eyes flicked back over to Smithy, who stood rigid, his face implacable. 'I should also not have to remind you all that this is a separate investigation, and should be treated as such. I will not have any vigilantes thinking they can point-score on this.' He looked pointedly at Smithy, and then at me. I felt my face suffuse with heat as people turned around to see who was getting all the attention. 'I don't want anyone cocking this up,' he said. 'This may be our one and only opportunity to get this animal behind bars, so we will be doing everything by the book. No mistakes.'

14

'You haven't said a thing since the meeting,' I said to Smithy as I handed him his cup of crap instant coffee with the requisite three teaspoonfuls of sugar.

'What's there to say?' He nodded his thanks.

'Anything would be better than this silence.'

Some people seemed sad when they were silent, some people contemplative. Smithy struck me as dangerous. Maybe I was reading too much into it. He wasn't the only one who had an emotional investment in the outcome of this case.

'Okay, how about I say 'yippee, the bastard who had me shot up and my mate killed is finally going to get what he deserves, may he rot in hell'. Does that make you feel better?'

'A little bit, yes, thank you.'

He managed a tic you could take as a smile. We were twiddling our thumbs in the squad-room, waiting while DI Johns and Paul led the crews off in search of Gideon Powell, or Mr Big — or, as we plebs not so fondly referred to him, Fat Bastard — and Jacob Sandhurst, The Cockroach, so called because he was filthy and no one seemed to be able to kill him. It wasn't through lack of trying. These men were at the heart of the organised-crime scene in Dunedin, running one of the factions that, alongside the gangs, found illegal ways of making a hell of a lot of money. Fat Bastard seemed to have his finger in every dodgy pie in the city and beyond, but until now his Teflon coating had kept him from being indicted for anything. It looked like his luck was about to change. It would be interesting to see how slick he was when he was brought in for questioning.

I decided to tackle another issue. Hopefully the coffee would be kicking in by now and improving Smithy's mood.

'You're not going to sulk because you've been bumped off heading the case, are you?' He'd been replaced by Paul, which, considering Smithy's lack of fondness for him, would not have gone down well.

'What do you think I am? A two-year-old?' Actually yes I did — the biggest, grumpiest and most belligerent one ever, but I wasn't about to mention it.

'I know this is personal for you.' Hell, it was for all of us. 'But this is one instance where, in the interests of justice, you need to take a back seat and let other people sort it out.'

'If you're referring to your little boyfriend, he hasn't done anything to convince me that he's got the ability to sort out a lolly scramble in a sweet factory, let alone this.'

I winced. Paul was a damn good detective and, in this case, had the advantage of being an outsider. He was still working in Gore last year when the shooting went down, and had only met Reihana in passing. He would be a little more objective than the rest of us and didn't have any conflicts of interest, which was why DI Johns had put him in charge. The logic didn't seem to hold any sway with Smithy, though; he hadn't appreciated being usurped and had let everyone know it. He was not a happy camper.

'Look, Smithy,' I said. I was getting heartily sick of having to tiptoe around his moods, and with all of the other shit happening in my life, I was at the limits of my tolerance. 'I know it's not an ideal situation for any of us, but do us a favour and don't be an arsehole about it.'

15

Fat Bastard Powell walked down the corridor like he owned the place. His swagger and smirk said 'I am untouchable, throw what you want at me, nothing will stick'. We'd see about that. He was a big unit and used every inch of his six-foot-four frame to intimidate. Despite being overweight, you could tell that under the excess was hard-earned muscle and power. You wouldn't want to mess with this man. Everything about him screamed bad bastard, from his long blond hair, pulled back into a ratty ponytail, to the stud earring in his right ear, to the hint of a snake tattoo that peeked from the top of his T-shirt and the glimpse of skulls on his biceps, to the jagged scar above his left cheekbone and the look of superiority in his eyes. He dressed and acted with the machismo of a man far younger than his forty-eight years.

He had an honour guard of sorts. A collection of officers and detectives lined the corridor, their silence and threatening stances providing a surreal moment. The man in question seemed impervious to the show of strength. I stood next to Smithy, poised to act, knowing full well that if he decided to have a go there wouldn't be a damn thing I could do to stop him. He didn't move; instead he glared, liquid venom streaming from his eyes. Their gazes locked, and whether Powell recognised Smithy, or merely recognised enmity when he saw it, he flicked his head with an 'up yours' and a sneer. I sensed Smithy's muscles tense, but he held his ground. He must have realised that while getting a cheap shot in here might feel good, the hangover wouldn't be worth it. Paul, who was guiding Powell to the interview room, eyed Smithy with caution, then, when he realised no challenge would eventuate, his eyes found mine. *Trust me,* was the silent communication. It wasn't necessary.

DI Johns followed up as rearguard.

'That's enough people, get back to work,' he said as they disappeared into the interview room and the door shut behind them with a sharp clank. The moment it closed there was a stampede for the adjacent viewing room. They had chosen to conduct the interview in a room with a two-way mirror. Smithy cleared a path in front of him and no one argued when he occupied the middle position. I sidled in next to him.

DI Johns was in charge of the interview, with Paul riding shotgun. Their voices crackled tinny over the speaker. They undertook the formalities while Fat Bastard Powell regarded them like they were minion scum. Just looking at him repulsed me, with his jowls and beer gut monuments to excess, his lank, long hair pulled back into a ponytail like some middle-aged greaser trying to reclaim his youth. Add to that the knowledge of the type of life he led, and he was truly loathsome. He was utterly sure of himself, so much so that he had waived his right to legal representation.

'Where were you on the night of Monday the eleventh?'

'I was at home fucking my wife. Where were you?'

The DI didn't bat an eyelid. 'I was at a crime scene actually, at the home of John Henderson. You may have heard about it.'

'That the one out at Seacliff? Lucky you.'

He didn't have a care in the world. His arrogance made him even uglier, if that was possible. He was one of those people where the ugliness on the inside seeped through to tarnish the outside. I doubted even a mother could love this man.

'Yes, but not so lucky for you.'

'Is that right? And why would that be?' He checked his watch and yawned. 'And can you hurry, I've got a haircut in an hour.' He needed it.

'We have evidence that puts you at the scene of the crime.'

Fat Bastard Powell laughed and leaned back in his chair. 'What did you do, pull it out of your arse? You can't have any evidence because I wasn't there. As I said, I was at home with the missus.' He gave the DI an up-and-down look. 'I bet she's a better lay than yours, if you've even got a wife. Or do you prefer the blokes? Would you rather fuck this dickhead beside you?'

To their credit, neither the DI nor Paul rose to the bait; in fact the two of them wore an expression that rather resembled boredom. They also didn't answer, so the silence hung there and got heavier by the second. Powell took a few moments to realise his goading wasn't working. His face underwent a subtle transition from full-on boast and bluff to slightly uncertain boast and bluff. After a few moments more, it was him who broke the spell.

'What do you mean you've got evidence that puts me at the scene of the crime? What evidence?' He sat forward, arms on the table. Someone had decided to take an interest.

'We have your fingerprints.'

He snorted. 'Well you can't have. Because, as I said earlier, I wasn't there.'

'We have your fingerprints from inside a rubber glove, one that happened to be worn when you shot John Henderson's head off. We know this because it is covered in his blood. You obviously haven't been watching enough TV, because if you did you would realise we can get prints off gloves, easy, prints like yours.' It wasn't actually that easy, but no one quibbled.

'Well it's a crock of shit. You can't possibly have my prints. I'm being stitched up. Is this how you do your policing nowadays, plant evidence? Make an innocent man look guilty? Well, it's a load of fucking crap. I'm not saying another word to you fucking arseholes until I get my lawyer.'

16

Jacob Sandhurst, aka The Cockroach, looked like he'd prefer to scuttle back under the dung heap where he belonged. Compared to Fat Bastard Powell, he was a string bean. In fact, I imagined side by side they would resemble Laurel and Hardy, except The Cockroach had really bad skin, and neither of them wore bowler hats. Also, The Cockroach's skinniness reflected overall ill health — self-inflicted ill health. His mere presence seemed to make a room feel grubbier. Unlike Fat Bastard, Sandhurst didn't look overconfident; in fact he looked pathologically suspicious, his eyes constantly darting around, his body a ball of nervous energy. My guess would have been that he was picked up pretty close to the time he would normally be due to top up his bloodstream with his chemical of choice. Oh dear, how sad. The viewing room wasn't quite as full as it had been for the big guy, although Smithy was still here, rumbling away like some dormant volcano preparing for a revival.

The questioning seemed to take a similar path to Fat Bastard's, and mimicking his boss's initial strategy, The Cockroach had waived his right to any representation. You had to admire the conceit of these sods, they thought they were untouchable. We had news for them, however, and were all looking forward to seeing them take a fall. This time it was Paul in the driving seat. From what I'd seen, his questioning style was quite laid-back in that 'lull you into a false sense of security then deftly rip your throat out' kind of a way. Seeing Paul there, so professional, so authoritative, so masterful, gave me the overwhelming urge to drag him off somewhere private and give him a thorough interrogation of my own.

'So, where were you on the night of Monday, the eleventh of April?'

'What's it to you?' The sneer on his face with his pursed little mouth reminded me more of a fly than a roach — still a filthy critter though.

'Shall I repeat the question for you? Where were you on the night . . . '

'I'm not deaf, or stupid. Why should I tell you?'

'Well, Mr Sandhurst, considering we're conducting a murder inquiry, and we've gone to all the trouble of bringing you in, I thought it might be in your best interests to answer any questions in order to eliminate yourself from the list of suspects. Unless, of course, you were involved in some way.'

'Who got done?'

Paul folded his arms and looked at him like he was some errant ten-year-old. 'Jacob, now you're treating us like we're stupid, because if my memory serves me correctly, I informed you of who had been killed when we popped by your house to pick you up, so don't bother trying that one. Where were you?'

'I was at home.'

'And is there anybody who can corroborate that?'

'The missus will.'

'Will she now?' I imagined the womenfolk in their organisation were all accustomed to saying they were at home on the sofa with a cup of tea watching TV, or shagging wildly in bed, whenever a cop asked their partner's whereabouts. I didn't have any doubt as to the consequences for them if they decided to be awkward and say they didn't have the foggiest.

'Yes she will, because that's where I was.' His leg was jiggling away, and even though his hands were clasped together on the table, he still managed to tap his thumbs together at a furious tempo. A gleam of sweat glistened on his pock-marked face.

'That's curious, because, you see, I have a few issues with you saying you were at home. We have evidence that just so happens to put you at the scene of John Henderson's murder. How do you explain that?'

The other leg started jiggling too. 'I have no idea what you're talking about.'

'Well, we have fingerprints, your fingerprints, which proves you were there when it happened, and the evidence doesn't lie.'

'Well you've got it all wrong, because I had nothing to do with that man getting done. How could I? I wasn't there, so don't you try and pin this one on me. That's police corruption, that is. I want my lawyer, and I want him now.'

And so they scuttled for cover.

17

The background *bleep, bleep* of a heart-rate monitor punctuated the eerie silence in the room. Dad looked peaceful as he slept. As I sat there, I found my eyes naturally drawn to his chest, making sure it was still rising and falling with the rhythm of life. I'd snuck down for a quick visit during my lunch hour and had timed it nicely as Mum and Sheryl had popped out for some food, so I could forgo the usual eggshell-walking, and just sit and watch. He looked so small, draped with the white cotton hospital blanket, his limbs bird-like forms with no substance. There was something about the clutter of cords, drips and monitors that diminished what was left of the man. The skin of his hand felt dry and papery in my grasp, the bones and tendons palpable under my touch. I felt a big, fat tear loll its way down my cheek.

18

'Bastard's still denying it,' Smithy said, his hand gripped around an industrial-sized mug of his disgusting brew of coffee. I looked at his white knuckles and feared for the mug's safety.

'Well, he's hardly going to turn around and say, 'Yeah, of course I did it, I confess, now lock me up and throw away the key,' is he?' I refused to stoop to instant coffee and had picked up a takeaway flat white from The Fix on the way back from the hospital. Standards had to be maintained, after all. 'He must realise his usual non-stick coating isn't going to wash this time. He's got everything to lose, so of course he'll go down fighting. And if that fighting involves pulling out the old police-planted-the-evidence card, and other such bullshit, then that's what he'll do.' It was amazing how often that defence reared its ugly head. You'd think the crooks would get a little more inventive and come up with something more imaginative, or at least realise it was the quickest road to pissing us off.

'He's going to walk.'

I looked up at Smithy. Disgust marred his already craggy face.

'What do you mean, he's going to walk?' I said.

'The evidence isn't conclusive enough to arrest him and remand him in custody, so he gets to go and enjoy the sunshine for a while.'

Smithy's voice was carefully even, but even the least attuned person in the universe would have been able to sense his displeasure.

'How was it not conclusive enough?'

'Because the gloves and protective clothing weren't found at the actual scene, and we have to wait for confirmation that the blood all over them was John Henderson's before we can go and do the bizzo.'

'So the fact they were found in a wheelie bin within a kilometre of the scene isn't sufficient to keep him in custody? God, DNA will take weeks to come through. Who decided this?'

'Their lawyers made a song and dance, so your boyfriend and Dickhead Johns backed off.' I tried to ignore the enmity in his voice.

'Well, maybe they were right to.' The look I got from Smithy wasn't very polite. I threw him a 'grow up' look in return. 'If you think about it, we are all desperate to nail Powell after what he did to you and Reihana. This is probably our one and only shot at getting him. The stakes are high. We've got to do this right, so maybe that's the best course of action. That will give us time to examine all the other evidence and make sure that when we do get a warrant for their arrests, the case is cast-iron, rock solid, absolutely crystal-clear perfect, and there will be no way in hell either of them will be able to worm their way out of it. They'll go down for good.'

Smithy drained the last of his coffee then banged the mug on the table with such force the handle sheared straight off. He stood there looking at the now defunct handle gripped in his hand. 'They won't walk away from this one, I'll make sure of it,' he said and stormed out of the room.

19

Gideon Powell was going to be tied up for another hour or two, so we grabbed the opportunity to pop around and visit Mrs Fat Bastard before he had the chance to come home and coach her. Powell's home was a blatant show of wealth that was designed to give a big up-yours to anyone and everyone. It was a grand, flashy affair on the Otago Peninsula perched up on Highcliff Rd, with a stunning view down the harbour towards Port Chalmers. The surrounding countryside was quintessential New Zealand, with the mop-top crowns of cabbage trees standing sentinel above a swathe of flax and toitoi. In stark contrast to the natural beauty, Powell's home was a McMansion straight out of Tackyville with bronzed horse heads on the stone plinth gateposts and Grecian-style urns lining the sweeping car entrance. I wondered if the horse heads were a nod to an infamous Hollywood gangster. Then again, I didn't think Mr Powell was that sophisticated. His security system was, though, with electronic gates topped with cameras barring the way. I half expected to see a couple of semi-rabid Dobermans come running up to snarl and salivate behind the bars. None did though. I pressed the buzzer and waited for a response.

'Who is it?' The accent was Kiwi, but it had a definite plum.

'Detective Shephard and Detective Constable

Richardson of the Dunedin Police.' I held my identification card up to the camera. Smithy was no longer allowed near this case, so I had brought along the latest newbie for company. She was a quiet kind of a girl, the observing kind, but very likeable. 'We'd like to speak with Mrs Angela Powell, please.'

There was a pause.

'Why?'

'We need to ask her a few questions regarding a police investigation.'

Another pause.

'You've already got Gideon. What do you need with me?'

She was direct, I'd give her that, and polite. If it had been her husband talking to us there would have been a string of expletives that would have curled anyone's toes by now.

'We need to verify his whereabouts on Monday, the eleventh of April. Can we come up to the house please?'

There was an even longer pause, and I didn't like our chances.

'Do you have a warrant?' Now those chances looked even more remote.

'No we don't have a warrant. But your cooperation would be helpful, for our investigation and for your husband.'

We waited. After a few minutes the security speaker gave that strange tik-a-tik-a-tik-a noise my computer gave when someone near to it was sending or receiving a text message. Not long afterwards it happened again.

There was a loud buzz and the automatic

gates swung open. She'd acted under advice, then. We drove up to the house, the driveway arcing around the circular lawn with its central cherubic fountain, the spouts of water originating from the parts of the anatomy that small boys loved seeing how far they can shoot from. Classy. We pulled in under the expansive portico protecting the front door.

When I rang the doorbell I wouldn't have been at all surprised if a zoot-suited butler had answered. Instead a beautifully coiffed woman and a pair of ankle-biter Pomeranians did. So there were guard dogs of a sort, but somehow I couldn't bring myself to feel intimidated by these two. They looked like a mobile tripping hazard.

'Hello Mrs Powell, I'm Detective Shephard, and this is Detective Constable Richardson. May we come in?'

She looked down her nose at us, made easier by the fact that she was taller than both of us and had the strategic advantage of higher ground. 'I'd prefer it if you didn't. We can have this conversation here, if you don't mind.'

At least standing on the front doorstep was preferable to having this conversation over the intercom. Angela Powell looked like she paid homage to the Coco Chanel school of personal grooming. She wore a modern take on the little pink suit, a ruffle-necked blouse, unbuttoned enough to show plenty of cleavage, with a long strand of pearls knotted at about nipple level, white sheer tights and white six-inch stilettos. A cigarette in one of those fancy long holders would have completed the look perfectly, as would a pearl barrette in her hair, but she hadn't gone that far. More remarkable was the fact that she looked barely thirty. What the hell was a woman that young and beautiful doing with a revolting piece of humanity like Gideon Powell? Mind you, all you needed to do was look around and you'd see what the attraction was. Many women overlooked glaring physical and emotional relationship inadequacies for the sake of a lifestyle and plenty of baubles. Angela Powell was clearly of that ilk.

'Well, can we get on with it please? I do have other things to do.' She held up her hands and made a show of checking her manicure. What she lacked in foul language she made up for with condescension, and she was very good at it.

'As you are aware, your husband has been helping us with our enquiries into the murder of John Henderson, which occurred on Monday night.' It sometimes amazed me how easily I could slip into cop speak, especially when I had an observer.

'It's not like he had any choice; and I wouldn't exactly call it helping, would you?' she shot back at me.

I smiled. Well, actually, it was more of a grimace. 'He has been answering our questions . . .'

'Until his lawyers told him to stop.' I could see she wasn't going to make this easy so I got straight to the point.

'Where was your husband on Monday night?'

'He was here with me.'

'For the entire evening?'

'Yes.'

'Can you give me more details about what you were doing?'

'Well, seeing as you asked, I was fucking him.' She smiled a smarmy smile. 'So if you have finished, I am busy.' With that she shut the door. I could hear the clip, clip, clip of her heels moving across the polished stone floor.

'Well,' I said to Sonia, who stood gawping beside me. 'What do you think of her?'

'Besides the fact that she's covering up for her husband?' she asked, turning towards me. I nodded. 'That lady is seriously up herself.'

20

Whereas Mrs Angela Powell had aspirations of grandeur, Mrs Sheila Sandhurst was far more what I expected from the wife of a low-life gangster. She looked as hard as nails, with mean, narrow eyes and lank-looking, long, dark hair stringed with grey. When she opened her mouth to speak I could see she was missing a lower front tooth, and those she did possess didn't look too healthy. She was dressed in a pair of jeans that accentuated her skinniness and a black ribbed jersey that did nothing to expel the impression of a junkie. She lit up a cigarette and dragged on it compulsively, her hands fidgeting the whole time.

The Sandhurst house was also quite a grand affair in Roslyn, or at least had been once, before they had managed to put their taint of shabbiness on to it. It looked like the home of people trying to be something they were not.

'What do youse want with me?' she asked. She was trying to act cool and calm, but I could see the flickering of her eyes and I could smell her tension.

'Jacob has been helping us with our investigations, but we need to confirm his whereabouts on the night of Monday, the eleventh of April.'

'Well why don't you just go and ask him?' She took another drag on the ciggy. Her hand had a slight tremor.

'We have, but we need someone to confirm where he was.'

'Well, he was at home with me, so you can bloody well put that down in your notebook.'

Where had we heard this before?

'And you are certain he was home for the entire night? He couldn't have slipped out at any point without your noticing?'

'Are you calling me a bloody liar? God, youse cops are all the same. I told you, he was at home the whole time.'

A likely story, but I didn't push it, because it didn't take a fancy-degree-laden psychologist to figure out that the woman was dead scared of her husband.

21

'Okay, the shotgun information has come through,' Sonia said as she waved at me from across the room. I don't know why she felt the need to wave, but I automatically did a double thumbs up back at her. Any distraction was welcome from my favourite pursuit of report writing.

'Fire away,' I said.

She rolled her eyes at my lame joke. 'It was a Winchester Defender 1300 twelve-gauge pump-action shotgun. Eighteen-inch barrel.'

'Eighteen-inch? That's short. Was it sawn off?'

'No, manufactured length.'

It wasn't for hunting then. 'No wonder it did so much damage,' I said. 'I suppose, with a name like Defender it was probably designed for gun-toting Americans to protect their properties from all those crazies out there, you know, neighbours, humans, pretty much anything that breathes.' I could never fathom the mentality that saw every-thing as a threat, and that the best response was to shoot first, and don't even bother with the questions later.

'Well, this particular weapon was reported stolen in 2010 from a hunting store in Invercargill that was ram-raided.'

'That's a long time for a stolen shotgun to be hanging around before making an appearance.'

'Yeah, you're right. It could have been someone's pet favourite.'

'Could have been. What about the ammunition?' I asked.

'Winchester two-and-three-quarter-inch buckshot. There were still three rounds in the magazine.'

I guessed when you'd just blown someone's head off, there wasn't much need for another go.

'Someone was a little brand conscious, weren't they? Matching the ammo to the brand of gun? A bit like matching your shoes and handbag.'

Sonia laughed. At least someone around here appreciated my sense of humour.

'So the shotgun was found further down on Coast Road than the wheelie bin with the clothing, wasn't it? So they were dumping evidence as they returned to Dunedin,' I said. 'I wonder, if we keep looking along the road, if we'll find the iPhone?'

'Could be worth sending someone out for a look,' Sonia said.

'You volunteering?'

'Nah,' she said, with a big grin. I was really beginning to like her.

'But you're right. I'll mention it to Paul.' He could make that call and run it by the head honcho if necessary. One less chance for me to have my throat ripped out by The Boss. 'I don't know why they just didn't get rid of it all in town. It would be a lot further away from the crime scene for a start, and a lot more places to hide it.'

'Unless they were worried about getting pulled over on the way.'

'Nothing like a healthy paranoia to keep you

out of clink. So, anything linking the gun to the scene?' I asked.

'There was blood evidence on the gun, back spatter on the barrel. It must have been fired close.'

'You've seen the pictures.'

'Urghhh, yes. I can't unsee them.'

'I'll bet you the blood will match that of John Henderson.'

'Not taking you up on that bet,' she said. 'I'm not into losing money. Now if we could only find out who stole that gun in the first place.'

'You'll be lucky. That's one trail that will be stone, cold dead.'

22

This was turning out to be the day of the women, and you couldn't have had a more diverse bunch if you tried. Astrid Allen was turning heads as she walked down the green-carpeted hallway to the interview room. She oozed Audrey Hepburnish elegance, with a figure-hugging, black turtleneck sweater, and a knee-length patterned skirt with a pair of slim, shapely legs poking out of the bottom of it. I was walking behind her, so got to observe every guy coming towards us look first at her chest, then her face, and then turn back for a second look at her butt once they were past her. She was also one of those people who, as she walked, swung her hips in a natural way that declared 'I am Woman', so when the blokes turned back to gawk, I had to dodge around them so they didn't walk into me. I wondered if she ever got tired of the attention. Surely it would wear thin after a while. While they were busy lusting after her, I was busy lusting after her shoes, which were an apple green, with chunky, laminated wooden three-inch heels. I had recently discovered my inner Imelda.

'Thanks for coming in, Astrid,' I said as we settled into our chairs on opposite sides of the interview-room table.

'Have you heard how Jill is today?' she asked. 'I thought I might go along to the hospital and visit her after this.'

'She's having a pretty hard time of it,' I said. 'They operated on her shoulder yesterday. And she's still very upset about everything, probably even more so now it has had time to sink in.'

'I can't even imagine how hard it must be for her,' she said. 'I can't get my head around the idea that John is gone, and in such violent and awful circumstances. I can't stop thinking about it. How would you ever feel safe again after something like that?' It was a damn good question. Your home was supposed to be your castle, a sanctuary. What with the rising number of home invasions over recent years, and a few unpleasant personal experiences, I realised that feeling safe in your home wasn't something you could take for granted.

'The reason I asked you in today is that we have a couple of potential suspects, and we're trying to work out their exact relationship with John. I was wondering if John had ever dealt with a man called Gideon Powell, and another named Jacob Sandhurst.' I could tell by her furrowed brow that he had.

'Mr Powell did come to see John on occasion, every few months or so, nothing regular. I guess his last visit would have been three, four weeks ago.'

'Would you be able to check on the exact date in your appointments diary?'

'He never made an appointment, he would just show up and demand to see John.' The way she said 'demand' suggested the same sort of feelings I'd felt when watching Fat Bastard Powell in the interview room. I could just imagine how arrogant he would have been.

'I'm guessing he wasn't very pleasant.'

'No.' It was a tight-lipped 'no'.

I played a hunch. 'And I'm guessing he made some improper comments or advances towards you.'

'Yes, you could say that.' I imagined it was an occupational hazard and that she had a well-rehearsed arsenal of fend-offs prepared to deal with it. 'He was grubbier than most.'

'Oddly, I have no difficulty in believing that.' In the brief encounter I'd had with him at the station I'd realised he was the kind of man that looked at a woman, mentally stripped her down, assessed her, and then gave her the type of leer that made her feel like going and taking a shower in disinfectant. Well, that was the effect he had on me. I imagined the response he gave the blonde goddess here would have been truly repugnant.

'Do you know what his business was with John?'

'I don't know specifically, and I am well aware of his reputation and supposed business activities.' She looked me in the eye, and it reminded me of the look Jill Henderson had given me, with a sigh of resignation, a few days earlier. 'I respected John, and he was a good employer, but I'm not so stupid as not to realise some of the things he dealt in weren't entirely legitimate. The fact that someone like Powell came to visit at all was evidence enough, but as far as I was concerned, it wasn't any of my business, and he kept me out of anything that wasn't his core trade.'

'So he didn't ask you to do anything that would compromise your ethics?' I asked.

'No,' she said. There wasn't any change in her face, or in the inflection of her voice, no tangible sign, but I knew there was a little undertone of something not quite ringing true there.

'What about Blair Harvey-Boyd? Was he involved in any of these dealings with Powell?'

'Not as far as I'm aware. Powell was clearly a homophobe and antagonistic towards him, so anytime he showed up at work Blair made himself scarce.'

Fat Bastard Powell struck me as the kind of Neanderthal man who saw all homosexual people as deviants and rampant perverts. One who openly flaunted his individuality, like Blair Harvey-Boyd, would have offended his sensibilities. I found it quite gratifying to know that a small and effeminate, well-groomed man probably threatened the hardened criminal mastermind more than any gang-related thug or mob-like henchman, although Powell would never admit to being bothered by him.

'And how did John react to Powell's visits? Did he seem threatened by Powell at all? What kind of relationship did they have?'

'I don't think I ever saw John Henderson threatened by anyone, if that's what you're asking. He was just as businesslike and pleasant with Gideon Powell as he was with anyone else, and his demeanour was the same after Powell left. He didn't seem relieved to see the back of him, or anything like that, so I had the impression they did business as equals.'

My stomach lurched. Given Astrid's calm and astute observations so far I had no reason to doubt this one, which raised a very important question. What sort of business was John Henderson into if he dealt with someone like super-scum-crim Fat Bastard Powell as an equal? And how far into the spectrum of illegal enterprise had he delved? Accounts so far from his friends and colleagues had John Henderson pegged as a well-regarded entrepreneur, a clean-living, suit-and-tie kind of a man. This information forced me to reexamine that impression because, as far as I was concerned, anyone who was even a slight acquaintance of Gideon Powell's was tainted by his nefarious stink and therefore set off alarm bells.

It also helped with the question of motive, because we knew all too well that Gideon Powell was a ruthless kind of a man, and anyone who did something against his wishes, or potentially damaging to his cause, seemed to wind up very, very dead, or at least permanently maimed.

'How did they seem towards each other after their last encounter? Was there any sign of animosity there, any tension you were aware of?' I asked.

'None that I can recall. They were always very cordial towards each other. Although, I have to say that Mr Powell was always a lot better mannered towards me when John saw him out of the office.' The expression on her face said it all.

'Did you mention his inappropriate behaviour to John?'

'Yes, and he responded by saying that dealing with it professionally was part of my job and a good skill to learn, as — how did he put it? — life's full of shits.' She must have seen my eyebrows take a climb up my forehead. 'In his defence, though, after I complained, John always walked Mr Powell out to the front door, so he didn't get the opportunity to be crude.'

'Was Mr Powell always alone when he came calling?'

'Not always. I was going to say before that Mr Sandhurst occasionally came with him.' She visibly shuddered at the mention of that name. My body joined in. I wondered if Sandhurst came along for the ride as the heavy on those occasions? Or the skinny, in his case.

'How did that work? Were those meetings still as cordial or did Sandhurst's presence change the dynamics?'

'I'd say those meetings were as relaxed as the others. If John was bothered by Sandhurst being there, he didn't show it. The overall impression I got was that they had dealings, they seemed to be on an equal footing, and they all got along. Mind you, with Powell's reputation, you'd go out of your way to make sure you got along.'

I wondered how a twenty-something young thing even knew what Powell's reputation was. He was clever enough to keep himself squeaky clean and under the media radar. The vast majority of Dunedin residents would have been blissfully unaware that he and his ilk even existed. We were only too familiar with his operations, however.

I looked her in the eye. 'I'm curious, Astrid. How is it that you're aware of Mr Powell's reputation?'

'It's common knowledge, isn't it?' she said. She looked calm, but a slight blush brushed her cheeks.

'No, not really. Most people wouldn't know anything about that. Had you come across him before?' I asked.

'No, but a few friends of mine who move in different circles were familiar with him. He'd come up in conversation.' She must have some interesting friends, then.

'So you didn't have the impression of any animosity between John and either Powell or Sandhurst?'

'No, none at all. They all seemed very cordial.'

'And had John seemed different, or did he seem concerned with anything in the time leading up to his death?'

'No, nothing out of the ordinary. He seemed relaxed. Everything seemed perfectly normal.'

23

'Okay. So what do we know?' I posed it as a rhetorical question. 'We know there was a definite connection between John Henderson and both Powell and Sandhurst. We know they'd both been regular visitors at John Henderson's business, and these visits were on an unofficial basis. Henderson's PA said these visits were never booked as appointments so weren't logged as such. She also said the men seemed to be on equal terms, which in itself should raise some questions, because I'm buggered if I know of anyone who would be brave or ballsy enough to be on equal terms with those two unless they were just as involved in the criminal underworld. And judging by the fact Henderson is now dead, and that the evidence is pointing straight at the other two, the relationship must have soured for whatever reason.'

Paul and I were sitting with our takeaways, looking down at a fuel ship being guided into the oil jetty from the vantage point of the Unity Park lookout. Daylight savings had recently finished, so we got to enjoy a beautiful dusk with the added bonus of the sparkle of city lights. It was a favourite place to chill and take in the gorgeous expanse of the Dunedin harbour spreading out below. Although it was relatively warm, the southerly wind wasn't very friendly so we were enjoying our dinner in the confines of Paul's car.

Glad it was his, not mine, because he would have to put up with the stunning aroma of stale curry in the morning, not me. Of course the bottom line of all this also meant we were doing that one thing we swore we'd never do — the inevitable pitfall of screwing the crew: talking shop out of hours.

'Did you want the last onion bhajee?' he asked. The question came as he was stuffing it in his mouth.

'No, you have it. Knock yourself out. You can skive off back to your own place later so I don't have to put up with the bhajee farts.'

'Bum.'

'Indeed.' I smiled sweetly at him, and then got back to the matter at hand. 'So we can take it that Powell and Sandhurst's visits weren't social calls.'

'Yeah, well, I don't think they were in there selling Tupperware,' Paul said.

'Er, no.' I smiled and finished the last of my share of the garlic naan. I looked down at the floor of the car and the random scattering of rice and a significant blob of chicken Afghani, and once again gave thanks this was Paul's car and not mine. I also made a mental note, next time we ate dinner in the car, to go for pizza, or fish and chips.

'So why the hell were they there then? I was talking to Billy Thorne from the drug squad, and John Henderson has never featured in any of their dealings; in fact he hasn't so much as blipped on the radar. Billy was just as surprised as we were about the possibility of him being involved in the trade in some way.'

'Perhaps his involvement is relatively new,' I said. 'Astrid Allen had only been working for Henderson for eight months or so. You could check with Blair Harvey-Boyd if the visits had been going on for longer than that.'

'People in that industry are naturally suspicious of newcomers, and from your description of what Astrid said, they had been on pretty friendly terms.'

'Can't have been that friendly — one of them is dead.'

'True. I guess that's a pretty obvious sign you're no longer popular. Perhaps he became a risk, or did something to offend them, which I'm certain wouldn't be difficult to do. It would be a bit like living with a pit bull, or your mother. You never know when they're going to turn and rip your throat out.'

I pretended indignation at the aspersions he cast on my mother, but couldn't keep it up, because they were true. The comment did cause a little pang though. After this, we were heading on down to the hospital to visit Dad. Paul sensed the change and gave me a pat on the knee.

'Sorry,' he said.

'That's okay, and anyway, you're absolutely right, on both counts. There is an element of danger in dealing with these kinds of men that I'm sure John Henderson would have been aware of. I just wish we knew how deep that connection went.'

'Well, it's our job to find out.'

24

The extras were filing into our squadroom for the morning's briefing. Smithy limped past me on the way to his desk. He was moving slowly, even for him, and his face was looking a bit pale.

'You okay?' I asked.

'Yeah. Just the old war wounds giving me gyp today,' He made a half-hearted attempt at a smile. The shadows of his craggy face contrasted with the pallor of his skin, making him look at least ten years older. Courtesy of the potshots taken at him by the minions of Fat Bastard Powell, Smithy had a nice, new artificial kneecap and a seriously munted shoulder. The patch-up job on both injuries hadn't returned him to one hundred per cent fitness, or anything even near it.

'You know, you can stay at home if it's that bad. The last thing we need is a flaming hero pretending to be stoic.' Why was it guys seemed to go to extremes when it came to illness or injury? Either they were complete wimps, like when they got man flu, or they soldiered on regardless of the fact they were bleeding internally, missing a limb, or had an axe sticking out of the back of their head.

'Never give in, never surrender,' he whispered as DI Johns entered the room.

It amazed me how the entrance of DI Johns could silence a room and ratchet up the tension.

I imagined Darth Vader had a similar effect when he arrived somewhere. I half expected someone to start clutching their throat, wrestling with the invisible vice grip. I had to suppress a chortle when he strode to the centre of the room and spun around theatrically. All he needed was the cape. Unfortunately that thought arrived just as he turned to look at me, and it must have manifested on my face.

'What's so funny, Detective Shephard?'

'Nothing, sir,' I said. All eyes turned to me. 'Just something I had been talking about with Detective Smith.'

His eyes flicked to Smithy, who just shrugged.

Bugger. I cursed myself for sticking my head above radar level. Paul gave me a cross-eyed look from the other side of the room and I almost laughed again.

'Right,' said the DI. 'Down to business. Best news of the day: we have confirmation from ESR that the blood found on the gloves and protective clothing recovered from the wheelie bin at Seacliff was of the same type as that of John Henderson. The same blood type and antigens, so as close as we can get until the DNA test results come in.' A collective murmur rippled around the room. I couldn't help but turn and look at Smithy, and neither could half the squad. This time he was sporting a proper smile. 'Likewise, the blood found on the shotgun recovered from the culvert on Coast Road was also confirmed to be the same type as that of John Henderson. The fingerprint and blood evidence is conclusive enough to keep the lawyers happy.'

He held his hand up to quieten the room. 'When we have the required warrant we will be sending out a party to arrest Gideon Powell and Jacob Sandhurst for the murder of John Henderson. I have requested that the Armed Offenders Squad back us up for this as we all know what these men are capable of. We will be making an arrest in this case, but . . . ' he paused for effect; ' . . . this is not the time to get complacent. We still have plenty of work to do. We need to gather further supporting evidence of their involvement in the murder for their day in court. We can assume they will plead 'not guilty'. At this point we have compelling forensic evidence, but we need to establish the whys. The biggest hole we have is motive. We know Henderson had some dealings with Powell and Sandhurst, but we do not know their exact nature. All of you will be aware what is at stake here. In the past we have thought we had Powell nailed, only to have him slip away. He is well resourced and will have the best legal advice his money can afford.' He turned his head to look at me. 'Therefore, we cannot afford any mistakes.' Naturally other people's gazes followed suit.

I looked down at the floor. My little good-news high plummeted. What always made him pick me out for special attention when making comments like that? I had enough trouble being Miss Unpopular around here, without him adding to it. I had been bumped up the detective training ladder a few years back ahead of some police officers who thought they were more deserving. It hadn't gone down too well. Was Dickhead Johns ever going to let me forget it? Probably not. The man sure as hell knew how to hold a grudge. It also appeared he'd taken it upon himself to be chairman of the Anti-Sam Uncharitable Trust.

'We want to see these men behind bars, where they belong, and for a very long time. I am aware one or two here have a very personal stake in this.' I sensed Smithy tense up. 'So don't take offence if you are excluded from elements of the investigation. We have to get this right.' Okay, that was different, he was on a charm offensive, then. He never apologised in advance, which could only mean one thing. I was going to get the shit jobs again.

25

'You can't take it personally, Smithy.'

'That's great coming from you,' he said.

Considering how much I'd been pouting, he had a point. Smithy had been left out of the arrest party. As a matter of fact, we'd both been sidelined by DI Johns. Perhaps he was worried Smithy's elbow might just come into contact with the suspects' faces and my pepper spray might accidentally deploy. Whatever his reasoning, even I had to admit there may have been a rather enormous conflict of interest on Smithy's part, and — just for a change — I'd drawn the short straw and had to babysit him.

'Hey, you were warned, remember. Surely you can't say you're surprised?'

He muttered something very rude about the parentage of the DI that I couldn't argue with. But I suspected that what grated the most for him was that Paul had been included. His whole Paul-hating routine was starting to get a bit tired.

We had pulled up outside the house of some two-bit thug who had poked his head above radar level by allegedly — God I hated that politically correct, lawyer-pandering word — breaking into a pharmacy to steal pseudoephedrine, used for making P, aka Crystal Meth. Unfortunately for our rocket scientist here, he'd hit two problems. Firstly, security systems are there for a reason, and if you're going to hit a business only five hundred metres from the alarm-monitoring centre, people are going to be on the scene pretty damn fast. And — probably more annoying for him — like most places, the pharmacy didn't stock products containing pseudoephedrine anyway, because they were sick of their staff being hassled by druggie scum trying to acquire it, and sick of having dumb-nuts smash their windows to get to it. So he got caught for nothing. Real bright. He was, by all accounts, trying to wiggle into the drug scene, although from outside the gangs. More by luck than design, he hadn't actually done anything to end up in clink for the past few years. That was about to change shortly, courtesy of his latest display of poor job planning.

For the purposes of DI Johns' current agenda, we'd been loaned to the drug squad for the morning. Whoop-de-doo.

'Why are we here again?' Smithy asked.

'Because the Dickhead hates us,' I replied.

'Oh, that's right. Thanks for reminding me.'

The moment we stepped onto the property, some scungy-looking, underfed excuse for a dog came charging around the corner. It looked like the usual pit bull-Staffordshire terrier cross kept by people who wanted a friendly family pet but with an intimidation factor and a mad-as-a-meat-axe mentality. It came bounding up to Smithy, snarling and barking, saliva dripping off of its canines. I hovered back by the gate, figuring out where I was going to run. Smithy looked unmoved and responded by giving it a swift kick right on the chest bone. The thing yelped and scuttled back around the house. So much for the big scary guard dog.

The house was your classic wooden state house, the two-storeyed type they generously described as an English bungalow. The lawns had been mowed recently, well within the last few months, because the grass under the festering car body was a foot tall, as opposed to the rest of the place where it was only three or four inches high. There was some washing on the line, hanging limp. It was one of those Dunedin days where the laundry would be as wet when you brought it in as it was when you hung it out.

Smithy strode up and banged on the front door. He chose the frosted-glass panel that wasn't already cracked.

The figure that came to the door picked us for cops immediately. I could see his posture change from 'yeah, what?' to 'what the fuck do you want?'. He was a very fit-looking man in his forties, as evidenced by the muscular body underneath the tight, white singlet top. He also wore blue jeans and boots, and with his clean-shaven face and slicked-back black hair, looked like a man who cared about his grooming. He was a cowboy minus the Stetson.

'Jimmy Clarke?'

'Yeah, what of it?'

'Detectives Smith and Shephard.'

His eyes narrowed and his lip curled up a fraction.

'What do you want? I've already made my statement to the cops and got my court date. I've got nothing else to say.'

'Oh, I would have thought that a guy with a court case looming and jail term inevitable would be a little more polite than that.'

Smithy was going in a bit hard. The guy hadn't sworn at us yet, so I was thinking he'd been perfectly well mannered.

'Well what do you want, then?'

'We want to know what you can tell us about Mikey Chadwick's activities?'

'Who's Mikey Chadwick when he's at home?'

'Who's Mikey Chadwick? You're funny. Now, don't mess with me, you know bloody well who Mikey Chadwick is. Don't even consider fucking me around.'

Jesus, Smithy was playing it tough. I was dying to give him a sideways look, but I didn't dare. You never undermined your colleague's authority by questioning their business practice. Well, not in front of the thugs, anyway.

'Hey, there's no need to speak to me like that, bro. Like I said, I have no idea who you are talking about.'

'You're lying. I don't appreciate being lied to. So I'm going to ask you again, and if you aren't going to cooperate, I'll haul your sorry arse down to the station and then we'll see how good your bloody memory is.' Smithy had stepped forward and pretty much filled the doorway.

To his credit, Mr Muscles stood his ground, and stayed civil, although that was looking like it might well change.

'Look, mate,' he said, crossing his arms, 'I know my rights, and you can't just come around here and talk to me like that. So you get yourself off my property before I ring your superiors and complain about harassment, because this is not on. I do not know who Mikey Chadwick is. Good day, officers.' With that he calmly swung the door closed, an inch from Smithy's nose.

'That fucking piece of shit,' Smithy said, and banged his fist hard against the door frame. I saw a crack in the window pane snake a little further up the glass.

'Smithy, come away.' I pulled his arm, and it was a few seconds before he budged.

When I thought we were well out of earshot I said my piece. 'What is wrong with you? There was no need to talk to him like that. Any chance we had of him talking went out the window when you went in hard.'

'He knew damn well who Mikey Chadwick was.'

'Probably, but you didn't help matters any. You're so grumpy.' I looked at the sheen of sweat across his forehead and the ginger way he was walking. 'If you're that flaming sore, you should have stayed at home instead of coming in and taking it out on everyone. At least go take a pill or something.'

It was a very frosty drive back to the station.

26

It was a relief to get away from the walking storm cloud that was Smithy, even if it meant doing something I didn't exactly relish. The Boss had sent me back along to the hospital to harangue our witness. I wouldn't have blamed her if she hated the sight of me by now. Still, it was better than the alternative with grumpy-guts.

Jill Henderson was, to be honest, looking worse than the last time I'd visited. She'd had her shoulder surgery, which had gone well, and her bruises were starting to yellow and fade, but I couldn't help but think she seemed more fragile than ever. The emotional wounds were taking their toll. I hoped the hospital had arranged some sort of counselling for her, because she looked like she needed it.

'I'm sorry to be back here again with some more questions, Jill,' I said, as I lowered myself onto the chair next to her bed. 'But I can tell you we are making great progress on John's case. In fact, they are making arrests as we speak.'

Her face brightened at the same time as two big tears tracked down her face. I reached behind the bouquet of flowers on her bedside table to the tissue box and passed it over to her.

'Thank you, that's great news,' she said as she dabbed at her eyes, and then blew her nose.

'I need to ask you a few questions about the men we are arresting.'

'Yes, of course,' she said.

I could see her visibly steel herself for the questions and felt a momentary pang of guilt for putting her through this again, but in the long term the goal was to see justice done and to help her come to terms with the death of her husband.

'Did you or John know of a Gideon Powell or a Jacob Sandhurst?'

I could see a frown dart across her face. 'Are they the men you have arrested for John's murder?' she asked, her voice hoarse.

I nodded. 'We need to figure out what their connection was with John. Had you met them before, or had John mentioned them?'

'Their names seem familiar, but I don't think I have met them. Perhaps John had talked about them. Were they something to do with his business?' She shook her head, and looked even more miserable, if that was possible. 'I'm not entirely sure. I'm sorry, I'm not much help to you, am I?' She started quietly weeping again. I seemed to specialise in setting her off. I think I was as much over this whole questioning business as she was. Boy, those bastards had a lot to answer for. Them and Dickhead Johns.

'Look, Jill, you're doing fine. You've survived a horrendous experience, so don't expect too much of yourself. Let me show you some pictures of them, see if it jogs your memory.'

If she was already crying, what was a bit more? I placed the pictures down on the tray table, next to her cup of tea. They weren't particularly flattering shots — police mugshots never were.

111

Like passport photos; no one ever smiled in mugshots. In fact, most of the time people were pretty much pissed off with requiring a new and special portrait. In this case, the sheer malevolence on their faces, combined with a good amount of five o'clock shadow, made the two men look like gangsters or terrorists — take your pick. She glanced at them, then looked quickly away, her eyes scrunching closed.

'You recognise them?' I asked

'I have seen them before.'

'Where?'

'I'm sorry, I can't be sure, just somewhere. I can't think.' Her voice cracked and she raised her hand to shield her eyes from the pictures. I could see watery rivulets wend their way below her fingers. I picked the photos up, slid them back into my folder and put the whole thing beneath the bed, out of her view.

'I know this is really difficult for you, and I'm very sorry to have to keep asking you questions, but in order to ensure justice for John and for you we need information, as much information as we can get. Can you recall where you might have seen these men? And when? Was it at your home, at John's work, socially?'

She looked back around at me, her face haggard, eyes puffy and red. She looked like she'd aged ten years in the last few days. 'It must have been at John's work. They haven't been to the house, I'm sure of that. I'd remember if they had. I don't think we would have been out anywhere socially with them, not with men who could do a thing like that.'

112

She had no idea exactly what kind of men they were. If she had known she would have been appalled to think her husband had anything to do with them. But the fact remained that he did; he was doing some kind of business with them and it got him killed, and almost killed his wife. I just wished I knew what it was.

27

Paul strode into the office and threw his keys at his desk. It wasn't an underarm toss, it was a full-throttle, overarm pitch. The sharp clatter of metal on wood jolted all my senses. The keys ricocheted off the surface and then continued on their journey through the air and to the floor, via a big clunk against the wall. He'd got our attention. Smithy stared at where the keys landed, then slowly turned his gaze to the source.

'That was real grown-up. I take it things didn't go well?' I said.

'Bugger it.' I'd never seen him this agitated. 'Shit, bugger and fuck it.' He was pacing now. 'The bastard has done a runner.'

'Who?' I asked, although you didn't need a degree in crystal-ball-gazing to know what he was going to say next. Judging by the abrupt thrust of hands onto the desk next to me, Smithy's clairvoyant skills were as sharply honed as mine.

'Bloody Powell,' Paul said as he sat heavily on the corner of his desk.

There was a moment of silence before Smithy lumbered to his feet. 'You're telling me we've finally got the evidence to nail that murdering bastard, and you bunch of Nancy girls can't even find him?'

Going by the airborne keys incident and the look on Paul's face, I could tell that his normal unflappable composure had been marginally flapped. Smithy's face did not require further interpretation.

'Hey, it's no one's fault,' I said in an attempt to placate the two aggrieved egos. 'Powell has been in the business long enough and survived enough close calls to know when his number's up, so it's small wonder he's gone to ground. Did you actually think he was going to give up easy?'

Smithy gave me a scathing look. 'That would be right — defend your useless prick boyfriend, won't you? We all know where your loyalties lie.' God, his mood hadn't improved any from this morning — he was still as tetchy as hell. Paul looked like he was about to respond in kind, so I threw him a 'don't bother' look and returned my attention to Smithy.

'Don't be an ass, Smithy.' Just because he was sore and grumpy didn't mean he could take it out on everyone else. We were all as anxious as he was about this arrest. 'You know damn well this was a likelihood. If it were you in Powell's position, would you stick around? No, I didn't think so. We'll find him. He's too big and New Zealand is way too small for him to hide for long. And I'm sure there are plenty of his business opposition out there who would be only too pleased to dob him in should the occasion arise.' It was a dog-eat-dog world, after all, and Powell had amassed a lot of enemies. I turned back to Paul, who was still looking a bit dark on it. 'What about Sandhurst? Have they arrested him yet?'

He shook his head. 'That crew aren't back

with him yet, and it's been a while so I'd be guessing not.'

So the Fat Bastard and The Cockroach had scarpered.

Shit.

28

DI Johns was walking around with what seemed like a low-pressure weather system surging ahead of him. Even the big boys were making excuses to vacate the building and get out of his path. I decided this was a wise strategy so headed for the stairwell with a mind to escape. I had lugged open the fire escape door when I heard the heart-stopping call from behind me.

'Shephard!'

It was tempting to pretend I didn't hear him, but considering the staff in the watchhouse could probably hear him four floors down, I didn't think I'd get away with it. I let the door swing closed and turned around.

'Sir?'

'Where are you at with the Henderson woman?'

'I saw her this morning and enquired as to her knowledge of Powell and Sandhurst.'

'And?'

'She knew of them, recognised Powell from a photograph, but wasn't sure where from.'

'That's not good enough.' He hadn't lowered his voice any, despite our proximity. 'I need more certainty than that.'

'Well she is still in quite a fragile state, sir. I couldn't press her on it too much.' I was about to remind him of the fact she'd witnessed her husband being murdered and had just had surgery when he interjected.

'I don't care what state she is in. We need every bit of information we can get. You get back down there and find out more, Detective.' The way he spat out the last word left me in no doubt as to how much he felt I merited the title. 'Go down and question her again. Stay there until she gives us the information we need. I don't care how long it takes you. Go and do your bloody job properly this time.'

With that he turned and stormed off down the corridor.

I stared daggers into the space between his shoulder blades, willing them to twitch, until he disappeared out of sight around the corner.

'Heartless bastard,' I said as I flipped him the fingers.

I did go to the hospital, but I didn't obey orders. There was no way in hell I was about to go back into that woman's room and tell her that a) we hadn't managed to apprehend the bastards who killed her husband, and then b) The Boss was insisting that I stay there and grill her until her memory managed to cough up the right information. I'd already worked on my story in case Dickhead Johns decided to follow up on it. I was going to say that Jill Henderson had been taken down to the X-ray department and they didn't know how long she was going to be. I'd go back and talk to her in the morning. Easy. Hopefully a night of drug-induced sleep would help both her state of wellbeing and her memory.

For some stupid reason my other appointment at the hospital had given me a case of the butterflies in my stomach. However, they disappeared the moment I saw Mum, Steve and Sheryl waiting for me at a table in the foyer café.

Mum looked dead on her feet. She didn't have bags under her eyes, she had haversacks, and I felt a little pang inside at the thought of what she was going through right now. Steve stood up and gave me a crush of a man hug. It was good to see him.

'Hiya, sorry I'm late.' I leaned down and gave Mum a kiss on the cheek, then Sheryl, before I sat down. They'd already ordered coffees and looked like they'd been picking away at the muffins on their plates. Mum must have been feeling bad because she didn't make a comment about my tardiness.

'You made it?' I said to Steve. 'Have you got someone to look after the farm?'

'Just a day trip, I'm afraid. I'm heading back later.' That would make for a big day all around, and like the rest of us his eyes were bearing the hallmarks of tiredness.

'How's Dad doing this afternoon?' I asked.

Mum and Sheryl looked at each other before Sheryl spoke.

'They're transferring him over to the hospice later today. They've got a space there for him now.'

It wasn't unexpected — we all knew this was pretty much a one-way ticket for Dad now — but still, that seemed pretty final.

'Has he deteriorated?'

'He's not improving. He'll be a lot more comfortable there. The rooms are so much nicer

119

and more private than in the hospital, and they'll do a better job of controlling his pain, I think.'

'How's he feel about it? He understands what's going on?'

'You know your dad,' Mum said. 'He doesn't like to be a bother, so he's protesting a bit, but I think he's pleased at the thought of getting out of here.'

I looked at the sag of Mum's shoulders and the state of her normally immaculate hair, and felt a little guilty at my less-than-charitable thoughts about her earlier. I'd been here for a full two minutes and she hadn't fired a barb at me. It was all taking its toll.

'When are they transferring him?' I asked. If I kept asking about the details then I wouldn't run the risk of losing it myself.

'They said around four o'clock,' Sheryl said.

'Do they have set visiting hours, or can we come and go as we please?'

'They are completely flexible. Trust me, it will be so much better at the hospice. I know some of the staff there. They are wonderful.' For once I felt pleased Sheryl was there, and thankful for her gentle reassurance.

'So you're actually planning to visit us down there, are you?'

I turned, my heart sinking at Mum's question. 'Of course I am, why wouldn't I?'

'Well you seem so busy with your work I was beginning to think Dad wasn't a priority for you.'

I felt a wave of heat rush up into my face. Was that what she thought? That I didn't have the time to come and see my own dad? I was about to bite back when I saw the embarrassed look on Sheryl's face and realised that, no, this was just Mum projecting her own fears and I was the nearest live target. She was hurting. Don't bite.

'Hopefully you'll manage to spend a bit more time with us down there than you have here. Well, I hope so, because it's too hard having to try and explain to your dad why you don't want to see him,' Mum said as she looked away from me and in the general direction of the wards. She couldn't have orchestrated the tears better. Lavishing on the guilt. Knowing it was her fear and grief speaking didn't prevent the pang in my chest.

She just couldn't resist.

29

'Declan, how are you doing?' I noticed Henderson junior as I walked out of the hospital entranceway. I had to dodge around a couple of smokers to get to him. One of them was attired in his classy hospital gown and dragging his intravenous drip stand with him. He stopped and took up his post under the smoke-free zone sign. The definitive diehard smoker.

'All right, I suppose,' he said, shuffling his feet and looking embarrassed in the way only a gangly teenage boy could manage.

'You off to see your mum?' Rhetorical question really, but if I'd learned anything about teenagers, it paid to keep it simple and state the obvious. Well, to a point — there was a fine line between being friendly and communicative, and coming across as plain, old dumb.

'Yeah . . . ' He paused, like he was going to say something else and then changed his mind. He shoved his hands into his pockets and swayed backward and forward on his heels.

'Are you a bit worried about her?' I asked. 'I didn't think she seemed too good this morning. How'd she seem to you? You've been up already?'

'She seems to be getting worse, not better,' he said, the relief at the opportunity to voice the thought apparent in his eyes. I couldn't imagine how hard it must be for him right now. He'd stumbled across that appalling scene in his own home, seen his father's devastated body and was mourning that loss, and the one person he needed to turn to right now was too tied up coping with her own physical and emotional pain to be able to support him. 'The doctors don't seem to be helping her much. Well, they are with surgery and stuff, but it's like she's, well, I suppose it's like shellshock, isn't it? Like soldiers get? Or post-traumatic stress, or whatever? Whenever I see her she seems to cry more. Can't they give her something for that?'

A hell of a lot of Valium, wine and plenty of time was the thought that came to mind, but somehow I didn't think that was what the professionals would be prescribing.

'They'll be treating her the best they can. But if you're concerned, you should go and talk to one of the doctors. They will listen to you. Your grandad can ask them too. You don't have to just sit back and watch.' I wondered how much care he was getting. Those narrow shoulders seemed to be hefting a hell of a load. 'Have you been offered any counselling at all, to talk about everything that's happened?'

'They had this nice guy from Victim Support, and they've given me an appointment with a shrink. I don't know if I want to go, though.'

'I really think you should. It makes a difference. In fact, I'll check up on you and make sure you go. Believe me, the last thing you want is me nagging you and being on your case.'

He smiled at my playful threat. Even though he was only seventeen he was a good foot taller than me.

'S'pose so.'

A thought suddenly popped into my mind out of the blue. It happened occasionally. 'Actually, Declan, do you mind if I ask you a couple of quick questions about the case?'

He looked around at all the people coming in and out and shrugged. 'Okay.'

I ushered him further along the footpath, towards the children's pavilion, so we couldn't be overheard.

'I was wondering if you had heard of a couple of men: Jacob Sandhurst and Gideon Powell.'

He looked blank, as though nothing was clicking.

'Perhaps if I showed you some photographs of them?'

He nodded.

Fortunately I still had their mugshots in my satchel. I fossicked around before getting my hands on the right pieces of paper.

He pointed his fingers at both of them. 'They do look familiar,' he said. 'In fact I think they've been out to the house. I think Dad had them around once, or something.'

'Are you certain?' I asked. When I'd showed the pictures to Jill she'd said they had never been out to the house. Mind you, her memory probably wasn't that reliable at the moment. 'How long ago would that have been?'

'Recently. Within the last month or so.'

'Was your mum home then?'

'Ah, I don't know. Dad introduced them to me, but I didn't pay that much attention. I think I was on the X-Box at the time, so I couldn't say.'

Suitably vague. But it did confirm that both men had been at the house, and yet the two of them had denied ever being there. Bloody liars. These webs of deceit always caught up with you in the end, so it was another nail in the coffin for them, as it were.

'Thanks, Declan. That's great — really helpful. But I will need you to pop down to the station and make a formal statement about it. Can you do that later today?'

He looked embarrassed, yet also a little pleased to have been some help. 'Sure.'

30

Paul wasn't the only one in an almighty snit about the lack of arrests.

'What did that woman say?' The voice boomed from the doorway.

I jumped in my seat. I'd been concentrating so hard on the report before me, my anti-arsehole radar hadn't picked him up. Sonia started so badly I thought she'd get whiplash. Her wanker-watch defence systems clearly still needed fine-tuning.

'Sorry, sir?'

'What did Jill Henderson give us?' He said it real slow, like I was stupid.

'She wasn't there when I called in, they'd taken her down for some X-rays.' I hoped I was convincing.

He narrowed his eyes. 'You didn't wait?'

'She had only just gone, and the nurse said it could take up to an hour, so I thought it would be a better use of time to come back here and do some work.' I impressed myself with that line. Surely he couldn't argue with that. I briefly toyed with the idea of mentioning Declan's revelation, but decided in the interests of safety to wait until his statement was signed, sealed and delivered.

The Boss did some subterranean grumbling and then looked from me to Sonia and then back again. 'You two look like you need some real work to do. Go and find out where they bought those masks from.'

'Haven't the regulars done that already?' I asked.

'Sorry, was that you just answering back, Detective Shephard?' God, he was in a right shitty liver. 'I will repeat myself, for the sake of the stupid. Go and find out where those pieces of shit bought those masks.'

I looked at Sonia. She looked at me.

'Now!' he bellowed.

We listened as his footsteps diminished into the distance.

Sonia expelled a large breath. 'Boy, is he always such an arsehole?'

'Yes,' I said, and then added, 'but not so much to the men,' and left it at that.

★   ★   ★

We were down in Lucky Coins, the shop containing the biggest collection of cheap, mass-produced, made-in-China crap you could find on the streets of Dunedin. And as usual it was packed full of people who lived for cheap, mass-produced, made-in-China crap. They all looked glazed over and ecstatic, like they were in the grip of some religious trance, worshipping the almighty god of junk. Ooh, plastic. These shops weren't my most hated kinds of stores; my most hated were second-hand shops, but only just. I normally avoided these loose-change shops like the plague. There was something about the claustrophobic, teetering, packed-to-the-gunwales aisles, and the smell, with its hint of chemical acridity. You could almost smell the carcinogens.

Sonia was looking at a fluorescent-pink lei

garland. She held it up against her face.

'What do you think? Is it me?'

'Nah, I think you should go for the lime-green feather boa.'

On the shelf above the high-class neckwear was a selection of masks. They ranged from the political — Donald Trump and Vladimir Putin; to the cartoonish — Winnie-the-Pooh and Piglet; to the positively creepy — wart-ridden witches, eyeball-drooping zombies and a familiar and shudder-inducing clown.

'Eureka,' I said and pointed up to the clown. I could never look at clowns the same after reading Stephen King's *It*. That had spoiled them for good.

'There are at least a dozen of them there,' she said. 'I wonder how common they are.' She reached up and grabbed one, saving my short-arsed self the embarrassment of having to ask. I liked this woman.

'Time to have a wee chat to the shopkeeper.'

The Asian girl behind the counter looked all of fourteen years old, but I assumed that seeing as it was a school day, and the local truancy officers were pretty vigilant, she must have been at least eighteen.

'Can I help you?' she asked with a perfect Kiwi accent. I smiled at myself for being surprised.

'Hi. Detectives Shephard and Richardson, Dunedin Police.' I gave Sonia a promotion for the day. 'We were wondering if you would have kept a record of sales of this particular mask over, say, the last three months? We need the information for an ongoing investigation.'

She shook her head slowly. 'No, we wouldn't. Items like that just go under the 'costumes' button. So they wouldn't show up individually. We have too much variety to have every product entered individually.' Shop-speak for way too much crap.

'Do you sell many of them?'

'Actually, they're one of our most popular masks, after Trump. We'd probably sell a dozen or so a week. People seem to like them for kids' birthday parties.'

The sadistic sods must have liked scaring their kids then. It wasn't my idea of entertainment.

'I take it you have security cameras?' I had spotted two cameras on our little recce of the shop; one was pointed right down the costumes aisle. That one had the rather amusing, handwritten 'smile for the camera' sign pinned, crooked, to the wall immediately below it.

'Yes, there are; three I think. My boss is the one in charge of those and he's not in until tomorrow, but I'm sure he'd help you out if there was something specific you were looking for.'

That was great for us, and bad for us. Great as it meant there would be three different angles of the shop and months' worth of recordings, and bad for us because it meant we would have to sit through months' worth of recordings. But if those two thugs had been in here to get masks, we'd spot them. The boredom would be worth the evidence supporting the fact they planned this thing to the nth degree.

'Okay, thanks for your help. We'll call in

tomorrow, then. Does your boss have a card?'

'I think so.' She pulled open a drawer and started ferreting around, before producing a rather cheap-looking business card. I handed her one of my flash ones. I still got a buzz about seeing my name with 'Detective' in front of it, printed alongside the police insignia. One of those cheap thrills. The thrill didn't last long though, because this was only the first coin shop we'd been in, and there were several more to go.

31

I felt like I was tiptoeing down the hallway of the hospice. It was quiet, but in a peaceful kind of a way, not that horrid, echoey hospital-like way. This place felt light and airy and it seemed to ooze a calm solidity.

'Your dad is in here. Your mum and Sheryl are with him,' the nurse said as she guided me to his room.

'Thanks,' I said and poked my head around the corner.

I wasn't sure what I was expecting, but this wasn't it. It seemed too normal. If you didn't know you were in a hospice, this could have been mistaken for a cosy bedroom in anybody's house, with a view out to a garden, a couple of arm-chairs, pretty art prints on the walls, a bedside table, and a man looking like he was sleeping peacefully in the midst of it. The only giveaways were the occupants of the chairs: my mother, looking grim, and Sheryl, looking like she was trying to ungrim Mum.

'Hi guys,' I said and went over to give Mum a kiss on the cheek, then Sheryl, followed by Dad on the forehead. His skin felt papery under my lips and I noted a little frown furrowed between his brows.

'This is a nice room,' I said, by way of breaking the ice.

'It's a vast improvement on the hospital, that's

for sure,' Sheryl said.

'How is he?' I asked, looking at what seemed a tiny form tucked under the blankets. His days of being a strapping, strong farmer seemed a very distant memory. His spindly arms looked like they wouldn't have been capable of lifting a pillow, let alone throwing a hay bale. He hadn't been eating or drinking for a few days, and I noted they hadn't set up a drip for fluids. Since he was here, there wasn't any point.

'The move seems to have tired him out. He's been asleep the whole time here. He won't rouse,' Sheryl said, and I could plainly see the affection tinged with sadness in her expression. 'The staff are tweaking his medication because they think he is still in some pain. They've put him on a syringe driver so he gets twenty-four-hour coverage and they're increasing his morphine dose slightly. They're doing their best to make him comfortable.'

The thought of him being in pain was unbearable. I looked again at the marked furrow between his brows.

'Have you heard from Mike? When's he coming over?' It must have been hard for my brother to be getting updates second-hand. But I knew his work meant he had to leave off coming from Melbourne as late as possible. I only hoped he hadn't left it too late.

'Yeah, he's flying in tomorrow.'

I softened my voice. 'How are you going, Mum?'

She looked at me, went to open her mouth, and then closed it again before turning towards Dad, a big tear lolling its way down her cheek.

32

My first duty for Friday morning was to attend the funeral of John Henderson. I was there both to support Jill and to represent the New Zealand Police. It wasn't often I got to dust off my dress blues nowadays, and I always felt a special kind of pride when I pulled them on. A few of my colleagues were here too. Naturally DI Johns was one of them, in his dress uniform, because the media were certain to be here. Cynical, wasn't I? Dunedin had turned it on with a stunning autumn day, azure sky and a light, warm, scented breeze. It seemed incongruous with the occasion. Weddings should have sunshine, funerals should have rain, as far as I was concerned. In my experience the weather turned arse about face way too often. No amount of frantic praying from stressed-out brides had swung it in fair fortune's favour at the weddings I'd been to.

It was always interesting to observe who came out for these events, and events they were. High-profile murders always brought a huge crowd, and there were at least five hundred people here. The church was chocka. I didn't pick John Henderson as a religious man, particularly with his line of business, but then it was amazing how many people found a new reliance on God to get through dark times. If I was in Jill's position I would have clutched at every bit of comfort available, too, although personally I would have been expecting to be struck down by lightning for hypocrisy.

I looked around at the faces in the crowd. I often wondered if half as many people would have come out if the dearly departed had shuffled off this mortal coil courtesy of a heart attack, or choking on dinner. I also wondered how many professional mourners came along to these things just so they could get a free cup of tea and some savouries. I wouldn't have had the cheek. According to the newspaper one of the big local funeral homes had to have a wee word to a regular only recently, especially after he started filling his pockets with the food. There were a number of familiar faces. Blair Harvey-Boyd was here, resplendent in expensive black. The tall, bald chap on his arm must have been Mr Chingford-Owen — Gregory, not Greg.

Even though Astrid Allen's mourning attire was tasteful and demure, leaving only her hands and face uncovered, she still managed to turn every male head in the room. Well, with the exception of the Harvey-Boyd-Chingford-Owenses.

What did surprise me, though it shouldn't have really, was the presence of a few people of interest to our Organised Crime Squad. It could have been coincidence — Dunedin could be a small town and everyone seemed to know everyone — but I didn't think so. John had many secrets, it would seem. They would be followed up later — this wasn't quite the right time.

All eyes turned to Jill and Declan Henderson. Jill had only been discharged from hospital the previous day. She was putting on a brave face. It must have been a phenomenal effort for her to walk up that aisle, and she leaned heavily on her son. She looked very much the glamorous widow, but while the makeup hid the last of the bruises, it couldn't hide the gaunt and agonised appearance of her face. Declan stood tall and straight in his suit. I could see plenty of his mates in school uniform were here to support him too.

Everyone was asked to rise. It was time to pay our respects.

33

The hunt was still on for Gideon Powell and
Jacob Sandhurst. Declan's statement that they
had previously been to the Henderson house,
despite claiming otherwise, added to the growing
mountain of evidence against them. Regular
police were out door-knocking at their favourite
haunts again, and being a little more insistent
than they had been the day before. There was
nothing like the funeral of a murder victim being
plastered all over the television news to give
everyone a sense of urgency; that and having The
Boss giving us all a kick up the arse. According
to border control, neither of them had tried to
leave the country. Not that they needed to. There
were plenty of backwater places to lose yourself
in New Zealand, especially down this end of the
country. We were having a mild autumn, Indian
summerish, so it wouldn't even be too unpleasant if they decided to go bush for a while.

Paul had been busy interviewing Angela
Powell that morning, while some of us were off
funeraling. He gave me a rather entertaining
version of events. Surprise, surprise, she was still
playing the good little gangster wife: swearing
her husband's innocence and vowing not to have
any knowledge of where he was. Such dedication
in one so young. Most admirable. Paul had referred
to her as the Trumped-up Trophy Tramp. It actually suited her quite well.

I had the dubious pleasure of keeping Smithy out of people's way for the afternoon. Since when did I become the designated babysitter? I took him for a trot into town to see if the owner of Lucky Coins was in residence. Smithy was unusually quiet, and clearly out of sorts. He even missed the opportunity to hassle and move along his favourite unlicensed busker from Albion Lane. Two-tone, as we nicknamed him, couldn't believe his luck. He'd seen us coming and begun gathering up the coins scattered in the bottom of his dinged-in, moth-eaten excuse for a guitar case, but I don't think Smithy even noticed him. I could see the gap-toothed smile flit across the guy's face as we walked past him. He gave me a questioning look. I just shrugged and smiled. It was his lucky day. By the time Smithy and I reached George Street, the semi-rhythmic strumming and seriously flat singing had started up again, extra loud. Why the hell people gave him money, I'd never know. It only encouraged him, for heaven's sake. I was glad I wasn't a shop-keeper around there.

Lucky Coins had its usual throng of students and mums with pushchairs admiring the crap. The girl I'd talked to the previous day was on duty again, and as soon as she saw me she waved and reached over to press a buzzer. A few minutes later a man in his mid-twenties appeared from a room off to the right. The shopgirl pointed us out to him and he came straight over.

I did the introductions. 'Hi. Detectives Shephard and Smith. We would like to ask you a few questions that relate to an ongoing investigation.'

'Hi, I'm Robert Chang.' He reached out and shook our hands with a limp-fish grip. 'Susie told me you'd called by yesterday.' Unlike his employee, Robert had a very pronounced Chinese accent, but like Susie, he also seemed very young. Mind you, I thought, age was no barrier to an entrepreneurial streak, as long as you had the resources to set yourself up. I wondered if he'd started out as a student here at the university and then moved on to bigger, brighter things. It wouldn't have taken too much capital to set this up, and the stock value wouldn't be massive, it was all cheap junk anyway.

'Would you like to come into my office?' I followed him, but noticed I'd lost Smithy to the kids' toys section. He was probably better out of the way.

The office was as big a mess as the rest of the place. We sat at a cheap veneer table that was covered with an array of dirty, floral-patterned mugs.

'Sorry about the mess,' he said, but he didn't look it. 'What can I help you with?'

'We're trying to confirm the identity of a person or persons who may have come in here and purchased two of your clown masks. Susie explained to us yesterday that your till records are too general to help, but I was wondering about your video surveillance cameras and how far back your recordings go?'

Robert blushed and looked a little embarrassed.

'Is there a problem with that?' I asked.

'Yes, a little.' He wriggled in his seat. 'The cameras are there from the previous business, but I haven't actually connected them up to the computer system here yet. I am going to; in fact I have a man coming next week to do it. We have a bit of a shoplifting problem, you see. It's not too bad because I have a few staff who wander around, and big signs pointing out the cameras.'

I resisted the urge to roll my eyes.

'Is it for something serious?' he asked. Like we'd be here if it wasn't?

'Yes, it is actually,' I said.

The annoyance must have shown in my voice because he leaned forward and almost whispered, 'Really, very serious ?'

That little urge I got to slap dorks started my hand a-twitching.

'Yes, a murder inquiry.'

He looked at me intently, then got up and slowly closed the office door, but not before having a good look around the shop to see if he had been observed. It was very theatrical, very Secret Squirrel.

'I've got something that might help, but you can't tell anyone.'

'And why would that be?'

'Because I don't want staff to know.' The expression on my face spurred him to elaborate. 'Look, I haven't been having too many problems with shoplifting — everyone has that, it's small-time. But I have had a big problem with staff stealing.' I thought of freshfaced Susie out there and wondered if she'd had her hand in the till. 'I got a private detective in, and he's put in a secret camera, right above the till. That might be able to help; but the whole apparatus is hidden in the ceiling space, and I'd have to get him to come down after hours and get the footage.' That explained the secrecy.

'That could be very useful. Can you arrange that please, and then give me a call when you have it?'

'Of course.'

'Who did you use?'

'Private investigator?'

No, plumber, idiot, of course I meant private investigator. The words wanted so badly to fly out of my mouth, but instead I managed a restrained, 'Yes.'

'A guy called Fripp, Benny Fripp.'

None of us was particularly fond of the private detectives. Most were ex-police anyway, but one or two had crossed the line between a private investigation and police operation in recent years, hampering the real detectives, and causing a bit of a public furore. Fripp was okay though, he had a solid name for himself.

When I finally wandered out, Smithy was waiting by the door, clutching a white plastic bag bulging with bits.

'What did you get?' I asked.

He held it open for me to see. There was a tacky-looking mermaid costume for Katie and an almost realistic plastic gun for Luke. There was also some colourful-looking stuff with Chinese writing on the package that I guessed must be Asian candy. It was all very nice playing dad and getting the kids a few pressies, but I wasn't so sure his ex-wife Veronica would be that thrilled about this lot.

I looked at Smithy standing there — unshaven, sweaty, aromatic — and not in a good way, suit rumpled and with what looked like a sauce stain on the front of his shirt, and was struck yet again by how much his standards had slipped. In fact, it was downright sad. He'd slid from being a sharp, determined and valuable detective to this vision of slovenliness in front of me. Even though he'd had his trials — no one would deny that — it was still no excuse for giving up on, well, everything. Friends were supposed to tell people these things, weren't they?

'You look like crap, Smithy. You need to go home, have a shower, shave and do some washing.'

'What?' He turned and looked at me like I was a nutcase.

'What do you mean?'

'You look like shit, you stink, and you've got food all over your clothes.' I pointed to the stain. 'It's not professional — it's not a good look. Go home and do something about it.'

He gave his pit a bit of a sniff, looked down at the brownish spot, gave it a rub, then looked at me again.

'Why don't you just fuck off and mind your own bloody business?' he said and stalked off.

Ah well, his response was not unexpected. And I could have been a little more subtle about it, I supposed. But at least I tried.

34

The day was turning into one of those. It was Saturday morning, and I had been all settled in at the breakfast table with the morning paper, a big mug of tea and some toast and peanut butter, enjoying a chat with Maggs, when the phone rang. The day before we had been at a funeral, fare-thee-welling a murder victim, and now we were faced with the discovery of another one. It was a case of all hands on deck. Bye-bye day off, bye-bye Sudoku, bye-bye cryptic crossword, hello work.

Now here I was, standing in the chill morning air, not exactly feeling spiffing, when I would rather have been curled up at home in my PJs, towelling robe and fluffy slippers. Someone had discovered a body down by the Otago Yacht Club. Crass thought though it was, there was one positive thing about it. Considering how bad we all felt about the lack of progress on the Henderson case, the bustle of a new case might help to get some people out of the funk of arrests gone bad, and give them something constructive to do. Smithy being candidate number one. In fact, he had been assigned to the case and was already in attendance.

I had to look from a distance beyond the cordon on Magnet Street while the SOCOs did their thing. One less person to contaminate the scene. I spent the time gazing at Forsyth Barr

Stadium, which loomed in the background, and listening to the hum of traffic on the nearby State Highway 88.

Despite all the fuss and furore in Dunedin over the new stadium being built in the first place, there was no denying that it was an impressive edifice. I'd had a few trips up to Dunedin with Dad at the time it was being built, and watching the actual construction process had been fascinating, from its first skeletal bones, to the fleshing out of concrete-tiered seating, to filling it all in and finally the impressive roof. We weren't the only ones who kept regular tabs on the process: there was always an array of cars and spectators keeping up with the play. Every time they held an open day at the construction site the place had been inundated by the curious. Kids large and small had come out to ogle at the cranes and feel dwarfed by the damned impressive structure, including us. And being a Southern Man, once opened Dad had dragged us along to the stadium to join in the fever of supporting the Otago Highlanders, and best of all, seeing the All Blacks play. He was your typical rugby-mad Kiwi bloke. I couldn't help the sigh that escaped — I'd planned on popping into the hospice this morning to see if he was more comfortable and settled. I guessed that was on hold for now.

I watched as another unmarked car pulled up, and was relieved when a familiar face hopped out from behind the wheel. I'd half expected The Boss to turn up, but hey, it was Saturday, he could get away with ordering people around while he stayed at home in his PJs, dressing gown and fluffy slippers.

'Anything happening?'

'Waiting, waiting, waiting,' I said.

Paul sauntered over, then, after having a quick look around to make sure no one was watching, gave me a quick kiss. He followed it up with a surreptitious grope.

'You know, if someone looked over here right now and saw your hand where it is, they'd have you up on charges.'

'Are you complaining?'

He tickled somewhere rather private and I gasped.

'No.' I slapped his hand away all the same. 'You can save that thought for later.'

'Promise?' he said, then leaned in and gave me another kiss. He'd been on the job till late last night, chasing ghosts, so hadn't come over for a spot of entertainment. I'd spent the evening down at the station going over security-camera footage for Gold Strike, one of the other dollar shops, which turned out to be a complete and utter waste of time. No men had brought the butt-ugly and creepy clown masks. I would have thought women would have more sense. Then I'd had my visit to the hospice. The upside to that was a chance to see big bro Mike for the first time in years. Damn shitty reason for a catch-up but still, somehow his presence made me feel a little more calm about it all.

'Maybe,' I said. 'Maybe not. You'll have to take your chances.' To be perfectly honest, I felt like crap, so his chances weren't that great. 'Perhaps, seeing as we're on the job, we could talk about work stuff.'

'That would be a novel idea. Fire away. So what's new?'

He stood there looking expectant, and when I didn't immediately come up with something he became rather smug. 'See, I told you my idea for entertainment was better.' Even with a dead body lying a hundred metres away, all he could think about was sex. What was it with guys?

I rolled my eyes at him. 'Well no one's come back with any info on our victim yet,' I said, indicating over my shoulder, beyond the crime-scene tape, to the white-suited people and glimpse of a police tent that was being erected over the position of the body.

'You must know something. What about the Henderson case?'

I was so tempted to wipe the smug look off his face, but that was something else best saved for privacy.

'Actually, I do know something,' I said. 'You caught up with Declan Henderson's statement? That Powell and Sandhurst had been out to their house at Seacliff?'

Paul's demeanour changed immediately, the jokiness brushed aside and replaced with serious mode. 'Yeah, I heard that. And he's absolutely certain?'

'Wouldn't have made a statement if he wasn't. He was certain they had been there, but uncertain of the exact date.'

'Lying bastards. They both swore they'd never been to the Hendersons' home.'

'Exactly.'

'Has Jill Henderson corroborated that?'

'No, she hasn't. Declan couldn't remember if she was there at the time. Jill didn't think they had been out to the house; she said John very rarely brought business acquaintances home. She thought she might have met them out socially somewhere, but wasn't sure. She's extremely emotional and a little confused on some matters at the moment. I couldn't very well go and question her yesterday, what with the funeral and all.'

'That would have been a little insensitive, even for you.' I obliged that comment with a thump to his shoulder. He continued without even flinching. 'She could have been out when they were at the house. In fact that makes sense, because if Powell and Sandhurst had been to the house when she was there, I'm sure they wouldn't risk lying about it. It would look particularly bad for them, calling the widow a liar. It would be a he-said, she-said scenario, and we all know who everyone would believe. But if she was absent, and they only met the kid, then chances are they'd think a boy would never remember them.'

'Declan said he was playing on the X-Box at the time. They might have thought he was too tuned out and distracted to take any notice of them.'

'It's still a bit of a gamble on their part, but then, who'd believe some flaky video-game-obsessed teenager?' He must have caught the look I threw him. 'Making generalisations here, not talking about Declan specifically. What sort of timeframe did he give?'

'Sometime within the last month.'

'Excellent. That's one more thing to put to

them when we finally get them apprehended and in here. Whenever that might be.'

'It's not going to be anytime soon for Gideon Powell,' Smithy said as he approached us, pulling down his suit hood and removing his gloves. He looked visibly shaken. The scene must have been pretty bad for Smithy to look pale on it. He could usually stomach anything.

'What's happened?' I asked.

He turned and looked back towards the tent, just visible among the array of trailered yachts. 'Gideon Powell is otherwise occupied.'

'What?'

'He is out of commission.' He pointed his thumb in the general direction.

'The body? You're certain?'

'Saw it with my own eyes. Shot in the head and neck, by the looks of it.'

It was hard to read Smithy's expression right then: was it relief? If I was him, in a way I'd be feeling a mite pleased. The piece of shit that got him shot and Reihana murdered had met a similar fate, and there was one more crim off the streets, a pretty major crim at that. In many ways it was a good day for Dunedin, although it did mean Gideon Powell would miss out on facing proper justice. It looked like street justice had been meted out instead. I shuddered, and it wasn't just because of the bite in the wind.

'You're off the case then?' Paul asked.

Smithy's face immediately folded into a sulk. 'How'd you guess?' He limped over towards the car. 'Usual line about conflict of interest, rah, rah.'

Great. Smithy would be in an even worse mood. Just what we needed. And so would The Boss. It wasn't a good look to have the chief suspect in a high-profile murder case offed under your nose. The media would have a field day. He'd be in full-on damage control. The pressure he'd be under would be immense. Actually, that thought made me kind of pleased.

'Well,' I said, 'if that's why they haven't been able to find Powell, you've got to wonder if that means his mate Sandhurst is lying around somewhere, otherwise occupied as well — or if he shot his boss and did a runner.'

35

'Sam?' The voice on the end of the phone belonged to Laurie, the CIB receptionist, another poor person dragged away from their weekend.

'Sure is.'

'I need your help down here at the counter. There's a bit of a problem.'

Reception was only twenty metres or so down the hallway. I took the phone away from my ear for a few moments and listened. I became aware of a raised and insistent voice.

'On my way, Laurie.'

Angela Powell was a vision of grief, anger and thwarted purpose. She had already donned the black uniform of the grieving widow, although hers was probably a little more flashy than most. The miniskirt was worn with barely there hose and six-inch black heels. She wore a black fascinator, complete with net veil, that artfully followed the contours of her jaw. The low-cut neckline on her designer black top was accented with a large, black crystal crucifix that hung between the ample mounds of her very visible cleavage. I'm sure she thought she looked good, but in my conservative and biased opinion she was a little lacking in taste, considering her recent bereavement. Call me old-fashioned, but I didn't think mourning was the best time for dressing in an alluring way. Unless, of course, you planned to replace your dearly departed as soon as possible.

'I want to speak to your boss right now. I'm not leaving until I do.'

Seeing her in full-on rant mode, I understood that she had more in common with her husband than perhaps I had given her credit for. She was quite formidable. Laurie spotted my approach and looked relieved.

'Mrs Powell.' She turned and I took her outstretched, previously pointing hand and shook it. 'I'm very sorry for your loss.'

The offer of sympathy quite disarmed her and she lost track of her argument for the moment.

'Was there something I could help you with?'

'Well, yes,' she said, in a far more civil voice. 'I want to know what you people are doing to find whoever murdered my husband. I want to talk to whoever is in charge.'

'Actually most of us are out working on the case. Why don't you come along to one of the rooms and I can fill you in on where we're at and what we are doing.' I guided her along towards one of the interview rooms. As we moved past Laurie, she mouthed the words 'thank you'. I grimaced.

Interview rooms aren't comfortable at the best of times, but it was the only private space I had to offer. She sat on the bog-standard office chair, like it was the best Chippendale, legs crossed at the ankles, hands in her lap, like she'd been taught at some posh ladies' finishing school in Europe. She was trying to do classy, but somehow it just didn't sit right on her. She was trying to do grief too, with about as much success as she did class.

'I know you police had it in for Gideon, you

always have. I know you all hate him and you were just looking for a way to bring him down. Always picking away at him, watching him, persecuting him. Then you tried to frame him for that cop getting killed last year, when he had nothing to do with it — nothing. I know he didn't.' Yeah right, I thought. 'And then there was this whole business with that man being murdered out at Seacliff. Another opportunity to set him up, make it look like he did it.' Her finger was out again, poking holes in the air in front of me like I was personally responsible for the alleged slurs against her husband. Angela Powell came from the school of 'attack is the best defence', and she was doing a good job of it. 'You people owe him; you owe him big time. So you better bloody well make sure you give him the same respect you give any other victim when it comes to finding out who killed him, or, so help me God, I'll take you all up to the highest authority I can go to, to the prime minister if I have to, the media and whoever will listen. I'll tell them how you framed him and how none of you gave a stuff about my Gideon.'

I sat, startled for a moment.

Now she'd said her piece, she visibly deflated, like some blowup doll, head hanging forward, shoulders hunching over. I watched as her body began to shake and she uttered low, gasping howls of misery. These weren't the put-on tears of someone garnering sympathy, or the lady-like tears of someone trying to maintain her dignity. These were full-on, gut-wrenching, heartfelt sobs. The kind of sobs that ripped at your soul and made you want to gather the poor person up in your arms and hug them, to soothe away their pain. My eyes couldn't help but mist up, and I felt an almost physical ache on her behalf. I felt a pang of guilt at my previous uncharitable thoughts. She was, after all, a woman who had just lost her husband in horrific circumstances, and was still dealing with the shock of it all. And she was right. Gideon Powell had just as much right to justice as John Henderson. Justice wasn't a popularity contest.

'Angela,' I said, gently. She didn't respond. 'Angela.' This time she looked up, her veil failing to mask her shattered face. I handed over a box of tissues. 'We will be working our damnedest to find out who killed Gideon, you can count on that.'

'Can I really?' The way she said it, low, laced with sarcasm and looking directly into my eyes, was like a challenge — to my profession and to me.

'Yes, of course you can.' I actually meant it. Despite the fact Gideon Powell had been what I considered one of the basest creatures on the planet, rating down there with rats and cockroaches, I couldn't escape the fact he had been a man, and a man with a family who cared for him. Angela Powell must have accepted my sincerity because she nodded.

'Thank you,' she said.

'You may be able to help us.'

'How?' She'd blown her nose, but now that she'd started crying, she didn't seem to be able to stop.

152

'Jacob Sandhurst has disappeared. We wonder if he and Gideon had a falling out and if Sandhurst might be responsible for killing your husband.'

She shook her head vehemently. 'No. There's no way.'

'Then why would he have run?'

'Why do you think?' she said. 'You guys stitched him up for the Seacliff murder too. Of course he ran. Wouldn't you?' Valid point — well, the running away bit, anyway.

'Did Gideon plan on running?'

She shook her head. 'He was not the kind of man to run away. Gideon would have made a stand.' That wasn't so hard to imagine. It would have been a loud and belligerent stand, too.

'Why don't you think Sandhurst could have killed him?'

'They were mates. They started out together when they were only twenty or so. They'd been through everything together and had a great respect for each other. They were more like brothers. Jacob would never have killed Gideon. Not for anything.'

I couldn't help but think there were plenty of mates and brothers who had killed each other, especially when it came to money, or women, but I didn't think the women thing applied in this case. I didn't think Angela Powell would have gone near anything as reprehensible as Jacob Sandhurst. And I didn't think Sandhurst's wife was Powell's style: not young enough and certainly not enough teeth, glam and cleavage.

'Do you have any thoughts on who might have wanted him dead?'

She laughed, which seemed to help stem the crying. 'Sorry, that's the funniest question. Don't you know who my husband was? There are quite probably hundreds of people who would have wanted to see the back of him.'

'Any in particular?'

'Well, you could start with the heads of all of the gangs. Those left after the police had that big clear-out. He mentioned there were a few new players in town who he had chosen to visit and have a business discussion with.' I could well imagine how that would have gone. 'Then you could move on to a few disgruntled people who were under him. Chuck in his kids' schoolteachers, who didn't like him asking questions about their progress. Oh, and you can't forget the police. So, yeah, there are a few people who could have done it.'

I ignored the last little throwaway dig. 'Do you know the names of some of these people?'

'No, you'd have to ask Jacob about that. But that's right, you can't, he's run away from you guys.'

She seemed to be quite open with her answers, if sarcastic, although I hadn't asked directly about Powell's drug empire business activities, and she hadn't directly mentioned it. We'd skirted the specifics nicely. I decided to risk another line of questioning.

'When did you last see Gideon?'

'Wednesday night. He was pretty livid after having been questioned by your lot all day, and especially pissed off you'd been to visit me. His lawyer did a good job though, and you couldn't

154

keep him in custody.'

'So he went out that night, and you hadn't seen him since?'

'That's right. And no, before you ask, he didn't say where he was going. I told as much to your goons the other day.'

The goon in question was Paul, and I couldn't help a slight smile. So he leaves Wednesday night, turns up dead on Saturday morning. Time of death would be interesting. Was his Wednesday-night appointment a fatal one, or did he live for another day or two? Either way, if I was the missus, I'd have been wondering where the hell he was.

'It didn't concern you that he was gone for a few days?'

'Well of course it concerned me, but I was hardly going to go to the police and report him missing, was I? I'm not that stupid.'

'Was it unusual for him to be gone that long?'

'Yes, it was, and I was getting worried. He'd usually always be home for bed — he liked his comforts, you know. So when he didn't come home for a few nights I rang around a bit, and no one had seen him. And I couldn't get hold of Jacob.'

'You didn't think he might have run?'

'No, not once. Like I said, he was the type of man to make a stand. He was no coward.' She picked away at the enamel at the corner of her thumbnail. 'And he wouldn't have just left me without properly saying goodbye. It was so unlike him. I was worried sick.'

'And on the Wednesday night, did he receive any phone calls at home?'

'Yes, a couple, I think. And his cellphone was always going too. He was a very busy man.'

'Did he mention any of them to you?'

'No, I was watching TV, so I didn't take much notice.'

'How would you feel if we looked at all your phone calls and his cellphone calls for that night, to see if we can find out where he was going?' It was worth a try, but I expected the standard, well-rehearsed, 'not without a warrant' response.

She looked up, tiredness framing the edges of her eyes. 'Just do what you have to do,' she said.

I had to push a little further.

'I know I've asked you before, but I do need to ask this again. What were you doing on the eleventh of April, the night John Henderson was murdered?'

'Oh, for God's sake,' she said. 'I've already answered that question. I was at home, with Gideon. I know you don't want to believe that, but it's the truth. Gideon did not murder that man. He was at home with me.'

'All night?'

'Yes.'

'You'd swear to that in court.'

'Yes.'

I sighed. Either she was a very devoted wife, or she was telling the truth. My thoughts tended towards devotion.

'I need you to promise me something,' Angela said, her voice sober.

I looked at her, wondering what was coming

next. 'What?' Even I could hear the suspicion in my voice.

'That you'll find out who did this. And I don't mean you, the police, I mean you, personally. I think I can trust you, you seem okay.' A compliment? 'I need you to clear my husband's name, and find out who killed him.' A primer.

I looked at this woman, eroded by the weight of grief — grief for someone I considered to be a monster, on the lowest rung of humanity — and realised with a lurch that this was a pledge I couldn't refuse.

36

'Who the hell are you and how did you get into my house?'

'Funny, ha, ha, ha.' I reached down and grabbed the nearest cushion off the sofa and hiffed it at Maggie, who was ensconced on the other sofa, reading what looked like a textbook. She'd turned into a girly swot. She deflected the cushion with the ease of someone who had years of practice. 'I haven't been that AWOL,' I said, which was a bit of a porky really.

'Oh yes you have. You were supposed to cook dinner tonight, but I guess you forgot.' She put on a mock stern look.

'Shit, sorry.' I looked at the coffee table and saw a breakfast bowl with what looked like traces of Weet-Bix in it. 'But I see you've dined anyway.'

She smiled. 'Breakfast of champions, for when only the best will do.' Maggs had lived with me long enough to know my turns on dinner duty occasionally resulted in an impromptu scavenge-for-yourself night. Fortunately she was the kind of girl who thought breakfast was fine dining at any time of day. In fact, sometimes she'd even get all fancy and cook herself porridge, with lashings of brown sugar and, if truly decadent, some cream. The thought made me salivate.

Maggie had put her book on her lap and was looking at me funny. I looked down to make sure

I didn't have anything stuck to my front and had done my fly up.

'What?'

'What, what?'

'You're looking at me like I've done something.'

'Am I?' she said. 'Well I think you owe me a mug of Milo at least, seeing as you failed in your duties as *chef du jour*. I need something to wash the stodge down with.'

'Fair enough.' I wandered across to the kitchen, filled up the jug and flipped it on. 'Do you want Toffee Pops with that?' She didn't reply. I heard a heavy clomp on the floor that I recognised as the textbook crash-landing, and then footsteps approaching me.

'What now?' I asked, and turned around. Maggie was standing there, smiling at me, looking sheepish. 'Something's up. Is it Rudy? He's proposed, hasn't he? Has he asked you to marry him?'

I saw a little flicker cross her eyes, but she was shaking her head. 'No, no, don't be silly. He wouldn't do a thing like that.' She blushed an elegant shade of red.

Oh yes, he would, and it was only a matter of time. I didn't want to think about the changes to our lives that event would bring, but knew it was a certainty, because the two of them were happy and perfect together. Mr Tall and Handsome French Aristocrat and Ms Tall and Gorgeous Queen of Serenity. Of course I'd be thrilled for them, but I still experienced a little pang of jealousy at the thought of some guy stealing my best friend away.

'Well, what then?'

She was hedging, and stalling. Maggie never hedged and stalled. She always shot from the hip, albeit in a friendly and loving kind of a way. My suspicion-o-meter cranked up to full alert.

'You're moving out, is that it? You're abandoning me and moving in with Rudy!'

'No, no, no,' she said, and laughed. 'It's nothing to do with Rudy, or me.'

'Well, what is it then?'

She took a big breath. She looked at me with her head cocked to the side, then straightened up and smiled. 'I don't quite know how to tell you this, and I don't know that you're going to like it.'

'But?'

'But, you're pregnant.'

I gave her a look that seriously questioned her sanity. 'Don't be so bloody daft. Me? Pregnant?'

'Yup. Pregnant.'

'Are you sure?' Maggie was one of those women who could tell from a sideways glance across a crowded room that a woman was in the family way. She'd never been wrong. Her track record was one hundred per cent bang on, banged-up accurate.

'Certain.'

I felt the blood drain out of my face. 'Oh shit.'

37

I was trying to keep my mind on the job but was suffering a severe lack of sleep due to churning over everything going on with Dad, and the bombshell Maggie had dropped on me the night before, confirmed emphatically by a do-it-yourself pregnancy test kit hurriedly bought from the urgent pharmacy. All in all it meant my mind was in la-la land and it was very much a case of lights on but no one home. Unfortunately, my lack of concentration had been noted by some of my colleagues.

'Shephard.' My head snapped to attention as DI Johns' voice cut through the air. 'Are you going to bother to listen to this, or is there something else more important you'd like to share?' I felt every set of eyes in the room zero in on my face. Well it was important, but nothing I was about to share.

'No, sir,' I mumbled, and looked down at the floor. I felt my eyes well up, and blinked hard. God knew I didn't need that kind of attention right now. And morning briefing wasn't the time or place for a girly breakdown.

'Well, keep up then. That goes for all of you. We have two murder investigations on the go, people, and a lot of public scrutiny. We can't have anyone dropping the ball. I expect everyone's A-game, nothing less.' Would he continue with the Sunday sermon or would he relinquish the pulpit so we could actually get on with our work? 'The media is already all over it. This is fine fodder for them — a warrant issued for Powell's arrest, and then he turns up dead. No one, but no one . . . ' he paused and I didn't have to glance up to know he was looking at me; ' . . . is to talk to the media, understood? Media liaison officer only. Right.' He clapped his hands twice, just like Miss McAllister in standard one. 'First up, Detective Frost. What is there to report on the Henderson case?'

Paul moved from his desk into the centre of the room. The burden I was carrying meant I couldn't bring myself to look him in the eye. God, what would he think? What did I think, for that matter? My thought processes were swinging wildly from total bewilderment, to vague wonderment, to outright terror.

'At present all of our energies are targeted on locating and arresting Jacob Sandhurst. We've put out an alert nationwide and informed border control. We are also talking with all of his known associates in an effort to find him, and are checking all properties he has a connection with. So far there has been no word as to his whereabouts and we haven't located his vehicle, a late-model BMW X5 SUV, black.'

'What about news from the drug squad, organised crime? Have there been any whispers in the criminal underworld?' the DI asked.

'Not as to his location. There is speculation that he was responsible for the murder of Gideon Powell, and also speculation that the reason we can't locate him is because he has

162

been murdered too and hasn't turned up yet. None of it is backed up by an ounce of proof, so none of it is helpful. We have had more forensic evidence results back from the crime scene at Seacliff. Hairs found inside the hood of the bloodied disposable boiler suit recovered from the township provided DNA that matched Gideon Powell. With that and his fingerprints recovered from the latex gloves, and Sandhurst's fingerprints, it gives conclusive evidence that Powell and Sandhurst were responsible for the murder of John Henderson. We also have eyewitness evidence from Declan Henderson that both Powell and Sandhurst had in fact been to the Henderson home in the month prior to the attack, something they both denied during questioning.'

'Thank you, Detective.' Paul caught my eye as he returned to his spot. I could see the question, 'you okay?' I gave a barely discernible nod. The fact was I was far from okay. Funny how easy it was to lie.

'Right, Detective Van Rij, the Powell case.'

Otto took centre stage. His South African accent had been diluted enough by years of living in New Zealand to be soft and mildly lyrical.

'Gideon Powell's body was discovered by a dog walker yesterday morning, down at the Otago Yacht Club on Magnet Street, in among the parked and stored boats. Preliminary post-mortem results show cause of death was gunshot wounds to the neck and head, most likely fired at a distance of one to two metres from the victim. It was a nine-millimetre calibre weapon, a pistol. Blood evidence indicates he died several metres from where he was found and was dragged feet first to where he could be hidden from easy view. The killer kicked dirt over the trail of blood and ripped up and threw grass over the scene. Time of death is estimated to have been around Wednesday night or early Thursday morning. Bear in mind, Powell had been here at the station until mid-afternoon on Wednesday for questioning.'

That fit with his wife's testimony about when she last saw him. It also meant the police may have been among the last people to see him alive. I bet the media would have something to say about that, too.

'No one from the general public has reported hearing gunshots, but there is a construction site nearby that is doing a lot of riveting at the moment, which could have disguised any noise; also, the quarry had been blasting around that time. Also the killer could have used a silencer.'

That made sense. The murder scene was also in an industrial area, with no residences nearby. There was a cycleway in the vicinity, so perhaps some cyclists or walkers would come forward now the case was in the media.

'One interesting thing from the post-mortem: there appears to have been a struggle — this wasn't a straight-out execution. Powell had some bruising to his face and torso. He didn't appear to have any defensive wounds on his hands, though. Also, we found the sheath of a knife in his right coat pocket. The blade would have been fifteen centimetres long, a hunting knife, but there was no sign of a knife at the scene. We have to assume the killer took the weapon. Powell may have stabbed at his killer, and even wounded him. We've taken blood samples from everywhere at the scene and from the body, in the hope of finding evidence of the other person, but as you can imagine, there was quite a lot of it. Also, the way he was dragged, his hands through his own blood, any other contributing blood evidence would have been masked. But you never know, we might get lucky.'

'Luck will have nothing to do with it. We can't afford to rely on luck. Thank you, Detective.'

Otto shot the DI a dark look, and then returned to his place next to Smithy, who was looking just as dark.

'Right, people. You all know what you've got to do. Get busy.'

Sermon was over. Church was out.

38

It was Sunday afternoon. I was supposed to be working, but was only managing a poor impression of it. My concentration levels had bottomed out and I was having fond thoughts of caffeine. I had spent the last hour looking over Gideon Powell's telephone and cellphone records on his last Wednesday as a living and breathing citizen of planet Earth. The long lists of numbers had phased in and out, with the digits seeming to move around on the page like one of those freaky optical illusions, evading my focus and blurring just as I thought I had a grasp on them. Thus, a job that should have taken half an hour took at least twice that.

Powell's home phone had received several calls, including one from a number that belonged to his mother. I couldn't get my head around such a despicable specimen actually having a mother. But I supposed, like all of us, he had been born, not somehow spawned. When imagining the kind of woman who would breed something like him, the words battle-axe jumped to mind, rather than an image of someone in the 'little old lady from *Tweety Pie and Sylvester*' mould. But I could have been wrong.

His mother might be a perfectly lovely woman. Yeah, right.

More significant was a call from the home phone number of a Mr Jacob Sandhurst. Mr

Sandhurst who was still at large. What had they discussed? Damage control? An appointment with fate? Somehow I didn't think they had been swapping casserole recipes. We had no direct evidence to say that Sandhurst had killed Powell, but this piece of information added to the overall picture of his actions on the night in question.

Powell's cellphone reflected the level of paranoia required to survive as a criminal. It was some android thing, as gadgety as you could get, and he had it loaded with every application known to man: games, weather, currency converter, this funny little thing that was like flicking a cigarette lighter, even a spirit level. What it was lacking was phone numbers. His cellphone logs only went back to the day before. It would appear that he cleared them all daily, in case of theft or seizure, I imagined. We could get all of his previous call numbers from his service provider; that was no problem. His contacts list was minimal: his wife, mother, children, children's school, what turned out to be immediate family, his lawyer, and Jacob Sandhurst. Considering my contacts list had at least fifty people on it, and I didn't consider myself to be flush with acquaintances, that was pretty spartan. Of the five calls logged that night, none was from those in his address book. Most were from unidentified pre-paid numbers. What a surprise. Powell probably owned a couple of those himself, for those little occasions where you didn't want to leave a trace. There was one exception to the pre-paid epidemic, and that was from an unlisted landline that, with some digging, turned out to belong to a public telephone on Hanover Street.

As far as I was aware there weren't any surveillance cameras in the area that could be used to try and identify the caller — Dunedin wasn't that Big Brotherish, thank God — but in the day of cellphones, it was decidedly dodgy for someone to call from a public payphone at nine o'clock at night. Especially when a few hours later the recipient was rather dead.

As I struggled to process this information, while simultaneously trying to cope with the Dad situation, the surprise Paul and progeny situation, and the lack of sleep situation, I came to realise my brain had actually frozen; it was doing the human equivalent to the computer blue screen of death, or the funny little spinning beachball if you were a Mac girl. It was a case of information overload, you have too many windows open, the system is not responding, please shut down. It was time to force quit.

39

It was Monday morning and I was feeling a tiny bit more human after an evening at home with Maggs and a date with the DVD player. Maggs had chosen a movie about some drop-dead gorgeous chick who got knocked up by some slovenly dweeb. Was she trying to tell me something? Whatever her motive, it backfired, because on that front I was just as confused as ever.

One of the fun things The Boss had instructed me to do today was have another little chat with that king of the paper shredder, Blair Harvey-Boyd. I didn't really mind as I would have taken on any task, no matter how menial, if only it would help take my mind off life, the universe and everything. Hell, I would have even cleaned the toilets if he'd asked me, and thanked him for the opportunity.

The forensic accountants had been busy doing their thing, going over the books of Eros Global, and had found one or two major discrepancies, and several hundred minor ones. The upshot of it was that Mr Harvey-Boyd had been a very bad boy and had been biting the hand that fed him. In fact, not only had he bitten the hand, he had eaten halfway up the arm. It also explained his behaviour when Smithy and I found him busy destroying documents at an alarming rate when we first visited John Henderson's offices. Documents that had all been re-pieced together. It was the behaviour of someone with something to hide, and Blair Harvey-Boyd most certainly did. So far the tally was at three hundred thousand dollars, and rising. If there had been any question as to the perpetrators of John Henderson's murder, we would have been having a very serious look at Blair Harvey-Boyd. Nevertheless, I suspected we'd still need to investigate the possibility of him being in cahoots with Powell and Sandhurst, though I doubted that was likely, going by Astrid's testimony.

The kind of greed that could lead a man to embezzle funds could also make him kill. His motive factor had just shot up. But that was all by the by, seeing as all the evidence pointed to Gideon Powell and Jacob Sandhurst — one of whom was safely under refrigeration at the morgue and was no loss to the world, the other of whom was at large. I felt a twinge of unease, the image of Angela Powell delivering her impassioned plea heavy in my mind.

Blair Harvey-Boyd was attired in his sartorial best. A threepiece suit, silk cravat and shoes that screamed expensive. At least we knew how he managed to fund his wardrobe and taste in footwear. He also knew we knew. At least he had the grace to look uncomfortable. The decor of the interrogation room didn't do anything to flatter the green of his suit.

'How long have you been stealing from John Henderson, Mr Harvey-Boyd?'

'Well I wouldn't call it stealing, as such,' he said.

I had to cover my scepticism with a cough.

'What precisely would you call it then?' I asked.

There was no reply. At least he didn't try to talk it away as creative accounting, or collecting what was due, or — my personal favourite — just borrowing it and intending to pay it back. As often happened with someone who had no reasonable defence, he mounted an offensive.

'Was it Astrid who dobbed me in? I bet it was. She always was a bit jealous, you know.'

I couldn't imagine a woman like Astrid feeling remotely jealous about any aspect of Blair Harvey-Boyd's life, except for maybe some of his jewellery. It appeared she had been just as deceived as John Henderson by this thief's charms.

'Jealous of what?'

'Oh, the fact that I earned more than she did, that I had a more active role in the business, whereas she was just the secretary.' I could think of some very hardworking, knowledgeable and highly esteemed women downstairs here at the station who would have gladly clubbed the man across the lug-hole if they'd heard that comment. I was tempted to give him one on their behalf. 'And I had a better relationship with John than she did.'

My mind did a few tired flip-flops at that statement, adding one plus one and coming up with five. 'Sorry, are you trying to tell me that you had a relationship with John Henderson — a sexual relationship?' Stranger things had happened. There I was thinking Jill Henderson was probably feeling a bit threatened by John's stunning secretary; I had never considered she might be more threatened by this particular man.

171

Blair spluttered a bit and then, with an extravagant hand wave, said, 'No, no, no, you've got me all wrong. Oh no, John was definitely a ladies' man; you only need to ask Astrid about that.'

'So you're implying that he had a sexual relationship with Astrid?'

'No, no, not that either. No.'

'Then what are you trying to say here?' I was not in the mood to be messed around. He was now in serious danger of a lecture of ear-withering proportions.

'I was just trying to say that John Henderson confided in me about things that he wouldn't discuss with her.'

'What kind of things?'

Blair Harvey-Boyd seemed to be on a roll. It was as if he realised his number was up so he might as well totally spill the beans. He was positively garrulous.

'Like the fact that he rescued Astrid from a life of prostitution. The way he described it was like something out of *Pretty Woman*, except in Dunedin, and he didn't win the girl in the end, if you see what I mean.' He seemed to think this was really funny. 'No, he and his wife kind of made her their pet project. In fact, that guy Powell who was found shot yesterday, down by the stadium, I'm sure he had something to do with her or her pimp.' My face must have looked shocked, because he sat there looking as pleased as Punch. 'So you didn't know that, huh? Interesting, don't you think?'

'Actually, Mr Harvey-Boyd, I'm less interested in scurrilous gossip about other people's past lives than I am about information on John Henderson's life and business that may have led to his murder. And the fact you have been found to have been robbing him blind makes me far more interested in you.' That wiped the smug look off his face. 'Let's start with anything you may know about John's dealings with Mr Powell, or anything he may have confided in you about the relationship.'

'Oh, of course. You know, I didn't mean to offend you with what I said about Astrid. I mean, she is a very capable and nice young lady.' My, we were changing our tune rapidly. It appeared to have dawned on him how much trouble he actually might be in. 'As for Mr. Powell, John did have some dealings with him.'

'What kind of dealings exactly?'

He looked a little uncomfortable. 'Well, he never said exactly.'

'But?'

Harvey-Boyd leaned forward, like he was about to expound some great secret. 'Between you and me,' and the video recorder, and the police constable in the corner, and most likely a court of law sometime soon, 'I actually think John was involved in something that wasn't quite legal there.' This coming from someone who had just been sprung for not-quite-legally pilfering from his boss.

'And what were your suspicions?'

'Well, I did overhear them once, talking about importing bulk liquids.'

'What kind of liquids?'

'I didn't hear the details exactly. It wasn't

173

exactly the kind of conversation one wanted to be caught out overhearing, if you catch my drift. And that dreadful Sandhurst man was there too. They weren't very nice people.'

It brought to mind what Astrid had said about Blair scuttling for cover every time they entered the building. It did get my mind whirring, though. On the one hand we had a kingpin of the criminal underworld suspected of being in charge of a very large drug operation, including the manufacture of P, and on the other hand we had a semi-respectable businessman involved in the manufacture of, as he called them, nutraceuticals, which still involved the importation of bulk ingredients. It didn't take a great stretch of the imagination to think that this could be a very beneficial partnership. A legitimate business to import a few choice ingredients, and a nice payout in return. It made a lot of sense. We had our link.

40

Jill Henderson was looking stronger than when I saw her last, and the physical evidence of her brush with violence was diminishing. The bruises were fading to yellow, and the stitches had been removed from the gash above her eye, but I suspected the psychological scars were anything but healing. Her eyes looked haunted and the dark-purple smears under them told of little sleep. Her mouth was pinched and tight. The poise and beauty I had noted upon first meeting her was being eroded. Well, at least the big hurdle of the funeral was over and they could now get on with figuring out what normal life entailed.

She and Declan had moved into a furnished upstairs apartment on Moray Place, unable to face the prospect of returning home as yet. By all accounts the cleaning firm had done a good job of the house at Seacliff, once the forensics team had finished their job; but the memories were still too raw and too strong for them to return. It wouldn't surprise me if they upped sticks and left. That house was forever tainted. There was plenty of time ahead for those kinds of decisions.

For the moment, though, they were by no means slumming it. I would have killed for the apartment. It had all the latest in appliances, designer furniture and, with that slightly industrial look to it, had an off-the-scale cool factor. Declan was back at school. I was pleased to hear that he'd gone back to the normal rhythm of life. It was also handy he wasn't going to be present for the upcoming conversation with his mum.

After I'd stopped ogling the decor and had made the requisite amount of small talk, I got straight to the point. 'Jill, I need to know why you didn't tell me about Astrid Allen's past life and your involvement with her. You told me you thought you may have met Gideon Powell socially, but I have been informed that you and John rescued her from a life in prostitution and that it was all linked with Powell. Why didn't you tell me about that association before?'

She turned her head away as tears welled from her eyes and drifted down her now reddening face, the change in her bearing instantaneous.

'I don't know,' she said, her voice quiet and childlike. 'So much had happened, and everything was just so hard. I couldn't think straight and I guess, in a way, I was just trying to protect everyone.' At least she didn't try to deny the association.

'What do you mean, protect everyone?'

'Well, I already knew you suspected John of having an affair with Astrid. I think everyone did — I mean, she's a beautiful young woman and you hear all the time about bosses and their secretaries. I didn't want anyone to think ill of John, not now, not with him being killed so horribly.' A sob burst out like a hiccup, and I could see her fight hard to suppress more. 'If everyone knew she had been a prostitute, they would assume John was, you know . . . I wanted to protect his memory.' She reached over, grabbed a tissue and blew her nose. Then she turned and looked at me, the image of utter misery. 'And I know everyone thought I was jealous of Astrid. I have to admit, I was a little bit. But mostly I felt sorry for her, for the life she was trapped in — we both did. She seemed to have so much potential, which is why we orchestrated things the way we did.' She took a sip of water from the glass on the coffee table in front of her, trying to steady herself. 'Look, I like Astrid. I didn't want the world to find out what she used to be — for our sake, and for her sake. I know she wouldn't have wanted it to be common knowledge, so I just kept that bit quiet. I couldn't have said anything to you about Gideon Powell without uncovering how I had met him, so I didn't. I'm sorry I couldn't.'

So she had lied — with reason, I supposed. As had Astrid Allen. But it was still a lie. Why did people do that? Withhold vital information so that they or others could save face? It never made sense to me. Honesty was so much simpler than lying. You didn't have to try and remember how you'd lied, and you didn't have to feel bad about it afterwards.

'So how exactly did you know Gideon Powell then? The full truth, please.'

'Okay. We met at this party out at Larnach Castle, in the ballroom. It was some big affair — formal dress — a fundraiser I think. I hadn't wanted to go to it, but John insisted. Astrid was there, looking amazing as you could imagine, but with this revolting guy who was supposed to be her boyfriend. He was drunk and bragging, you know, about how little he had to pay to be there with a woman who looked like that. It was so demeaning for her. Somehow we got talking with her while he was away getting a drink or something, and she was so pleasant and intelligent, and so incredibly sad. We decided we had to do something, and John came up with this idea. John said he needed to sort things out with Gideon Powell, though I didn't entirely understand what that meant, and he left me a while to go and work out the finer details. I didn't want to know about that side of things. But the end result was that we offered her the job.'

Taking a beautiful prostitute out of the working pool wouldn't have been a cheap exercise for John Henderson, and having met Gideon Powell before his untimely demise, I was certain he wouldn't have given her up in the grip of a charitable mood. It would have cost John plenty. Was this the beginning of their business venture together, or was that already firmly established? Did he have some leverage over John because of it? All things I needed to investigate further.

There was another inconsistency I needed to clear up with Jill.

'I need to ask you something else about other information you have given me. I'm sorry to have to ask again, but I need to know the honest truth.'

She looked downcast, like a schoolkid caught lying about why her homework wasn't done.

'You told me that Gideon Powell and Jacob

178

Sandhurst had never been out to your home at Seacliff, yet Declan told me that they had. What's the story?'

She looked away again for a bit as if collecting her thoughts, then turned back to me.

'You have to believe me, I had never seen them out at the house, I wouldn't lie about that. Did Declan say I was there?' She looked genuinely puzzled and upset, a deeper frown than usual creasing her forehead.

'Declan couldn't remember if you were there or not, but he certainly recalls them, and being introduced to them by John.'

'Well, I must have been out then, because I'd certainly remember that. John very rarely brought his business associates home; it was like his sanctuary out there. He kept work and his home life as separate as possible. But if Declan said they were there, then they must have been there, because he's such a good boy and wouldn't lie about something like that. But I certainly didn't see them. It must have been when I was out of the house.' She started shaking her head, as if trying to process what I'd just told her. 'I can't believe he would have brought men like that into our home. What was he thinking?'

I couldn't answer that for her. The poor woman looked so wretched, I felt guilty for even asking.

41

Astrid Allen was back at the interview table. Again she was the epitome of poise and calm, two attributes I felt sadly lacking in, especially at the moment. After Blair Harvey-Boyd's revelations about her past life, and confirmation from a far more reliable source, I hoped Astrid would be able to provide some valuable insights into Gideon Powell's operations — information that she might be more forthcoming with, now we knew about her background. Lying by omission was still lying as far as I was concerned, although I could see why she wouldn't have been eager to share her previous business experience.

'Thanks for coming back in, Astrid.'

'That's okay,' she said. 'Anything I can do to help.'

I wasn't about to beat around the bush, so got straight to the point. 'It has come to our attention that you had dealings with Gideon Powell in a professional capacity before you came to work for John Henderson.'

She frowned and then straightened herself up in the chair. 'Information from whom, may I ask?'

'I'm sorry, I can't tell you that. Would you like to describe your exact relationship with Gideon Powell?'

She gave a tight little smile. 'You don't need to tell me. I know it would have been Blair

Harvey-Boyd who told you. It would have been just the kind of thing he wouldn't have been able to resist divulging. You know, I can't understand for the life of me why John would have told him about it. It's very personal, and none of his business, for that matter. Unless perhaps Blair overheard something and quizzed John until he relented. I don't know. Blair is very good at accidentally overhearing things.'

I could believe that. 'So what happened? How did you get mixed up with that man?'

She leaned back in her chair and seemed to be choosing her words carefully. 'When I was younger, one of my boyfriends was in with the wrong crowd. I was probably a bit impressionable and trying hard to fit in, to be cool. I seemed to go for the bad boys. I had appalling taste back then.' We shared a coy smile. I could relate to that; I'd had one or two myself that I was rather keen to forget. 'The upshot of it is that I got into a rather difficult situation and found myself being manipulated by him. I . . . ' She appeared to be struggling to find the words, but I had a sinking premonition of what she was about to say; it was something I'd heard from many women before. 'I found myself trapped into providing services.' She looked me in the eye to make sure I got the gist of it, and then continued when she realised I did. 'I was young. I'm still not entirely sure how I got myself into that situation, but it happened. It was at that stage in life that I first learned about Gideon Powell. He had his own operations. I wasn't involved directly in any of it, although I suspect my boyfriend handed money on — protection, I guess. I didn't take that much notice of the details, I was just trying to get by.'

Well, that explained why Astrid had a depth and a maturity that seemed lacking in many of the scatterbrained young women of her age I saw. She had lived in a way that most of them couldn't even imagine, and had clearly survived to tell the tale. In fact she'd more than survived, she'd forged a better life. You had to admire her for it.

'Women who find themselves trapped in the prostitution business find it very difficult to get out. How did you manage it?' I assumed she'd managed to get out completely, unless she was supplementing her wages. She flinched at the p-word.

'That was where John Henderson came in.'

Despite Jill Henderson's assurances, my pathologically suspicious brain still wondered if John Henderson had more than philanthropy in mind when he helped her out.

The thought must have translated to the look on my face, as she immediately looked startled and leaned forward. 'No, no, it was nothing like that. He didn't, I didn't.' It was the first time I had seen her flustered.

She took a deep breath, and then continued. 'I met him at a party, well actually a ball, out at Larnach Castle. I was escorting some slime-bucket businessman. It was quite formal.' My imagination put a Roy Orbison soundtrack to it — tall, young, gorgeous blonde thing on the arm of some wannabe who would never manage to achieve that without paying for the privilege. 'He and John got to talking, and he couldn't help himself and bragged about me. I don't think I had ever felt so humiliated or cheap in my life, being talked about like that, like I was some prize piece of meat, and with me standing right there beside him when he did it. John must have seen how embarrassed and unhappy I was. One thing led to another, and he offered me a job — a legitimate job. It was my out.'

'And Jill Henderson was there?'

'Well, yes, she was there when it all happened. They both looked as embarrassed as I was and found a way to get away from us very quickly. But later on, when the creep was out of the way, they came over and talked with me alone, and offered me the job, gave me a chance.'

I still found it hard to believe Jill would have easily agreed to that arrangement. I couldn't picture any wife agreeing to a new, gorgeous young PA with a history like that.

'And there was no expectation from John, for anything outside of your job description?'

'No, not at all. I know you will find that hard to believe, but it's true.' I really had to work on disguising my thoughts. 'If it wasn't for them, who knows where I'd be by now? I saw what happened to the other girls around me. They all got hooked on drugs, and then had to sell themselves more and more to pay for it, and it just turned into a spiral of doom. I hadn't got into the drugs yet, but I was trapped by the arsehole pimp boyfriend I had. The Hendersons gave me work, a place to stay and got me away from the creep. I owe them everything; in fact I probably owe them my life.'

The way she said it was so matter-of-fact that I believed her. Courtesy of the job, I had seen, all too often, the pathway she'd described, and, although it amazed me, the number of beautiful and intelligent young women who'd slid down it. Invariably it started with a dodgy boyfriend and his gaslighting, that gradual and often purposeful erosion at their self-confidence and self-worth, until they found themselves doing things completely against their moral code. Most of them were tied in with drugs too. I wondered how on earth Astrid had managed to fend off that one. Mind you, from what I'd seen of her, there was a certain amount of steel behind that overtly feminine exterior.

'So, did you ever have any direct dealings with Gideon Powell?'

She shuddered and sat herself up straight again, a sickened expression on her face. 'He became one of the clients my boyfriend insisted on. Although he didn't pay.'

The thought of that man's hands anywhere near my body made me shudder in sympathy. It was simply beyond imagination. The poor girl. No wonder she had to put up with his leering and rude comments whenever he came to the office. You'd dread the visits.

None of this really helped in establishing a clear motive. Would resentment at John taking away one of his trophies be enough to make Gideon Powell commit murder? I doubted it. Men like that treated women like commodities

— yet another business transaction. But it might have swayed the decision. But, then, why would he have brought The Cockroach along for the ride?

'Was Jacob Sandhurst ever a client?'

'Oh, God no.' She looked so repulsed I thought she might be ill. 'I would have rather taken a beating, run away, anything to avoid that.' I seconded that motion.

'Is there anything at all you can give me about Powell that might shed light on why he killed John?'

'Sorry, like I said earlier, they seemed to have a solid, respectful relationship. But I don't know any details about what that relationship was. I didn't want to know. I wanted to keep as much distance between myself and that man as I could. He was a dangerous and despicable person. And you have to know that if I could help you I would, because I owe John Henderson everything . . . and Jill. If there was anything I could do to help you nail his killer, I would.'

I didn't doubt it for a second.

42

'Shephard.'

I'd heard his footsteps coming down the hall-way so had already assumed the brace position by the time he arrived at the door. I wasn't the only person in the squadroom. Sonia was there too. I noticed she had steeled herself too, so her radar must have finally tuned in to his frequency.

'Yes, sir?'

'What are you doing?'

There was a loaded question. My mood-o-meter hadn't had time to gauge his in the three seconds I'd seen of him. When in doubt, take the cautious approach, especially if you still wanted your throat intact at the end of the encounter. I chose my words carefully.

'Do you mean with regards to the case?'

'No, I mean with regards to what you plan to eat for lunch. Of course I mean the bloody case.' Bad mood confirmed.

'I was looking into the manufacturing side of John Henderson's business, seeing if there were any ingredients he imported for production that could also be used in the production of P. Trying to establish that link between Henderson and Powell.'

'So where is his manufacturing plant?' DI Johns asked.

'All of the nutraceuticals are manufactured in Auckland. So if there is any evidence of the bulk buying and importing of ingredients that could be used in the manufacture of P it would be up there, whether that was product actually awaiting delivery down here, or invoices and packing slips.'

He grumbled to himself a bit before coming back to look at me. I felt uncomfortable under his gaze. There was always something predatory about it. There weren't many people in this world who could make me feel vulnerable.

'Okay, you're on a plane tomorrow. Get it organised.'

'What?' I said, the word blurting out before I could rein it in.

He gave me a 'how dare you question me' look.

'You are going to sort it out up there.' He spoke slowly, like I was some idiot.

I thought of the beloved man lying in the bed in Otago Community Hospice. The thought of being that far away was unbearable. 'I'm sorry, I can't do that. My dad is very ill. I don't want to leave the city.'

'Well I'm sorry, Detective, but I have two murder investigations happening here, we are short-staffed as it is and I have to be very careful who I allocate where because of conflicts of interest. You are going to Auckland. End of story. I can't spare anyone else.'

'Can't one of the Auckland detectives go on our behalf?' Sonia asked.

'And who asked you? You can keep your opinions to yourself.' Shot down in flames. I appreciated her trying, though. 'I need someone from here to go. It's your job, Shephard. Now go and sort it out.'

With that he stormed off down the corridor, leaving two red-faced women in his wake.

'Fuckwit,' I heard Sonia say under her breath.

'Bastard,' I echoed.

43

'Sam, wait up.' Shit, it was Paul.

I was playing dodge the cruise-ship passengers walking through the alleyway of Albion Lane. They were a dead giveaway with their matching nylon tracksuits and big, expensive cameras.

'I feel like I haven't seen you for ages.' That might have been because I was avoiding him. 'You okay? You didn't look that happy this morning. How's your dad?'

He put his arm around my shoulder and drew me in close. I felt my body tense up for a moment before relaxing against him. Despite my inner turmoil I realised that a hug from him was precisely what I needed right now. I stopped walking and gripped his waist tightly.

'Whoa, you'll squeeze me to death there, girl,' he said.

I felt my eyes welling up and a wave of sheer exhaustion wash over me. I'd been staving it off all day, but his warmth released the flood and I felt my body start wracking with the sobs. He shuffled me over to the side of the footpath then discreetly turned me around so passersby couldn't see that I was having a moment; or, if they did. realise, they couldn't see who was having a moment. I felt his chin rest on my head and he didn't say anything, just gently rocked me from side to side.

'Has he died?' he asked quietly, after a time.

I shook my head. The mere mention of the

death word started me off again.

'Ah, Sammy, you're having a hard time of it, aren't you?'

I marvelled at how he managed to express his love, support and grief in so few words. How could I ever question the heart of this man? Here I was carrying his child, and instead of wanting to blurt it out and share the joy, and try not to let it be overshadowed by Dad, I couldn't; I had to conceal it, figure out how I felt about it, and if I even wanted this. I felt foolish, guilty and sick at heart all at the same time.

'How about we go get a coffee or something, hey? Unless you need something a little stronger than that?' God, what I would have given for a big glass of pinot noir right then, but that wasn't about to happen anytime soon.

'Coffee would be good.'

'I've got some news that will make you feel better,' he said.

Fortunately for me there was a café to hand, and it was dimly lit, so no one had to see what I was sure would be my beautiful, bloodshot eyes.

'So what's the good news?' I asked, when he came back from ordering the drinks. I'd opted for English Breakfast tea in the end. The thought of coffee had made my stomach turn a little.

'The good news is that we've tracked down Sandhurst's wife.'

'Really? But I'm taking it The Cockroach wasn't with her.'

'No, I didn't mention there was a bad news part too, did I? Either she's holding out, or she doesn't know where he is.'

'Where did they find her?' The family home had been notably empty since Wednesday.

'At a crib out at Karitane.'

'So she was that close. Was it theirs?'

'No, some friend's. Anyway, she didn't take too kindly to being told that Gideon Powell was dead and that we were very interested in having a chat with her husband.'

I could imagine some of the colourful language that would have flowed out of that dentally challenged mouth.

'I'm guessing she's standing by her man.'

'Yup. The usual 'he didn't do it' rubbish, along with 'the police framed him'. Bit tired of hearing that, really.'

'It is a little lacking in imagination.'

'Does that cheer you up a bit?' he asked, giving me the big, blue, crystalline doe eyes.

'Not as much as it would have if you told me they'd found Sandhurst, but it does, a little.' I managed a smile.

'Do you want to come over tonight? I could cook you something nice, we could crack open a good bottle of red and wash away our sorrows.' It sounded very appealing, but there were a myriad of reasons why I couldn't do that.

'Sorry, I'm on the early flight to Auckland in the morning.'

'Why?'

'Johns is sending me on a P hunt.'

'I didn't think you'd want to head out of town right now, not with Jock so sick.'

I felt the tears prick at the corner of my eyes again. 'The bastard didn't give me a choice.'

'Sod,' he said, and reached over for my hand. 'Is there anything I can do to help?'

I felt tired and confused and fraught, but despite that, or perhaps because of it, there was one special kind of comfort I needed that I knew damn well he could give.

'Well, you could come over later tonight, just for a while.'

44

I'd gone for a run after work. I had to blow out the cobwebs, relax into the rhythm of my feet on the road, try and make sense of the turmoil in my head. The cadence of left foot, right foot, left foot, right foot was so reassuring, so predictable and regular. I had run down through the green belt to the city and then across through the university, past its gloriously gothic-looking registry building, felt a momentary shudder for a murdered young woman as I ran past Gore Place, and then up through the lush greenness of Lovelock Ave. My feet took me towards the Northern Cemetery. I hadn't planned on going there, but it was as if something inside me knew better than my conscious self that I needed to come here, to acknowledge death, and the imminence of it, instead of skirting around its edges, not daring to look it in the eye. The simple and unavoidable fact was that my father was going to die.

I stood in front of the enormous folly that was the tomb of William Larnach, he of the landmark castle. His tomb was a miniature of Dunedin's First Church, as grandiose a monument to death as you could get, although one that was looking in dire need of repair right now.

'Dad is going to die.'

I said the words out loud.

The wind took them and swirled them around my head. They cut and hurt and stung my face, but they made a sad kind of sense.

I said them again.

'Dad is going to die.'

With a sigh I turned and started to run back down the hill.

My dad was going to die, and soon.

There was something he needed to know.

45

The only illumination in the room came from the low lighting in the hallway. It was late, and there was no one else there, just me and him. I watched the slow rise and fall of his chest, listened to the quiet wheeze of his breath. I smiled as I thought back to the times in the past when I'd quietly sidled up to him, when I'd needed a chat, advice, reassurance, and he'd taken me in his big, strong arms and told me that everything would be okay. Oh, how I wished for that right now. For him to say Sam-a-Lamb, you'll be fine. You're doing the right thing. It will all be okay.

I knelt down on the floor by his head, looked at the little crease between his brows and gently brushed a wisp of his greying hair aside.

'Hey Dad.' I felt my voice choke. 'I'm pregnant. I'm going to have a baby.'

I'm sure I saw the little crease soften.

46

Flying sucked. There was nothing comforting about being in a glorified tin-can ten thousand metres above sea level. There was nothing comforting about it when the turbulence made you feel slightly seedy. There was certainly nothing comforting about it when you were seated next to someone with a baby on their lap. To give the frazzled mother and restless child their due, the little girl was intolerably cute, with a mass of dark curls, and she didn't cry; but she was entertained with snacks, lots of snacks, and a number of them landed up on my clothes. By the time I disembarked, and resisted the urge to kiss the ground, I had a nice range of sticky fruit-fingers on my shirt and barbecue rice-cracker crumbs on my trousers. So much for landing in Auckland looking as fresh as a daisy.

Fortunately for me, I was met at the airport by Detective Tim Green from the Auckland Drug Squad. Unfortunately for both of us, we had to contend with morning rush-hour traffic. In Dunedin, rush-hour traffic was more like rush-minute traffic. In Dunedin you felt seriously, seriously miffed if you had to wait through more than one traffic-light cycle. In Dunedin, a long traffic queue was considered to be any amount over five cars. Auckland defied my southern logic. Whatever possessed the population of an entire city to hop in their individual cars and flood the roads at the same time? I actually laughed as we crawled past the hundred-kilometre-per-hour speed sign on the motorway at five kilometres per hour. I could have walked faster than this. Had anyone ever reached one hundred, or was that an aspiration?

We were coming up to the one part of the journey I was looking forward to — driving across the harbour bridge. I was a card-carrying anti-Aucklander, but even I had to admit that, with the sun glinting off the water, the boat masts in the marina and the backdrop of skyscrapers and the impressive silhouette of the Sky Tower, the central city harbour was a beautiful place. That pleasure was gone soon enough.

'Couldn't you just stick the siren and lights on and hop in the bus lane?' I asked. I was finding being stuck in traffic more claustrophobic than being stuck in the plane, and that was saying something.

'Well I could, but then I'd let you explain it to the powers that be why you decided to use them in a non-emergency situation.'

'No one would know, no one would tell.'

'Yes they would. These things have a way of coming back to bite you.'

'Well, it is an emergency. I'm feeling sick — sick of the traffic,' I looked either side of me at the cars, crawling in unison, the sole occupant behind each wheel. Everyone looked tense and miserable. 'Do you do this, drive to work?'

'Hell no,' he said. 'I've got more sense. I take the train.'

We pulled up outside the manufacturing plant for Eros Global, which was in an industrial area in Rosedale, on the North Shore. It went under the slightly more socially acceptable title of Global Nutritional. The whole thing oozed respectability and higher purpose. The reception area was immaculate, with modern office furniture and lush plants, hired no doubt.

'Detectives Green and Shephard to see Mr Langford please.'

The young woman behind the counter blushed slightly and it didn't take a rocket scientist to realise she was more than impressed with my colleague. He could have been the original template for tall, dark and handsome. His suit looked high-street tailor-made rather than something off the rack from Hallensteins, like most of my co-workers wore. He oozed Auckland. He also oozed charm.

'I'm afraid Mr Langford has just popped out. Was there something I could help you with?'

'Did he say when he was coming back?' I asked.

She looked disappointed that I'd spoken, and still directed her answers to Green.

'No, he just said something had come up. Would you like me to try and call him for you?'

'That would be good, thank you.'

She went about trying to ring the boss, and Green and I stood in the corner speculating.

'What do you reckon. Done a runner?' he asked.

'It could just be an overwhelming urge for coffee. But I doubt it. I'm with you. What's the bet he doesn't answer his phone.'

We smiled at each other as the reception chick announced: 'He's not answering his phone — he must be driving. I've left a message. Do you want to wait?'

'Actually, we've got a warrant to search the premises, so we won't wait, if you don't mind,' Green said.

'Oh,' she said, looking confused. 'Was there anything in particular you were looking for? Can I help you with that?'

I had to give her full points for holding her poise. I imagined part of her being so helpful was for Detective Green's benefit, not mine.

'You could give us a quick tour of the premises and then show us where Mr Langford's office is. When he went out, did he take anything with him? Did you notice?' Green said.

'Well no, I didn't notice anything, so I guess not.'

Receptionist Chick's voice was overshadowed by the sound of an engine revving. I looked out the window and saw the brake lights of an Audi glowing red as the car jerked forward, trying to inch its way into the traffic.

'Jesus, is that him?'

Receptionist Chick stammered something vaguely affirmative while Tim Green grabbed me by the arm and hauled me bodily out the door and in the direction of the car.

'Get in,' he yelled.

I was fumbling with my seatbelt as Tim threw our unmarked Holden into reverse. I swung my head around in time to see Audi Guy screech out into the traffic and head north up the road.

'Get onto comms, call for back-up,' Tim yelled as he too screeched into the flow of traffic.

At least we had the advantage of flashing lights and a bloody loud siren. Some officers loved the sound of those sirens. I loathed them; they seemed to trigger some primeval response in me that made me want to curl up and hide. That and high-speed driving. I grew up on a farm — the tractor barely made it to twenty. With one hand I clung on to the door handle for dear life. The other was messing around with the radio. The communication centre wanted to know our exact location, but how the hell was I supposed to know? I tried to read the street signs, but being thrown about so much in the car made this rather difficult.

'Call out the road names,' I said to Tim and then relayed them as best I could. Being tossed around in a swerving, weaving car wasn't what I was expecting when I woke up this morning, and it certainly wasn't my idea of a fun way to get a guided tour of Auckland. I felt a sudden urge to pray. I also wished I'd worn my Hanes self-cleaning underwear.

My sense of direction was thoroughly screwed, as Langford's tactic for escape seemed to involve taking every turn he could, and so many of them involved roundabouts it wasn't funny. He also seemed to be avoiding the main roads, which helped us as there was less chance of getting caught by traffic. Green was matching each twist and turn and was slowly gaining on him. The grim determination on his face told me we were going to be seeing this one out to the end; there would be no backing off unless absolutely in the interests of safety.

Langford must have noticed the trend and realised the futility, because as we approached yet another roundabout at a speed I really wouldn't recommend for the average punter, a rectangular projectile flew out of his car window — well, not so much flew as arched and then exploded in a sea of paper. The bastard had biffed the file boxes. I had to admit that in a surreal kind of way they looked really rather pretty, pages of paper flying across the road and being carried up on the breeze like a flock of oversized white cabbage moths. Driving though them felt akin to ploughing through an A4 blizzard. Unfortunately for us, a traffic sign leapt out from behind one of them and we glanced off it, the hit making a hideous metallic scraping noise that put my teeth on edge, like fingernails down a blackboard. The force dragged the car sideways briefly until Green wrestled it back under control. My heart was pounding so hard in my chest I thought I was going to throw up.

'Jesus Christ,' I yelled, the words flying out of my mouth before I could stop them.

'Well if you've got any complaints, you drive,' Green fired back at me.

I shut my mouth.

A number of other cars fell prey to the unique driving conditions too, and I saw a startled-looking woman end up parked smack in the middle of the roundabout, with a large, new arrow-sign bonnet decoration. There was going to be one hell of a mess to clean up, and I felt a bit sorry for the constables who would end up out there scouring the streets of Albany, trying to locate every last document. The diversion had slowed us down momentarily, and Langford had jumped forward an extra fifty metres and was still accelerating. Green wasted no time in trying to catch him up. Where the hell was the back-up? They hadn't made an appearance yet.

'Go left, go left,' Green yelled. He was the one holding the steering wheel, so I don't know why the hell he was giving me directions. Then I realised it was Langford he was shouting instructions at, as if he could send out thought waves, and remote-control the man. My mind automatically took up the chant: *Go left, go left.* The Audi veered sharply left at the next intersection, straight in front of a red Honda that slammed on the anchors and ended up stalled on the middle of the road. Green shot me a grin and I gave him a mental high five.

'Yes,' Green shouted. 'Yes, yes, yes, you sucker. That's a deadend street, dickwad. Gotcha.' I don't know how the hell he managed to swing around the Honda at speed without collecting it, because I had my eyes closed at the time. All I know is there was a lot of tyre squealing involved and my head hit the side window with a clunk.

'Shit.'

'Sorry.'

When we got halfway down the street it was apparent Langford had figured out his error: his car was now slowed, turned and pointing directly towards ours, and I had a nasty thought that the silly bugger was going to try and ram his way past us; but I had underestimated his sense of self-preservation, because it lurched to a halt, the driver door swung open and he shot out and across the road like a rabbit with a dog up its arse.

'Oh Jesus, he's gonna run,' Green said, the resignation heavy in his voice. 'I hate running.'

'The suspect has taken off on foot through the back of, ah what's this street?' I asked Green, as he was heading out the door.

'Northcross Drive.'

'Northcross Drive. The suspect is approximately five foot ten, brown greying hair, wearing a navy-blue suit, apple-green tie and heading through the back of what looks like apartment blocks. We're pursuing on foot.'

I took off after Green. Desperation must have given Langford wings because he'd made short work of the back fence, and was nowhere to be seen. Great, fences. The guys had a definite advantage there, and Green managed it without too much difficulty, other than a tearing noise. But where I may have been short, I was also quick, and with a decent run-up and not too much of a loss of decorum, I scrabbled over the top of the thing. From the elevated view I could see Langford had made a lot of ground on us, a surprising amount. Just our luck: we had a runner, in all senses of the word. It soon became apparent that Green was not, and it wasn't long before I had overtaken him.

'Can you run him down?' he called from behind.

'Yes,' I called back. I might have lacked the pace, but I more than made up for it in stamina. I knew that as long as I kept him in sight, he'd tire before I did. Well, that was the theory, unless he happened to be a national rep, or something equally over-achieving.

It didn't take long before I was gaining. We'd also gained a bloody dog, which ran alongside me, barking its head off like it was a great game. The barking seemed to spur Langford to run faster.

We'd been running across a park, but were now getting up towards built-up residential streets again and a busy road. I was getting closer.

Forty metres.

Thirty metres.

Twenty.

Ten.

'Give it up, Langford,' I yelled between gulps of air. 'You may as well stop. Can't you hear the sirens? They're coming for you.'

He probably couldn't hear them over the bloody dog. The stupid bugger kept running.

'Don't make me tackle you.'

He started weaving from side to side. Bloody marvellous.

I could see the grass was going to be ending sometime soon, so, if I wanted any kind of cushioned landing, I was going to have to do something fast. I threw on a burst of speed and so, dammit, did he. It was just as we reached the joy of asphalt that I was finally in range to throw myself at his legs, the words of my sixth-form phys-ed teacher echoing in my ears: 'Go low and hard.' I felt the thwack as my shoulder hit the back of his thighs, and the two of us pitched forward, my arms wrapping around his waist.

In a tackle that would have done the All Blacks proud, I brought him to the ground.

'Oh fuck,' was all he said, and lay there like a beached fish, all the run gone out of him.

The dog still pranced around, making pretend growls, interspersed with delighted yelps. Stupid mutt. I wasn't sure whether I was feeling exhilarated or pissed off, and there was an overwhelming urge to smack Langford around the side of the head for being such an idiot; but ultimately, there was something inordinately satisfying about having left Detective Green in my wake and brought down the bad guy myself. It even overcame the sting of grazed knuckles and knees.

47

Rowan Langford was looking decidedly shitty. But not half as shitty as Detective Tim Green. Although the car chase had only been short-lived, Tim was annoyed by the fact he'd scraped the car, even more rattled by the fact that in the rush to get over the fence he had ripped the pocket on his flash suit, and hideously upset by all the grief he was getting from his colleagues because he'd been outrun by a girl. Langford was not attuned to the general mood. If he was he might have been a little more cooperative.

'Why did you decide to run from us when we arrived at your workplace, Mr Langford?' Green asked.

'I wasn't running from you. I had just realised I was late for an important appointment, so I was in a hurry.'

'In such a hurry that you failed to notice the vehicle following you with the flashing lights and the siren going?'

'I had the radio on, sorry. I didn't hear it.'

'Ah, so it's normal driving practice for you to cut dangerously across lanes and travel thirty kilometres per hour above the speed limit, is it?'

He didn't get a reply to that one.

'And running away on foot? Not stopping for an officer?'

Silence.

'Maybe you can answer this question then.

Why did you feel the need to throw a carton full of documents out the window while you were rushing to your appointment?'

'Fine me for littering then.'

Tim Green put his face very close to that of our designated clown. The clown looked uncomfortable about the proximity. 'You might want to think twice about getting cute with us, Mr Langford. This isn't some little chat about a minor misdemeanour. We are in the process of investigating a homicide. So it is in your best interests to lay off the funny talk and start answering some questions.' It was always amazing how the word homicide could coax people into being more reasonable. 'So how about we start again, and you tell us why you ran and why you threw away all of those documents?'

'I'm not saying anything until I speak to my lawyer.'

Or not. Why did the bastards always hide behind their lawyers?

'I'm pretty sure your lawyer would recommend telling the truth, considering today's debacle.'

'I haven't done anything wrong.'

'So why did you run?'

'Because you chased me.'

'Oh, so you're saying it's our fault that you sped off and raced through city streets, putting innocent people at risk?' That was always the way the media portrayed it.

Langford shut up and didn't say another word.

48

After five hours of searching the manufacturing plant and going through endless files of documents, both hard copy and on computer, we hit some pay dirt. The bulk storage room contained a number of drums of ingredients that could be used in the manufacture of methamphetamine. Not pseudoephedrine, or anything that required the strictest registration and accountability, but there were some of the other ingredients that would be a little difficult to explain if you weren't involved in a legitimate pharmaceutical manufacturing plant. Most households didn't need bulk lots of hypophosphorous acid, or iodine, for instance. Yes, sir, my kid grazes himself a lot. Yeah, right. These products didn't appear to have any legitimate purpose on the manufacturing schedules we checked, so I was guessing they were destined for shipping to underhand enterprises, including those of Gideon Powell in Dunedin.

We'd stopped for a welcome bite to eat, thank God, because I was feeling ravenous, seedy and mildly faint all at the same time. Mr Auckland was eating sushi with that strange combination of delicacy and macho that only men can manage. I'd succumbed to an urge for a mince-and-cheese pie and a cream donut. Apparently I wasn't supposed to eat cream, according to the pregnant people police, but, what the hell; tell that to my hormones.

'You know, for some time we've been aware of a mystery man, someone quite respectable, who was involved in the supply chain for manufacture. We'd nicknamed him Mr Clean. The drug-squad boys in Dunedin would have been aware of this. I'm beginning to wonder if your John Henderson was our Mr Clean, or perhaps the manager here, Langford.'

'Could be,' I said, my mind whirring ahead. 'Although, I'd wager that John would be more likely. Firstly, he owned the business — although he'd need an insider, a Johnny-on-the-spot up here: Mr I've-done-a-runner-with-a-box-of-goodies Langford. But we'd established he had a good relationship with Gideon Powell, his client. With him living in Dunedin, there's also a nice degree of separation for both sides of the business. For the CIB in Dunedin, we've been looking local, but the actual supply chain comes from Auckland; and for you guys, the supply chain is here, but the owner is out of town. Quite neat and tidy really.'

'Yes, he'd be someone quite useful, especially if he was quiet, professional and flew under the radar. He'd be an asset to any organisation.'

Yes, he would, which raised a very significant question.

'He'd be a terrific asset, which makes me ask myself why on earth Gideon Powell would have killed the hand that supplied him?'

49

How's Dad? I typed into the cellphone. I had learned to double check everything before I hit send, courtesy of a few unfortunate incidents with autocorrect. This would not be the time to inadvertently send 'who's dead'.

The departure lounge at Auckland airport had lost its charm. Normally I would have said the best thing about Auckland was the departure lounge, or being on the motorway heading south; but having been herded like sheep through security and then left to sit here for hours, courtesy of fog temporarily closing Dunedin airport, I was well and truly sick of it. By the time I got to Dunners and then into the city, it would be after eleven o'clock at night. A bit late to sneak in a visit to Dad.

Even though I was expecting it, the bleep-bleep text reply nearly gave me a coronary. I felt the knot of anxiety screw a little tighter. Between worrying about Dad and then worrying about the imminent pleasure of being stuck like a sardine in a winged tin-can projectile way too high above the ground, and then worrying that Dunedin airport would close again and we'd end up flying to Invercargill and get chucked on a bus for a fun two-and-a-half hour ride back to the city, I was turning into a basket case. I longed for either a lot of wine or diazepam, and wasn't in any condition to have either.

I worked up the courage to look at the reply from Sheryl:

Not good. Unconscious but groaning. In pain. Staff tweaking morphine. Travel safe xx.

I turned off my phone and headed towards the bar.

50

The morning's squad meeting drifted by in a tired and sleep-deprived daze. My worst-case scenario had eventuated the previous night, and after two aborted attempts at landing, the aircraft had been diverted to Invercargill because of the fog. The ear-splitting roar of engines and the sensation of being thrown back into my seat not once, but twice as we got to within a hundred and fifty metres of the tarmac in Dunedin hadn't done anything for my nervous system or my constitution, and I'd had to acquaint myself with the greaseproof bag provided in the seat pocket in front of me. Between airplane rollercoaster rides and bus trips, I had finally got home at three o'clock in the morning a little the worse for wear.

I should have pulled a sickie. Well, actually, I wouldn't have been faking it, but I was expected to give a full report on yesterday's events to the group. I managed to get through it, although I was feeling a bit wobbly on my pins. I must have looked bad, because even Dickhead Johns asked if I was feeling all right, which was unheard of.

At least the day before hadn't been wasted from a case perspective. We had managed to uncover the paper trail that followed several barrel-loads of ingredients used in the manufacture of P from legitimate suppliers in China, to John Henderson's Global Nutritional in Auckland, to a Dunedin address we knew to be linked to Gideon Powell. Langford's little attempt at ditching the evidence hadn't worked after all, the slightly road-soiled documents providing a concrete connection. We also uncovered a bit of double-handling that brought the products to Dunedin, to Eros Global, and then back to Auckland, to another business for distribution to the drug trade. Everything ran through genuine businesses, with what seemed to be proper documentation, which kept it all above board and off the police radar. John Henderson, as it turned out, was definitely Mr Clean.

'You look like a girl who needs some food and a coffee.'

That was the understatement of the year. Paul had tracked me down immediately after the meeting. No amount of makeup could hide the attack of the pale and sicklies I was suffering this morning. I could see the concern on his face.

'God, yes,' I said. 'Get me out of here.'

'I've got a car, for a meeting at ten. We've got time to grab something, then we could head over to the beach for some fresh air.' It was a bit out of the way, but the idea of looking at the wide-open expanses of the Pacific Ocean held a lot of appeal. It was even a reasonable enough day to consider a quick wander.

'Sounds perfect,' I said.

It was a quiet car ride, with me content to sit, warming my hands around the takeaway hot chocolate, head leaning against the window, ruminating about life. I still couldn't face coffee for some reason. Paul had enough sense to leave me to my thoughts. The background chatter on the police radio punctuating the hum of the engine and tyre noise provided the ambience.

I had to tell him. There was so much going on in my life right now that this was getting to be too big a thing to bear alone. For me this was the elephant in the room, and it felt like the walls of that room were closing in and the elephant was having a growth spurt. But how did you break that kind of news to a man? *Hey Paul, you're going to be a daddy! I'm pregnant, but I don't know what I'm going to do yet or how much I want you involved, just thought you should know.* Did I drop that bombshell on him and then cruise back to work, whistling a happy tune because I'd got it off my chest while he went off to his meeting in shock? There you go, love, have a nice rest of your day.

Paul pulled up beyond the surf life-saving club at St Kilda, near to the bollards the DCC had put across the road to close John Wilson Drive to vehicles. It was apparent from the sideways rocking motion and the insistent whistling noise that it was way too windy over here to get out of the car, not unless you enjoyed being sand-blasted and frozen all at the same time. Still, it was good to look out at the whitecaps and the occasional masochist out walking their dog along the beach. It had to be one of the windiest, and thus coldest places in the city, which is why they built a big children's playground out here. It didn't seem to stop the punters, though, with little rugged-up figures doing their best on the swings, and running up the stairs of the dinosaur slide.

Paul turned off the engine and then, like a teenager parked up at the beach with a fresh driver's licence and his girlfriend, he leaned over and took matters to hand in the time-honoured tradition of making out in the car. It was a while before we surfaced for air, and I was amazed at how fast you could steam up the windows.

'Hi,' he said.

'Hi, yourself,' I replied, grinning, despite my preoccupations. What was it about cars, especially work ones, that made kissing feel somehow gloriously wicked? He reached for his giant-sized coffee from the cup-holder. The waft of it made me wince. Even the smell of coffee wasn't doing it for me today.

'So how are you really holding up?' he asked. 'Are you sure you should be working with your dad so ill? You could take some time, you know. No one would blame you.'

'I know, but I think I'm better to be working,' I said, my eyes giving their automatic response to any words or thoughts that involved Dad. 'I couldn't bear to just sit there and wait for him to die. God, if he was one of the critters from the farm, we'd just put him out of his misery. The waiting is horrific. And I certainly don't think it would be a good thing if Mum and I were there doing it together. That would be a recipe for disaster.' He laughed at the understatement. 'We'd probably end up killing each other, which is not what the family needs right now.'

'I thought as much,' he said, giving me a pained smile. 'Just make sure you don't put yourself under too much pressure. You've been looking really pale and tired lately.'

'Gee, thanks a lot,' I said.

'But still beautiful, of course,' he added.

'Nice save.'

'Thanks.'

I took a long drink of my hot chocolate, finishing off the last sweet globs of melted marshmallow from the bottom.

'You know, Paul, there's something I need to talk to you about, something serious.'

'How serious?'

'Seriously serious.'

'Hold that thought, will you.' A burst of chatter had started on the police radio, the tone of the voice grabbing both of our attentions — that and the fact they'd called Paul's name.

'Frost here,' he responded.

'Central. Be advised Jacob Sandhurst has been located at a residence on Riverside Road, Taieri Mouth. He appears to be armed, but is contained in the area by police. Armed Offenders Squad back-up is on the way. Where are you situated?'

'St Kilda. On my way. Be advised I have Detective Shephard with me too.'

'Roger that.'

Well that sure killed the moment. All hopes of a deep and meaningful just flew out the window.

51

Taieri Mouth was a small coastal settlement south of Dunedin. It was popular with boaties, and mostly only drew attention to itself when some dumb-nut got their boat stuck on the sand bar and had to be rescued. It happened with monotonous regularity, due to the shifting nature of the bar and that age-old problem of boaties underestimating the power of the sea. On the odd occasion the results had been tragic.

The wind wasn't any kinder out here, and I could see wisps of sand being thrown up like puffs of smoke. Jacob Sandhurst was holed up in a crib on Riverside Road and he wasn't about to go anywhere — well, not unless he felt like a swim or a bushwalk up the hill. He was on a dead-end road. We knew he was armed, but so far no shots had been fired. We stopped at the safe forward point set up by the regulars at the foot of the bridge that stretched across the Taieri River. They'd barred civilian traffic from each end as they didn't want a ducks-in-a-row fairground attraction thing going on. A bit further back a small crowd of locals huddled, bracing themselves against the wind. One or two had their cameras. It always amazed me that people considered a police operation a spectator sport. It made you want to shoo them away: *Go home, you nosey buggers, go find something safer and useful to do.* The Armed Offenders Squad had arrived before us and they looked set up and like they were close to moving in.

'You wait back here. I'll be following them up — I've got my vest in the back. There's none for you, so don't bother arguing.'

I wasn't about to argue. If they had a spare vest anywhere it would be way too big anyway. We got out of the car and I watched as he opened the boot and geared up. Paul was something else when he was all business. It sent shivers down my spine.

'Don't do anything heroic,' I said.

'I'll be in the back row with the cowards,' he said. 'There to do the business once the big boys have got it under control, don't you worry.' He checked no one was watching then bent down and gave me a quick kiss, a wink, and ran over to where the squad was being briefed.

I pulled my jacket zip up as high as it would go and went over to where the communications were set up.

It wasn't an ideal situation they were heading into — not that any situation involving a killer holed up in a house with guns was ideal. I was certain every officer out here would have thoughts of the Aramoana massacre hanging about in the back of their mind. But that was a long time ago, a different beach, and Jacob Sandhurst wasn't a paranoid loner who had snapped. No, he was a desperate criminal with his back to the wall. Somehow the thought wasn't all that comforting.

This wasn't going to be an easy extraction for the AOS. The lay of the land would be difficult. The houses ran along the left-hand side of the

218

road from this vantage point. The right-hand side was completely open, with a narrow grass verge, a sprinkling of trees and then just sand and river. And all of the houses down that end backed up to a bush-clad hill. The only approach for them would be through the bush, or weaving through the neighbours' properties. We could only hope Sandhurst would realise there was no chance of escape, see sense and give himself up. That would be the intelligent thing to do. That would be the thing anyone with a modicum of self-preservation would do.

The AOS moved out, an exercise in furtiveness and stealth. Paul was at the back, and I noted he was now armed. The rest of us, except for the armed guys on watch and the chap on crowd control, gathered around DI Johns. He was calling the shots. He watched as the technician finished setting up the comms. I'd tried to hover at the back, out of view, but the DI spotted me and frowned. He looked like he was about to protest my presence here, when he was interrupted.

'Okay, we're getting him on line.'

I had to concentrate hard to hear the sound of the phone ringing over the top of the wind. After four rings it picked up.

'What?' the voice said. Even with the acoustic challenges I could recognise the sound of stress when I heard it.

'Jacob Sandhurst, this is Detective Inspector Johns of the Dunedin CIB.'

'Fuck off,' the voice yelled down the phone.

'Is there anyone there with you, or are you alone?'

'Fuck you.'

We knew he was alone. I'd learned from one of the other guys that we'd been tipped off to Sandhurst's whereabouts by someone at the neighbouring house. He had recognised his photo in the morning newspaper. The Cockroach didn't own this place, and the neighbour hadn't seen him here before. He put two and two together and made a telephone call. The house happened to be owned by one James Clarke. Surely that couldn't be a coincidence? It had to be our Jimmy Clarke, him of the tight shirt and mangy dog. Dunedin was too small for that to be a coincidence, and anyway, I didn't believe in coincidences. Suddenly some connections were coming clear. Jimmy was a new player in the drug business, Cockroach an old hand, looking for a new business partner perhaps. Knock off the old one? Disappear with some help from a friend?

DI Johns pressed on. 'You need to know that you are surrounded and cannot escape. We have a warrant for your arrest for the murder of John Henderson, and would like to question you about the murder of Gideon Powell.'

'I didn't fucking kill either of them.' His voice sounded puffed, like he was running. I could hear the sound of curtains being pulled, old ones on metal runners. He was obviously rushing from window to window, seeing who was coming.

'That is something we can only clear up if you come in. Give yourself up, Jacob, and you can give us your side of the story.'

'No fucking way. You guys have stitched me up over Henderson, and now you're going to do the same over Gid. You're all the bloody same.'

DI Johns kept on in the same calm, even voice. The look on his face didn't match the tone. 'No one is stitching you up. We are only interested in establishing the truth. We can't do that unless you hand yourself in and come and talk about it.'

There was no response, but I could still hear the panting breath, and the sound of scraping furniture. He was barricading himself in.

'Jacob, you need to know you are surrounded, and our officers are armed. You cannot escape. The best thing you can do right now is lay down your weapons, put your hands above your head and walk out the front door, onto the road and lie face down. I promise you won't get hurt.'

'No fucking way. Why should I trust you? You've been setting me up all along. You tell your men to get back, you hear? Tell them to back off right fucking now.'

This wasn't sounding good. Did he honestly think we were about to back down and walk away? I had a sudden thought. I bet he was high — high as a kite. I remembered his twitchiness when he'd first been brought in for questioning, which seemed like an eternity ago, but was in reality only a little over a week since. I wondered what substance was making his decisions for him? If it was P he was probably thinking he was a caped superhero and invincible about now. Bulletproof.

I heard a familiar sound, a shotgun being primed, and then another, and another. Jesus, how many weapons did he have? Behind me I heard the low warning murmur of the AOS communicator.

'Jacob, it's not too late to surrender.'

There was a smashing of glass, and then the boom of a shotgun blast from over the phone speaker. A split second later the report echoed in the distance. Then all hell broke loose as return fire came from the AOS and Taieri Mouth started to sound like a battlefield.

'Fuck,' DI Johns said as the phone connection terminated.

I felt fingers of ice spread through my veins and blocks crystallise in my belly. There was only one thought going around in my head.

Paul.

52

It felt like an eternity before news started filtering back, an eternity where I could do nothing but sit on the ground and wait. I would have stood, but the strength in my legs had deserted me. The gunfight had been brief, but intense, and then the all-clears and the headcounts came in. I'd never felt such relief in my life as I did when I heard Paul's name and the word 'safe' used in the same sentence.

It felt like another eternity before I saw him trudging back down the road towards me, flanked by two AOS guys. As he approached I threw caution to the wind and ran to throw my arms around his waist. I didn't give a flying fuck who saw it.

'Thank God you're safe.'

'Well of course I am, you funny little lady. I was hiding in the back, remember?' He leaned down and gave me a big kiss. Apparently he'd given up caring too.

'Still, when I heard all the shots.'

'Yeah, well, I'd have preferred it if that hadn't happened.'

Him and everyone else. It was amazing how fast the spectators had scuttled away once the guns got blazing, even though we were all well and truly out of harm's way.

Again, the shadow of Aramoana played its part there, I suspected. It got me back to thinking about the idiot down at the house.

'The dumb bugger. It would have been much easier to give himself up. Why did he have to open fire?'

'Good question. Bit late to ask him now, though. Sandhurst's well and truly dead.'

53

The shit had hit the fan down outside Central Police Station. I'd been dropped off out front by one of the patrol cars, as Paul was still out at Taieri Mouth helping to sort out the mess. There appeared to be media swarming around the station, waiting for information. There were two camera crews, and they seemed to be concentrating on a little group of people standing under the central glass-covered entranceway.

Unfortunately I lacked the height to see who it was they were preying on.

The media and I had a testy relationship, to say the least. They seemed to have a knack of catching me when I wasn't at my best. A walk along the driveway side of the building and down to the back entrance suddenly seemed like a very good idea, and I felt grateful I was dressed in my civvies and not clearly labelled 'cop'. I had almost made it to cover when I heard a woman screech out at the top of her lungs, 'You!'

As I swung my head around to see who the scream had come from and who it was directed at, I realised in horror that all of the cameras and media people were swinging around to look at me. They parted like the Red Sea and there, standing at the apex, pointing at me, like some wild witch ready to unleash a curse, was Sheila Sandhurst.

Oh, bloody hell.

My first instinct was to bolt for cover, but common sense told me that would be a bad move, so I took the 'stand and look bewildered' approach. She took the 'I'm coming to get you' approach, and before my feet even had a chance to get walking again, Witchy Woman and her entourage were heading my way.

'You bastards killed my husband,' she said as she strode over, tears running down her face and hair streaming out behind her. The way the microphone-clutching reporters were scrabbling to keep up, and the camera flashes were going off, the media sharks were loving this. It was going to turn into a feeding frenzy in a second. I looked desperately into the foyer to see if the watch-house guys were keeping an eye out.

'You framed him for murder and then you killed him. You are all murderers, you are the murderers,' she screamed, and before I could react she had swung her arm around and punched me right smack in the face. A flare of white exploded in my eyes, followed by a wave of heat through my nose and I staggered back from the shock of the blow. A metallic tang rushed into my mouth and I could feel the warmth of blood running down my lip. I raised my hand up to wipe at it and it came away smeared in glistening red. I blinked away the sudden influx of water that had flooded my eyes just in time to see her arm swinging around for another shot.

Another wave flooded through me, and this time it was anger. The bitch had hit me. Why the hell had she done that? Jesus Christ. And not some girly slap either, but a full-on, closed-fist punch. And she wasn't done yet.

Bugger this. She didn't have the element of surprise this time, and as her fist came at me a second time I ducked under it at the last moment, reached up and, grabbing her by the wrist, let her own momentum carry her forward. I then pulled her arm up and around her back, at the same time stepping behind her. I gave a quick kick to the back of her legs and she fell forward onto her knees. I leaned my weight into her, pinning her down so she was trapped. I might have been smaller than her, but I had a few surprises up my sleeve as well.

'You fucking bitch,' she yelled.

The cameramen, photographers and reporters all swarmed around, forming a huddle, so when I looked up all I saw was a sea of lenses and microphones, and eager, expectant faces.

Sheila was still struggling for all she was worth, flailing her left hand around, trying to get at me. I leaned over onto her other shoulder to keep out of range, but she still managed to rake at my ribs with her fingernails. A sharp sting seared my side, to match the throb in my face. All the while the mob stood there and watched, eager for more. I could sense their need for blood, could feel their unspoken chant, egging her on. It was both terrifying and infuriating at the same time. Then one of them shoved a microphone into Sheila's face.

'Who is this woman, Sheila? And what has she done to you?'

What had I done to her? To her? It was pretty bloody obvious what she had done to me.

'Get her off me,' she yelled. 'Get her off. They're murderers, they're all murderers.' She was still writhing under me, struggling, and this time she managed to reach over her head and grab me by the hair, yanking for all she was worth.

Bloody hell. Were they all just going to stand there? I realised with a sinking heart that yes, they were, and they would enjoy the show. Where was my back-up? Where was the cavalry? Joe Public certainly hadn't come to my rescue.

It was time this was over.

'I'm an officer of the law, who has just been assaulted,' I yelled to anyone who would listen. 'And if you're just going to stand there and watch, you will be charged as accessories. Now is any one of you heartless wankers going to help me?'

54

I was sitting in the interview room, still holding a cold facecloth to my nose. The bleeding had stopped, but the hurting sure as hell hadn't. Fortunately my nose had taken the brunt of the attack, and even more fortunately I didn't think it was broken, as it was still pointing in the direction it should. That was lucky, and meant I wasn't sporting a couple of shiners. Instead there was just a little bruising beneath each eye and a touch of puffiness that could easily have been mistaken as the result of too many late nights. A little bit of concealer and no one would ever know.

The woman at the table opposite me sure as hell knew, though.

Sheila Sandhurst was slumped in the seat, hugging herself, a rocking and blubbering mess. All the impassioned fervour from earlier had gone and the Witchy Woman had been replaced by a hollowed, grief-stricken shell. I had a flashback to not that many days ago when it was Gideon Powell's wife in here. Although their grace and decorum differed, there was no mistaking the deepseated and heartfelt pain they both felt. They might have been married to criminal scum, but there was no questioning the love these women had for their men. In fact, seeing Sheila here, broken like this, I could almost forgive her for attacking me. I wouldn't forget it in a hurry though.

DC Richardson sat beside me, looking uncomfortable. I didn't know whether it was because she wasn't sure how to deal with the intense emotion on display, or because she wasn't relishing her role as my personal bodyguard. Normally the victim of an assault wouldn't have been allowed anywhere near the perpetrator, but in this instance I'd asked to be here, and Sheila Sandhurst had insisted she would only talk to me. It was an odd situation all round.

'Sheila, do you think you're able to answer a few questions now?' I asked. With my swollen, blocked nose and the facecloth partially covering my face, I sounded a bit like Daffy Duck. I put the cloth on the table.

She nodded and gave an almighty, chunky sniff that made my stomach turn.

'Did you know that Jacob was out at Taieri Mouth?'

She shook her head.

'But you'd been in contact?'

'Yes. I knew he was safe, but not where.' The word 'safe' seemed pretty redundant now. 'If I didn't know where he was, I wouldn't have to lie to anyone who asked.'

'What did he tell you about Gideon Powell?'

'You mean about his death?'

'Yes.'

'Nothing.' She gave another stomach-churning sniff. 'I told him.'

'What do you mean?'

'He didn't know Gid was dead. When I rang and told him, that was the first he knew of it. He was really, really upset and crying and stuff.

230

Then after youse guys told me you thought my Jacob did it, and I told him that, he was fair shitting himself.'

'He said he didn't do it?'

'Of course he didn't do it. Gid was his mate, they'd been mates forever, they looked out for each other. Someone else got to Gid and did that — it wasn't my Jacob.'

'So where was he on the night Gideon Powell died — on Wednesday the thirteenth of April?'

She took on a dejected, almost resigned look. 'I don't know. He'd already buggered off because youse guys were trying to pin the Seacliff man's murder on them. He packed up and left straight after he got back from the cop shop. Said he wasn't going to hang around to get arrested for something he didn't do. Like I said before, he never told me where any of his boltholes were. He was probably already out at Taieri Mouth, where you guys . . .'

The words were left unspoken, and she took a big drink from the white plastic cup of water on the table next to her, trying to get herself together. When she'd regained her composure she continued.

'I did talk to him that night, and he was all normal. I think there was someone else there too. Yeah, there was, because I remember hearing the telly on in the background, there was that big boxing match on. He was there watching telly, and someone was there with him, because he talked to him. He wasn't out killing anyone.'

'Do you know who was there?'

'No, I don't. And I wish I did because then he

could tell you, and you might believe him. It wasn't my Jacob.'

'The house we found him in out at Taieri Mouth, it belonged to someone called James Clarke. Do you know anyone by that name?'

'Jimmy — must be Jimmy Clarke. He's just a mate,' Sheila said.

'Is he one of Gideon and Jacob's associates? Part of their operations?'

'No. He's outside. New, I think.'

'But he let Jacob use his house? How well did Jacob know him? Did Gideon know he knew him?' It was too many questions at once, and Sheila looked a little bewildered, but to her credit, she picked up on what I was getting at. I guessed you didn't get to be the wife of a criminal king-pin without picking up a few wiles of your own.

'If you're saying that my Jacob was pulling the wool on Gid, then no way. Gid knew about Jimmy. Knew all about him. They were just testing the water, letting Jacob become friendly with him, keeping an eye out.'

It was a dog-eat-dog world. So Jimmy had got their attention enough that they were checking him out. Did Jimmy get too big for his boots? Or did Sandhurst decide he liked playing at Jimmy's house and with Jimmy's toys better than Powell's and the two of them colluded to get rid of the big guy? But then I remembered what Sheila had just said about Jacob not having known Powell was dead, and about his having the wind up about being a suspect. People who had survived in the drug industry for as long as Jacob Sandhurst had did not fair crap themselves about anything. They could roll with any punch. So maybe he didn't kill Powell after all and some other piece of vermin had taken care of it.

'Tell me, Sheila. With Gideon and Jacob gone, who would be next in their organisation? Who would step up to take the reins?'

She shook her head. 'No, I'm not going to talk about any of that stuff to youse. That was their business; I'm not going there. Enough is enough.'

'But Sheila, you were just telling me that Jacob didn't kill Gideon. If Jacob didn't then we have to find out who did. That's the only way we can clear Jacob's name, isn't it? Find out the identity of the real killer? We have to look at Gideon's enemies, but we also have to look at people closer to him.' The good old enemy within. 'Give us a name.'

'Are you serious? This could help clear Jacob?'

'It might.' Non-committal, but the best I could do.

She considered for a moment, then looked down at the desk and spoke quietly like she didn't want anyone to overhear.

'Mikey. Mikey Chadwick.'

That name rang a bell. And we just happened to have asked Jimmy Clarke about him the other day. The drug squad had been trying to figure out his exact place in the scheme of things and who he was aligned to. Well now we knew.

'Thank you,' I said. 'It gives us a good place to start looking.'

'What about that other business?' She leaned forward onto the table, imploring.

'What do you mean?'

'That other murder, the Seacliff one. Can you clear Jacob's name of that?'

I sighed. It had been a hell of a day, and the last thing I needed was yet another woman putting the onus on me to absolve the sins of her man.

'Look, Sheila. I know this is hard for you, and I am truly sorry for your loss today. But we have really good evidence — solid evidence that will stand up in a court of law — that says that Gideon Powell killed John Henderson and that Jacob was there too. We have their fingerprints, and we have DNA evidence that tells us they were at the scene of the crime. There is nothing we can do to change that.'

'But can't you see?' she said. 'Can't you see he didn't do it? He was with me, I swear he was. How can I prove that to you? Can't you see that was why he was forced to do what he did today? Why he opened fire on the cops? You backed him into a corner. He didn't have to do that, he didn't have to die, but he couldn't see any other way out. My Jacob didn't kill either of those men, but no one would listen, no one would believe him.'

I looked into her eyes and thought about the way events had turned and tried to ignore the little feeling of disquiet in my belly.

55

My mind wasn't being cooperative and kept swinging back to the rather pressing issues of new life and imminent death. In an attempt to drown out the head noise with other noise I'd plonked myself down in one of the interview rooms and was watching the original recorded interrogation of The Cockroach. DI Johns and Paul were doing the interviewing and were being persistent and repetitive, going back over what he'd said, trying to detect any change in his story, gaps, the unexplainable. Their quiet persistence was driving Sandhurst nuts; in fact he was vehemently denying having killed John Henderson.

'Can't you dumb fucks see? I've been stitched up. We both have been. There's no fucking way we killed Henderson.'

'The evidence doesn't lie, Mr Sandhurst.'

'Well it fucking well has this time, because I had nothing to do with it, I wasn't even there. You got it wrong. I've been framed. In fact, I bet it was you guys.' At which point he started pointing his fingers at the detectives. 'You fuckers planted the evidence, didn't you? Planted this crap to make it look like we did it. You been wanting to put us away for years. It's a fucking stitch-up.'

Sandhurst seriously needed to expand his repertoire of expletives. Also, if he had any idea how often we heard those words — 'framed', 'stitched up' and 'planted' — he'd have thought

235

of something else more original to say, or else he would have saved his breath. Unfortunately, he had the credibility of a kid with his hand caught in the cookie jar. He was such a repugnant and reprehensible excuse for a human being, with a string of priors longer than my arm, that he garnered as much sympathy from me as he did from the two detectives sitting across the table, hammering away at him. But, I did have to concede, he appeared a lot more sincere and convincing than most people who took the attack approach to defence. In fact, he was doing a good job of 'pleading and desperate', tempered with 'defiant and obnoxious'. Quite a skill.

I thought of the voice coming over the phone out at Taieri Mouth, again accusing us of planting evidence, of framing him and Powell, of killing John Henderson, and then of framing him for the murder of Powell. A voice desperate enough to go out guns blazing, into a certain death sentence. Suicide by cop. Desperation because of guilt? Or desperation because of innocence and the realisation that there was no hope of justice?

My mind entertained the unspeakable for a moment. Powell denied it, Sandhurst denied it. Their wives provided their alibis. Their wives also, in their own dramatic ways, fought for their husbands' innocence. What if they were telling the truth? Could they have been set up? I dismissed the thought pretty damn fast. It would have been impossible — the evidence was too strong. There was both fingerprint and DNA evidence linking them to the scene of John Henderson's murder. The only witness to the murder hadn't been able to make a positive identification, just a limited physical description because of the killers' protective clothing and disguise. So what if someone managed to find two people of similar stature to Gideon Powell and Jacob Sandhurst to do the deed, and somehow managed to have the evidence to plant, as it were? You would have to have some pretty determined and clever enemies to pull that one off. But then, God only knew, Gideon Powell and Jacob Sandhurst had amassed quite a collection of enemies.

56

'So what would you do?'

'You'll need to be a little more specific than that, I'm afraid,' Maggie said. We were parked at home at our small circular dining-room table, trying to eat, with some semblance of decorum, the smoked salmon linguine Maggs had created for dinner. So far I wasn't succeeding too well, and had the stain on the front of my shirt to prove it. At least it was her I was being piggy in front of, and not someone I was trying to impress. The dinner would have been washed down so much better with a good Riesling, but, due to a certain parasitic condition, I wasn't allowed any, and Maggie was abstaining in sympathy.

'If you're referring to the 'some crazed woman punched me today' thing, then yes, you have to press charges. No one can assault an officer and get away with it, especially when it was on the national news. What kind of message would that send?'

We'd watched the six o'clock news, me cringing with anticipation of what angle the media would have made of it. They didn't disappoint and managed to make out that I had somehow provoked the attack, and of course they played up the distraught widow, with the police having just brutally and wrongfully killed her angelic, model-citizen husband who the big nasty police had framed for a murder he didn't commit. My only consolation for enduring it was Maggie giving me a high five for what she referred to as the 'wild witchy woman hold' move.

'As much as I hated to do it, yes, she was charged with assault, which I'm sure made her day. And no, I'm not that big a bleeding heart.'

'Oh yes, you are,' she said as she noisily slurped up a mouthful of noodles.

'Classy.'

'Thank you.'

I smiled. 'No, I was thinking more of a conundrum that's come up at work.' I swirled the linguine around my fork but thought better of putting it in my mouth. I'd reached an elegant sufficiency, and, as my Gran would have put it, any more would have been a superfluity. So I played with it instead.

'I take it you're not referring to the pregnancy? You have told him, haven't you?'

'Well . . . '

'You're kidding me. You haven't told him yet? Why not?'

'I did try, but work got in the way, and then, with the whole shooting thing, I didn't get the chance. In fact, I haven't even seen Paul since this morning.'

'Sam, you've known for days. What's the issue?'

'There isn't an issue.'

She looked at me, suspicion curling the corners of her mouth. 'You are going through with it, aren't you? You are going to have this baby? You're not going to deprive me of a goddaughter, are you?'

That was a bit of an assumption, even if it was correct.

'Of course I am,' I said. 'And of course I wouldn't deprive you.' Although, to be honest, the alternative had crossed my mind. But somehow, especially with Dad being the way he was, it didn't seem right. I thought about the other thing she said. 'What makes you so sure it will be a girl?'

She just shrugged, and smiled that knowing smile of hers.

'Paul will make a great dad. He'll be fantastic, you know that, don't you?'

I looked at Maggie, a spark of shock forming in my mind. I had to admit something to myself that I didn't really like. In all of my thoughts so far on the new life I was carrying, I hadn't actually thought of it in terms of Paul being a dad, in the broader sense. Biologically speaking, yes, and in terms of how that would affect me, yes, but not from his perspective — of him being a little person's daddy. An image leapt into my mind of him tossing a giggling, tousle-haired little girl into the air, sheer joy sculpted into his face, and I realised with a gulp that she was right, he would be amazing. I felt a pang of guilt at how Sam-centric I'd been about all this. It wasn't all about me. With that realisation I felt a big funk descend upon me and my shoulders sagged under the combined load of tiredness, emotional drain and painful self-revelation.

'Okay,' she said, 'whatever went through your head just then looks like it blew something. You all right?'

'Not really, but I'll get over it,' I said.

'Have you told your mum?'

Bless her, Maggie knew that would make me laugh, and I did, borderline hysterically. 'Are you insane?'

'According to our self-testing in my psych labs, yes,' she said. 'But you won't hold that against me, will you?' I shook my head. 'So, what's really bugging you, besides all that other minor stuff in your life?'

How did I put this into words?

'You know this murder case I'm working on, the Seacliff one? And how we have good, solid evidence to put away two of the scummiest, most repugnant criminal individuals on the planet? The same people we think were responsible for Detective Reihana being killed?'

'Yes.'

'Well, I'm having my doubts.'

'Why? I thought you said the evidence was conclusive.'

'That's the thing, it is. We have solid fingerprint and DNA evidence that puts them at the scene; it's cut and dried as far as everyone is concerned. And God only knows we've been trying to put these guys away for years, but . . . '

'Why are you having doubts?'

'It's the women. Both the wives are the only alibis these guys have, and of course no one believes them. We all know that wives would say anything to help their husbands, especially if they know what's good for them. But, you know something? I'm actually starting to believe them.'

'This isn't just another one of your idealistic attacks of too much faith in human nature?'

'Maybe it is, maybe it isn't. But it's not just

that. I heard him, Maggie, I heard that man today when he was holed up in the house out Taieri Beach, backed into a corner and still proclaiming his innocence, and it haunts me. He sounded desperate — more than desperate. He sounded . . . God, I don't even know the word. Pleading? Resigned?'

'Innocent?'

'Innocent.' That was the word. 'And that's the thing I can't get my head around. These men were far from innocent; they were the biggest criminals this city had. They were responsible for providing the drugs that ruin so many lives and cause so many deaths. They ordered the beatings and killings of so many people, and only ever created mayhem and misery. They were despicable, wicked men, and here was our chance to put them inside and throw away the key, except we can't even do that now, because they're both dead. But we can lay all this at their feet — except that I think they're innocent. In my heart, I don't think they did this, and I don't know what to do. Part of me thinks I should let it go, that they are vermin, scum, the meanest bastards in the world, and they got what they deserved. But then this other part of me thinks this isn't right.'

There was a long pause before Maggie spoke.

'But what part of you do you think you can live with, Sam?' It was a simple question, asked quietly, but its power clarified everything. She knew it too.

'But they will hate me for it.'

'Who will?'

'My colleagues, especially The Boss . . . oh God, and Smithy. Everyone.'

'Why did you join the police, Sam?'

'To save the world, fight for the wronged, bring justice for all.'

'Justice for all?'

'Yeah, for all.' And that included vermin, scum and the meanest bastards in the world.

57

'I don't know why you're even bringing this
up, Shep. We've got the bastards.' Smithy was
looking none too pleased with my playing devil's
advocate. Paul was beside him, and judging by
the look on Paul's face, for the first time ever
— miracles and wonders — the two of them
were in total agreement.

'I know, I know,' I said, unaccustomed to the
show of unity, 'and the evidence is strong; but
what I'm trying to say here, is okay, what if yes,
the evidence is strong, but it is contrived? That
someone has engineered all this. And it's not like
either of them are able to defend themselves, are
they?'

'But who would go to that kind of trouble?
Because what you're suggesting is something so
fantastic, it's impossible. Someone managed to
orchestrate it so that two killers turned up who
just happened to be of a similar build to Powell
and Sandhurst, and not only did these mystery
people commit the murder, but they then actually had the evidence to plant and incriminate
with. How would they have been able to get hold
of a pair of latex gloves with the fingerprints?
And then manage to get them covered in gunshot
residue and John Henderson's blood? And how
would they have got hold of hair to provide
DNA?'

Normally I'd have felt betrayed by Paul

negating my argument, but he was right, this one was so fantastical that, for today, his questioning only mildly piqued me. My mind had to have a little grapple before it came up with a possible answer to that one.

'Well, the men were involved in the drug trade. They were manufacturing. They would often be wearing gloves, I would imagine, and masks to stop themselves from being permanently high. And probably the ugly little disposable caps, and in reality it's not that hard to get a hair sample off someone. So, what if it was someone in their own organisation? Someone high up their pecking order who decided they wanted a promotion to the top-dog position?' Smithy and Paul shared an incredulous look. 'Come on guys, think about it. What a perfect way for the next in line to assume the leadership role. They have cleverly managed to make it look like the top guys have committed a major crime that would see them put away for a very, very long time. They would have known them well enough to know their routines, so they could ensure that on the night in question neither of them had a decent alibi. So, to the rest of the organisation, it doesn't actually look like an overthrow or a coup. No one's toes get stepped on and no loyalties are divided. No one is forced to have to choose between the old guard and the new. It would be a bloody smart move.'

'Bloody impossible move,' Smithy said. 'Tell me this then, smart arse. If that was the case, why would Powell suddenly get shot?'

And that was where I felt my argument crumbled somewhat. 'Rival gang? I don't know.

245

Or maybe Powell suspected something or someone and they had to move to deal with it? It certainly could have been the person who orchestrated this.'

'I would be curious to know who has taken over as head of Powell's operations.'

I could have kissed Paul for that comment. It also made me aware that I had been standing with my hands folded over my belly. I dropped them down to my sides, hoping I didn't look self-conscious about it.

'According to Sheila Sandhurst, it's a guy named Mikey Chadwick. And we need to talk to Jimmy Clarke again — it was his place Sandhurst was holed up in.'

'Surely that can't be a coincidence.'

'Oh, for fuck's sake, you're not buying into this idea, are you?' Smithy was never good at hiding his disgust. 'This is all a load of crap. For a start, how the hell would the glove thing work?'

'Well, I've been thinking about that,' I said, as I pulled a few photographs off the pile on my desk. 'Remember in the evidence report they said the killers had double-gloved. I was wondering why they bothered. But then I realised — you would bother if you wanted the blood spatter and gunshot residue evidence on the outside pair of gloves, and the planted fingerprint evidence for the inside pair. So, two pairs.' I'd grabbed two boxes of latex gloves, sizes large and small, to give a demonstration. 'Come on guys, glove up.'

They looked at each other, then looked at me, one with distaste and one with mock long-suffering.

246

'Okay, I'll play the game, but I hope there's a point to this,' Paul said. He reached into the box that said large and proceeded to wriggle two pairs on. I did the same with my small ones.

Smithy stood still. He clearly wasn't in the mood for joining in.

'Okay, Paul. Now take them off.'

Now he looked at me like I was a stubbie short of a six-pack. 'I just put them on.'

'Humour me.'

He gave a big sigh and pulled the two pairs off in one go.

'Bingo.' I smiled to myself, then pointedly held out my hands and pulled off my gloves in one go, too.

'And your point is?' Paul asked.

I slid to him the scene photographs of the bloodied protective suits pulled out of the wheelie bin.

'What do you notice about the gloves in the photo?' I asked.

Paul cottoned on straight away. 'They have been pulled off individually, each layer separately, so they are all individual gloves.'

'Exactly; but the instinctive way to deglove yourself is to pull both gloves off in one go. So why would they do them individually? Because the real killers wanted the outer pair to link the evidence to the scene, the gunshot residue and blood spatter, and pocketed their inner pairs with their own fingerprints, and substituted them with the Powell and Sandhurst pairs they brought along to plant. So suddenly, it looks like Fat Bastard and The Cockroach were the killers. Easy.'

'Not exactly easy, and still pretty far-fetched,' sighed Paul.

'It's a load of utter tosh if you ask me. We've got solid evidence that tells us two of the biggest pieces of scum of the earth, the scum we know damn well killed Reihana,' Smithy's face was contorted with anger, and he was spitting out the words; ' . . . those pieces of shit murdered John Henderson, just like they murdered our friend. So don't you even dare suggest it was otherwise.' And with that he swept the boxes of gloves off the desk and stormed out of the room.

58

'Your mate is a little touchy, don't you think?'

Paul and I were in that Dunedin institution — The Best Café — sitting at a Formica table, grabbing a comfort-food lunch. Sometimes fish and chips at lunchtime was all a girl wanted. I wasn't about to tell Paul one of the reasons for this option was because of the magic a big feed of fat and cholesterol did for a squeamish stomach. Not that this was your ordinary plate of shark and taties — it was my all-time favourite, blue cod.

'If you're referring to Smithy, that wasn't grumpy. You haven't seen grumpy yet.'

Paul looked a tad sceptical at that statement. 'Well, he wasn't fond of your theory.'

'You wouldn't be either if it suggested someone you hated with a vengeance was actually not to blame, and could walk again. Not that Fat Bastard Powell is walking anywhere anymore. Can we talk about something else? I'm sure we can manage to have a meal without talking shop.'

'Okay,' he said with a chuckle. 'So I have to rely on wit and charm to entertain you?'

'True, that could be a challenge, considering you're so lacking in that department.'

He took a pretend swipe at me. 'Okay then, if we aren't allowed to discuss business, what shall we talk about? What's new? What do you know?'

When faced with the realities of my options

here — number one, talk about the imminent death of my father; or, number two, tell the man he was going to be a daddy — I had a sudden urge to talk about the intricacies of tear marks in insulation tape at crime scenes. Then there was the need to strip off a layer of clothing, because it was really quite hot and stuffy in here.

'Well,' he said, 'you must know something?'

I shook my head dumbly, hoping he didn't notice the fluorescent red I was certain my face was glowing. When in doubt, go on the offensive.

'Okay, your turn. What have you got to tell me about?'

He laughed, and my heart couldn't help but melt. If he had such an effect on me, what the hell was I holding back for? Did I want blissful cohabitation with baby? Was pregnancy really a valid reason to change my tune on the whole living-together thing? Was I such a vast commitment phobe?

'You look beautiful when you're scarlet.'

'I'm not scarlet.'

'You make beetroot look wan.'

'You have to admit it's rather stuffy in here.'

'It's not that bad.'

'Yes it is.'

'What's up? What are you hiding?'

'I'm not hiding anything. Why would you think I'm hiding something?'

'Because you're bright red, being cagey and acting all prickly.'

Sprung on all fronts. But the simple fact was that I wasn't ready for that conversation right now. At this exact moment my courage had deserted me. I went for diversion tactics.

'Well, it's about work and I thought we were trying to have a meal without shop talk. I don't want to come across as someone who can't go a moment without obsessing about work, and we don't want to turn into one of those sad couples who don't have anything to talk about other than work. But if you really want to know, I've been thinking about the Henderson and Powell case again.'

He laughed properly this time. 'You're right. We are sad, because now you've got my attention and I really want to know. What have you come up with this time? I just hope it doesn't involve a live demonstration or an experiment in a restaurant.'

I looked around at the happily munching groups at the tables around us and lowered my voice. The topic of conversation wasn't really suitable for mass consumption.

'No, I won't do that to you. But you might not like this anyway.'

He gave me a quizzical look, but he still had that annoying 'go on then, humour me' expression on his face. He was lucky it was kind of endearing. He was also lucky I was desperate for a diversion.

'You know I'm convinced that Powell and Sandhurst didn't kill John Henderson.'

'Yes. You've made that quite clear.'

'And you're with me on that one?'

'Not entirely, but I'm listening.'

'I'm also convinced that Sandhurst didn't kill Powell.'

'No one said that he did.'

'Yeah, but everyone thinks that was why he ran.'

'It's a popular theory.'

'But Powell's wife says there's no way he would have killed his mate, and Sandhurst's wife denies it too. And I mentioned this morning what Sandhurst's wife said about Jimmy Clarke, and who the 3IC is from the organisation.'

'Mikey Chadwick. Yes. And I'm wondering why you're suddenly so chummy with the wives, especially the one who gave you a hiding.'

My hand drifted up and touched my nose. It was true that I seemed to have a knack for attracting the hard-done-by and the underdogs, who invariably expected me to solve all their problems. I seemed to have a neon sign over my head flashing the word 'sucker' alternating with 'champion of hopeless causes'.

'We need to go and see Jimmy,' I said.

'Yes, that's a logical step. So why are you talking like that's a problem?'

'Because Dickhead Johns and almost everyone else is convinced they know who killed who, and they are happy to leave it at that. I'm not, and I need you to come with me, to get to the bottom of it properly.'

He looked at me, serious, his big blue eyes boring into mine. 'You know I love you, don't you?' he said.

'Yes.'

'So when I tell you you're a liability and a pain in the arse sometimes, you know I mean it in the nicest possible way.'

'Of course. So does that mean you're going to help me?'

'Does it mean I'll get sex?' he asked, a cheeky curl pulling at the corner of his mouth.

'Maybe.'

'Okay, that's good enough for me.'

59

Paul and I were getting quite inventive in finding reasons to be out of the building, and due to recent events, everyone else was too busy to notice. The Boss had been tied up with the internal investigation — inevitable when a police operation results in the death of a civilian. He was also reacquainting himself with the downside of being in the media spotlight. There was a beautiful satisfaction in seeing him squirm. It did mean he was in a fouler mood than usual, which was another good reason to be out of the building.

The last time I'd called on Jimmy Clarke I was with Smithy. And the last time I'd visited Jimmy, Smithy had dealt with his mangy mutt. Once again the manic critter came flying around the corner at us, frothing at the mouth — except this time it came with a companion, an equally feral-looking kid. The kid must have been about five years old, was wearing a white singlet top, jeans and bare feet. Considering it was only about eight degrees out, I thought he was perhaps a little underdressed.

By the time all this had gone through my mind the cur had reached Paul and looked like it was figuring out which bit of him it was going to eat first. Paul looked down at it unconcerned and proceeded to knee the bugger in the middle of the chest, just like Smithy had. There was a yelp and the dog turned tail and hurtled back past the kid, who looked a little surprised at this turn of events. The kid was made of sterner stuff, though. He stood his ground, with his hands on his hips, appraising us.

'Who are you?' he asked.

'We are here to see your dad,' I said, making an assumption.

'Yeah, but who are you?'

'We're detectives.'

'From the police?'

'Yes.'

'Do you have a warrant?'

I heard a stifled snort from beside me and tried not to burst out laughing myself. The way he stood there, serious and polite, guardian of the property, was almost too much.

'No, we don't have a warrant,' I said, 'but I can show you my identification.' I pulled my ID out of my wallet, bent down and held it out for him to see.

He came over and looked at it closely, comparing the photograph to my face, and then looked expectantly up at Paul. Paul obediently pulled his ID out and extended it for scrutiny.

'Can you please go and ask your dad if he will talk with us?'

We seemed to have passed his test. 'All right.' The little man turned on his heel and ran around the back of the house.

'Was it just me or was that intolerably cute?' I said.

'He was well coached.'

He certainly knew the drill.

A few moments later Jimmy Clarke opened the front door. He was wearing the same kind of singlet top and jeans as the boy, although he was wearing shoes, and he looked at us with the same level of suspicion.

'Hi, I'm Detective Shephard. I was here the other day.' He nodded in acknowledgement. 'This is Detective Frost. You have a very confident wee boy there.'

The child in question was standing behind his dad, mirroring his posture.

'He's a good kid.' Jimmy turned around and spoke to him quietly. 'Go on and play now.' Then he turned back to us. 'And what can I help you with this time, Detectives?' With that tone in his voice, I imagined it was a dig about the last visit, when Smithy had not been exactly civil.

'We've got some questions we'd like to ask you, about Jacob Sandhurst.'

'What do you want to know?' At least he didn't deny knowing him. It was a good start.

'He was killed yesterday at your property at Taieri Mouth. Were you aware that he was there?' Looking at this dump, I wondered how he could afford a place out that way.

'Yes.'

'Why were you hiding him?'

'I wasn't hiding him. He asked if he could have a place to stay for a few days, so I said yes.'

'Are you aware there was a warrant out for his arrest for the murder of John Henderson?'

'He just said he was in a bit of trouble, and that he needed a few days for it to blow over. After what happened out there yesterday, it's quite obvious it didn't blow over. I gather the house is a bit of a mess.'

'You haven't been out there yet?' Paul asked.

'No. This is my first official visit from any police. I was waiting to see when you would be in touch, when I'd get an invitation. I guess you've been busy.'

He stood there, calm and expressionless. I got a sudden feeling in my stomach. There was something more ominous to me about his calm assurance than there had been seeing Gideon Powell in full-on blow-hard cursing and arrogant flight, and Jacob Sandhurst in revolting Cockroach mode. There wasn't any sense of hostility, or even of concern on Jimmy's part, just a touch of sarcasm. It was the complete unreadability that made me uncomfortable. That, and his physical presence. He was of a similar build to Paul — tall, all lean muscle and sinew, with a wiry strength that would be unstoppable should he choose to use it.

'When did you talk to him last?' I said.

'Yesterday. He rang me when you guys had him pinned down.'

'Can you recall what he said?'

'He asked me what he should do. He was panicking. I told him he should put his guns down, walk out the front door, lie down and surrender, that it wasn't worth picking a fight. But he said he couldn't do that.'

'Why not?' Although I suspected I knew what the answer would be.

'His exact words were 'because the bastards aren't going to believe me'. He'd heard that you suspected him of killing Gid, and of course you had a warrant out for the other guy. As far as he was concerned the police were out to get him and he couldn't see any way out.'

He'd been candid up to this point. It was time to press it further.

'And do you believe he had anything to do with the death of Gideon Powell?'

'No, I'm positive he didn't.'

'How about you?'

He showed his first real sign of emotion then. He laughed.

I could sense Paul tensing up behind me.

'No. I had nothing to do with that either.'

'So where were you on the night of Wednesday, the thirteenth of April?'

'You're serious?' he asked.

I nodded.

He shrugged. 'If you must know, I was out at the Taieri Mouth house with Jaco. We had a few beers and were watching the fight.' Sheila Sandhurst had said her husband wasn't alone when she'd rung him that night. She'd mentioned the fight.

'Who won?' Paul asked.

Jimmy looked at him like he had been living in a vacuum. 'The home boy, of course. In the third round, if you want specifics, right upper cut, KO.'

'That just tells us you watched the fight. You could have seen that on the replay. Was there anyone else there who can confirm it?' Paul said. Paul's easy manner was a stark contrast to Smithy's style of questioning the other day. I could sense that Jimmy here wasn't about to take offence.

'No, but my missus will vouch that I was away for the night. And Sheila rang Jaco when the fight was on. I heard them talking.'

That didn't mean anything either. I didn't care much for this guy, but I needed to establish that Jacob Sandhurst couldn't have been anywhere else but out enjoying a boys' night at Taieri Mouth when Powell was busy meeting his demise. I did some mental gymnastics.

'The fight — it was on Sky, wasn't it?'

'Yeah.'

'On Pay Per View?'

'Yes.'

'So if we got your Sky decoder number out there, we'd be able to see if you were watching the match?'

I saw his shoulders relax, just a fraction. 'Yeah, you would. You go do that.'

'Do you have Sky here? A separate decoder? Or do you take the one unit to whichever house you're at?'

'Are you kidding? We've got two. My missus would go apeshit if I took off and left her without the Living Channel.' Judging by the state of this place, she watched it but didn't emulate.

'How well did you know Gideon Powell?' Paul changed tack.

The shoulders tensed up again. 'I didn't kill him, if that's what you are asking.' Jimmy was completely the wrong build, going from Jill's description, to have been on the business end of the murder, but it didn't mean he couldn't have orchestrated it. 'I met Gid a few times, through Jaco. He was an all-right guy. I know the two of them were keeping an eye on me, testing the ground.'

'You had aspirations to their business?'

'Let's just say I wouldn't have minded being part of their organisation, but I wasn't, not yet. Like I said, they were keeping an eye.'

'Which is why you let Sandhurst stay at your house?'

'A favour is a favour.'

'What about Mikey Chadwick?'

'Like I said the other day, I have no idea who Mikey Chadwick is.'

'What about John Henderson? Had you met him?'

'No, never met the guy.'

'Did Jacob talk about him at all?'

'He talked about this guy who got bulk ingredients for them, but not the pseudo. Said he was some flashy businessman, but never named him. He only said who he was after he was lumped with his murder.' He looked back, as if listening for someone in the hallway behind him, and then leaned forward like he was confiding. 'Look, if you want to know what I think, I reckon you guys have got the wrong men. Those two had nothing to do with that Seacliff guy dying, and Jaco certainly didn't kill Gid. I was with him the whole time. I'll stand up in court and swear it. They've been stitched up.' I looked at him sideways. 'And not by me either.' I had to believe him because someone who was stupid enough to fart up a pharmacy burglary so badly wouldn't have had the smarts to orchestrate this little affair. 'I reckon it was the police. Not necessarily you two, but someone.'

I didn't even bother entertaining that idea. We

had far more effective ways of dealing with criminals than pulling complicated stunts like that. And no one was going to put their career in jeopardy to get even with a few two-bit crooks.

'Stupid suggestion, Jimmy. Get real.'

'Well, you guys have got it all wrong anyway. You're barking up the wrong tree.'

60

'Do you believe me now?' I asked.

'It's gaining more traction,' Paul said. We were back at the station, having had a coffee, and figuring out where to head next. Well, he had coffee, I had tea. Paul was on his way out the door to check on a certain Sky decoder at Taieri Mouth. Hopefully it wouldn't have a bullet hole in a vital place.

It was almost lunchtime, and a visit to Dad was in order for me. In a way I didn't really want to see him. I'd kind of said my goodbyes, and this waiting around was killing me. It felt like every visit just picked at the scab of my grief and didn't actually achieve anything, other than heartache. The quietly groaning shell in the bed wasn't Dad as I wanted to remember him. But I had to do it. I had to put in an appearance for Mum's sake. Family politics only seemed to intensify at times like this and I knew all too well my mother would never forgive me if I didn't come. Dad would have just shrugged in his no-nonsense kind of way and said fair enough. He would have been mortified by all the bickering and backstabbing. I was glad he was oblivious to that side of things. I just prayed that deep down his subconscious was oblivious to his pain as well.

The phone on my desk started ringing, and I felt the little bite of anxiety that sound triggered in me nowadays.

'Shephard.'

'Detective? It's Angela Powell. We need to talk.'

★　★　★

We met in a seedy little Japanese restaurant down on George Street. I figured at this time of day the only people in there would be students taking advantage of the ten-dollar lunch special, so there was no risk of running into anyone from work. The ginger-beef bento box in front of me was huge — there was enough food there for two meals and it was delicious. It was clear why the students were fans.

I confessed to a certain amount of trepidation as well as curiosity when Angela asked for a get-together of the non-official kind — even more so when I saw she had turned up with Sheila Sandhurst. Some careful work with the concealer and the foundation had covered up her handiwork from yesterday, and I hoped there wouldn't be a repeat performance. Surely they weren't about to make a scene in a public place. The women's delegation was an unlikely pair: Powell wearing a new variation of her slut-in-mourning look, and Sandhurst looking more witchy than ever in the same clothes from yesterday. I think she'd slept in them too. They both carried the weary-worn look of people who were hurting.

'We have to know what's going on. No one will talk to us. Whenever the police come, it's just questions, questions, questions and all angling to try and make out our men were guilty. None of you believe us,' Angela said.

I lay my chopsticks down on the table beside the box. It was time to show my hand.

'I believe you,' I said quietly.

'Really? You honestly believe us? You're not having us on?' The misted-up look of gratitude on Sheila's face was incongruous with her hard image.

'Yes, I believe your husbands have been set up to look like they killed John Henderson. I don't know who by, yet, but I'm working on it. And I'm sure that Jacob had nothing to do with Gideon's death.'

They took a while to absorb what I was saying, as if they had never considered my acceptance of their stories a possibility.

'Does that mean their names will be cleared?' Angela asked.

'I'm sorry, I can't guarantee that. The thing is, most of my colleagues think they did these things, and, if I'm honest, I'd say they want them to be found guilty. Your husbands weren't saints and, because of things they did in the past, there are one or two people in the force who see it as a personal thing and want them done for it.'

'We know what they were into, and we know they were pretty hard men. I don't blame the cops for hating them. But the thing is, they didn't do this.'

I thought back to the reaction I got from Smithy for even suggesting the possibility. That sentiment would be echoed by many if word of my suspicions got out.

'It's going to take some serious evidence to

264

prove otherwise, and I don't know that it exists. Whoever did this planned everything so carefully, from the planted evidence to the general size and shape of the people who did the killing to match the men. They didn't make mistakes. Gideon's killing might hold the key. That one seems a little more spontaneous, less well planned. It may lead us to those responsible for the other. But I can't make any promises.'

'But you promise you will try?'

'I promise I will try.'

'What can we do?' Angela asked.

What could they do? I'd been thinking about that since I got the phone call. The physical evidence we had was too good for a jury to overlook. My only hope, besides a full confession from the guilty parties, was to prove their alibi. And not with the word of an easily influenced family member. The business with the Sky decoder had got me to thinking of other electronic devices that held a time record.

'Can either of you remember if Gideon or Jacob had used a computer on the night John Henderson was murdered?'

'No, I don't think so. We were watching a movie,' Sheila said.

'Gid always had his going. He was always on the internet, looking up stuff, or on Free Market.'

Free Market? The online trading website that was a perfect vehicle for getting rid of crap or acquiring crap. I imagined, for the career criminal, it was a handy means of offloading stolen goods. In fact, hard experience had told me it was widely used by all sorts of undesirables, as well as the bona fide, mumsy-dadsy traders out there.

'Do you know if he was buying or selling anything specific that night?'

I was sure I saw a glimmer of something — was it hope? — in her eyes. 'You know, he was always looking at model trains. He was really into them. We've got a room in our house that's one big train track — bridges, tunnels, everything. He was obsessed. He'd been trying to buy some train that week, and I'm pretty sure that was the night the auction finished. Something to do with the Queen's coronation. Some special-edition thing.'

My mind was trying to equate my image of Powell the criminal kingpin with one of a grown man playing with trains. I was struggling.

'The thing is,' I said, 'it may have left a trail, and it's a trail with a recorded time.' That was only if he'd been bidding. But then the web history would also have been logged — what pages had been looked at and when — and that could prove helpful. I got my hopes up for a moment before realising that surely the police computer guys would already have looked into this.

'When they came to arrest Gideon, I know he wasn't home, but did they take away his computer?'

'Yes, they did. They had a warrant to search the house and they took it away, along with a whole lot of other things.'

Which meant it should have been looked at. Although they were probably looking at files, rather than a time stamp that could prove his innocence.

266

'But he wasn't using his computer,' Angela said.

I looked up at her. 'What do you mean?'

'He was downstairs, so he was using my laptop. Had it on the table so he could pop out and check on things, then come back to watch TV.'

I felt a smile on my face. It felt alien and I realised how long it had been since I'd worn one.

'Did the police take your computer?'

'Well no, they didn't. They didn't take mine or the kids'.'

'Can I take it?'

A smile lit her face. 'Knock yourself out.'

61

'Shephard, what the hell do you think you are doing?'

I was walking down the hallway on the way back to the squadroom after my lunch with the widows' club and a quick visit down to Dad. Mum had been at her caustic best and managed to get in a few good pings. Accusing me of wanting Dad to die had been a barb too far, however, and I'd had to leave the building before I let fly with a few of my own. Even after the drive back and a walk around the block I was still seething. So when I heard that voice hollering down the hallway at me once more, I had to stand a few moments, count to five and consciously unclench my teeth before I turned around.

'Sir?'

He strode up and stood a little further into my personal space than I considered necessary.

'What the hell do you think you're up to? I hear you have this ridiculous notion that those two bastards didn't kill John Henderson.' Three guesses as to who he heard that from. I never thought I'd see the day when Smithy would side with The Boss against me. This whole damn affair was bringing out the worst in everyone. 'Well?'

'Well what?' I wasn't in the mood to pander to his outbursts today.

'Don't you talk like that to me, young lady. Explain yourself.'

268

I could see heads peeking around doorways down the corridor. We had an audience; great. Any chance of discreetly investigating my theory had just flown out the window. Perhaps in retrospect I should have altered my tone, but no, I wasn't in a sucking-up frame of mind. I stood straight, shoulders back, and looked him dead in the eye.

'I have reason to believe the evidence we found for the Henderson case was made to look like Powell and Sandhurst had done it. That it was a cleverly constructed plot to set them up.'

'And what reason would that be? Because of your feeble little idea about the gloves? That's ludicrous.'

'But it's enough to generate doubt. I have a duty to look into it.'

'Bullshit it is. And who the hell would do something like that? Don't be so bloody stupid. Those two men are the biggest pieces of shit this city has ever seen, and we have good, solid evidence that they did it. End of story. I don't want to hear a word more about it. In fact, if I find out you have been wasting any more police time on that ridiculous notion, then I'll see to it that the only job you are deemed fit for is cleaning the shit out of the cellblock toilets.' I could see the angry little red patches flaring on his cheeks and smell the stale coffee on his breath.

Then it dawned on me what he was saying. My God, he was threatening me. The overbearing, one-eyed, halitotic bastard was threatening me. And where the hell did he get off, thinking that every conversation he had with me had to be at 120 decibels? I felt the heat infusing my face and a little fist ball inside my stomach. I looked down the hallway at the collection of nosey faces and realised, actually, it was a bloody good thing to have an audience right now. I pulled myself up to my full height and prepared both barrels.

'You bastard. Are you telling me, sir,' — the 'sir' came out like a curse — 'are you formally instructing me to stop investigating this case, to stop searching for the real killers of John Henderson and to stop investigating what could be a huge miscarriage of justice? Is that what you are doing, sir, in front of all of these witnesses?'

The moment I said the word witnesses, all the people who had been rubbernecking the scene looked like they were suddenly keen to disappear. But it was too late, because he knew and I knew that they were there; and DI Johns wasn't the only person in the world who knew how to play to a crowd. I saw his eyes dart to the people who must have been behind me. He knew he'd been outwitted. They then settled back on me.

'No.' His lips were white with anger. 'I am not instructing you to stop investigating, Detective Shephard,' he said at volume for the benefit of the audience. Then he leaned down to my ear, and dropped his voice low, so only I could hear. 'But you should bear in mind, when you make me look bad, you little bitch, there is always a price to pay. Next time you decide you have something to say to me, Detective, you do it in private.'

I wasn't about to be kowtowed. 'And next time you have something to say to me, sir, maybe you should extend the same courtesy.'

I heard his sharp intake of breath, the snake-like hiss as he stood back up straight again.

'What are you all looking at ?' he roared at the spectators. 'Get back to work.' With that he stormed off down the hallway.

My glow of victory lasted about three seconds before the stares of my colleagues and the echo of his words gelled into a cold mass that sat like a stone in my belly.

62

In an attempt to ease my mind after the day's various encounters, I had pulled out one of the jobs that had been overshadowed by the tyranny of the urgent. The manager of Lucky Coins had dropped in the hidden security camera footage for the two weeks we had requested. It was one of those jobs that was mind-numbing to the point of being torturous, but that was precisely what my frazzled brain needed at that moment. The camera angle hadn't been much help. The lens had been placed directly above the till, so all you saw were the tops of people's heads, as well as the goods on the counter. It was a bit like those shots of cameras used to spy on croupiers at casinos — great to see what the hands were up to, but not so good for faces. The one consolation was a hideous, brightly coloured clown mask was going to be easy to spot, so I had been able to play through the recording on fast forward. Still, my head was pounding after an hour. After the three hours needed to watch the lot my eyes were all wonky and my head was hammering. But it wasn't an entirely pointless exercise, because it did tell me that neither Gideon Powell nor Jacob Sandhurst had been into the store to purchase the masks.

In fact, of all the eight masks purchased in the time surveyed, only one had been bought by a man — and he wasn't a man, strictly speaking, because he looked to have been all of seven years old. I was relieved.

I'd also taken the opportunity to note for Robert Chang the five occasions I saw staff members with their fingers in the till when they most definitely shouldn't have been. He'd been right to be suspicious. It just went to show, you had to be careful who you trusted.

63

As far as I was concerned, my brush with DI
Johns had given me a mandate — well, that was
the way I chose to interpret it. It was out in the
open. The way gossip travelled around here, I
was sure everyone in the building, right down to
the cleaner, knew I'd stood up to that arsehole.
It also meant, for better or worse, they knew I
was trying to prove two of the biggest, most
loathed crooks in the business were innocent.
That was the bit I was worried about. Would
people be a help or a hindrance? The vast
majority were still convinced by the evidence. I
knew of one for sure who would be blocking me
all the way, but as much as I liked Smithy, his
whole 'wounded warrior with a grudge' thing
had almost completely eaten away my 'give him
some space and time' cache. At least I had Paul
on side.

Angela Powell had dropped her laptop in to
me first thing that morning. I now stood at the
doors of Dunedin North Station, the home of
the Electronic Crime Lab. I took a deep breath
and walked in. This was going to be my first big
test, my first real chance to gauge the feel of
public sentiment.

Craig Todd, or Toddy as he was known by the
guys — or Hot Toddy as he was known by the
girls — was one of the resident computer nerds.
He was also the one who I hoped would be able

to prove beyond doubt that Gideon Powell was in fact home, bidding up a storm on Free Market the night that John Henderson had been killed, and couldn't possibly have been out at Seacliff. And if he couldn't have been there, then it was highly likely that Jacob Sandhurst hadn't been there either.

I handed over the computer to him and signed the evidence form.

'So what am I expected to do with this?' he asked.

'I need a time log of all the transactions, websites visited, anything at all that says when this computer was used by Gideon Powell.'

'The cop killer?'

'Alleged.' It wasn't looking good.

'The one who committed the Seacliff murder?'

'Allegedly.' I never thought I'd see the day when I'd be voluntarily using that dreaded word. He looked at me as if appraising something.

'Is that all you want done? You realise I'll have to take a good look through everything else too, all the other files and emails,' he said. To look for evidence to disprove my theory. I supposed it was his job to be thorough.

'Of course,' I said. 'Do whatever you have to.'

'And you do realise, even if I produce a time-line that shows it was in use at the time John Henderson was murdered, it only proves that someone used this computer, not Gideon Powell. It could have been his wife, or his kids, a visitor, anyone.'

'I know that. But I have an affidavit from his wife to say he was using it, and I hope the types of sites looked at would suggest his likes and preferences. I'm hoping Free Market was logged on with his personal ID. The computer has been dusted for his fingerprints. I can't do much more than that.'

'Hmm,' he said, like he was having a good think about it. 'I'll see what I can do. There are other things that are first in line though, so it probably won't be ready till next week.'

'That's okay. It's not urgent.' And it wasn't — the dead didn't have deadlines. 'I really appreciate your help.'

He looked down at me. A little smile played at the corners of his mouth. 'Did you really pull DI Johns up in front of everyone, over at Central? Call him a bastard to his face?'

News travelled fast. Sometimes I thought the police force was a bigger gossip generator than Aunt Aggie's knitting circle. Facebook schmacebook, word of mouth ruled.

'Yeah, I did.'

'In that case, I'll have this ready for you by tomorrow.'

64

The air had changed somehow. It wasn't to do with Dad. He was still the same. Same frown, same little groaning noises. If I had to pinpoint something different about him, though, it would perhaps be that he looked smaller than ever. No, the real change was with Mum. Sheryl had gone home to spend a bit of time with her kids. She and Steve were due back tomorrow morning. Mike had been in and out — he couldn't stand to just sit and wait — but still, I think his presence had been steadying. Also, I think the extra time alone with Dad had done Mum good. She seemed somehow calmer, less fragile. Perhaps she was coming to terms with this.

'How are you, Mum?' I asked after giving her a quick hug.

'I'm okay. How are you?' I couldn't remember the last time she'd asked me that. The answer was way too complex to even consider delivering honestly.

'I'm fine. Just tired. Work is insane.'

I realised as the words slipped out of my mouth that I had left myself open for a major pinging, and braced myself in anticipation. Much to my surprise, however, it didn't come. Instead we sat in semi-companionable silence. A silence that was punctuated by Dad's groans. I could sense Mum flinching with each one.

'I hope so much that he's unaware of all this,

that he feels nothing. The doctors tell me he can't, but still,' Mum said. 'Because honestly, if he was, he'd be lying there wishing someone would put a bullet between his eyes.'

'I know,' I said. 'But the simple fact is that they are doing everything they can to make him comfortable. We just have to wait, and it sucks.'

'You know, Sam,' she said, her voice quiet. 'Your dad is very proud of you.'

I looked at her in amazement, and, to be honest, confusion. I couldn't remember the last time she'd given me anything even remotely resembling approval. It was so unexpected I held my breath, waiting for the catch. But it didn't come.

'You think so?' I asked, my voice volume dropping to match hers.

'I know so,' she said. 'He understands why you haven't been here.' He understood? Or she understood? That would be typical of Mum, never one to admit outright what she was feeling. But all the same, it was an olive branch, and I clutched at it.

'Thank you,' I said, a lump forming in my throat.

'You should go, go and do what you do best.'

65

I loved Dunedin. How many cities in the world boasted the offer to walk, or, in my case, run, pretty much from one side to the other through a greenbelt of trees? And it wasn't just the trees, their texture and colour, shape and form, and that wonderful damp, earthy smell of humus that came from the bush that made it special. It wasn't only the shush and rustle of leaves being caressed by the breeze that sang to my senses. Or the little glimpses you got of the harbour and the ocean. Most of all, I loved the birdsong. From the operatic notes of the bellbirds, the two-tone cries of the tui, to the titters of the piwakawaka. It made the bush come to life. Just to prove the point, my body ducked instinctively at the low *whoosh, whoosh* of a kererū lumbering overhead. I was running along the path that threaded between Maori Road and Serpentine Avenue. When I got to the bottom, I'd just head where my feet took me. I didn't really care where they went as long as their cadence numbed my hyperactive emotional state into some semblance of manageability. I also hoped the fresh air would clear my headache. So far it wasn't quite working.

My thoughts turned back to work. Maybe work could blot out the mental image of my father fading away before my eyes, and maybe work could overshadow the enormity of that other development I couldn't quite bring myself to face head on. Work was a balm, albeit a gritty one. I always found running and the thrum of feet on road helped to corral my thoughts, allow my subconscious to process the mass of information we gathered in a case, from the minutiae to the monstrous. It seemed to help solidify the connections, make the pieces relate, weave the threads to create a pattern, a picture.

My memory pulled up the images I'd been looking at this afternoon. I'd been going over the cellphone video Declan had taken at the house before the police arrived. My head still found it hard to accept there was a generation of kids out there who were so au fait with technology and communication they would actually think to record an event like this on a cellphone. But I supposed there was many a YouTube clip that originated from that very fact. It was a new kind of voyeurism and a type of sharing that would never have occurred to me. *Look, I saw these girls having a fight at school so I filmed it and I'll stick it on YouTube.* Or, *Here's a photo of so-and-so Hollywood starlet getting out of a car with no knickers on, I'll share it on Facebook.* Well, actually, they'd probably sell that one to the highest, grubbiest bidder and make their fortune. But it was a similar thing. Mind you, I didn't think that was Declan's motive. I think he was being damn smart and realised every little thing counted towards finding who did this god-awful thing to his family. Little did he know I had been looking at his pictures and thinking they were perhaps evidence to get two of the biggest scumbags in the country off the hook for killing his father and just falling short of killing his mother. In fact, he'd probably be mortified.

But the simple fact was, no matter how despicable and unlikable they were, Fat Bastard Powell and The Cockroach deserved justice as much as anyone else. Someone had set them up right and proper. Trouble was, I was having a hell of a job convincing anyone else; and ultimately the only way to convince them would be to front up with the real killers.

What was puzzling me the most right now was the real murderers' treatment of Jill Henderson. She'd been up making a cup of tea when the intruders came door knocking. I recalled the crime-scene photos of two forlorn-looking mugs with the tea bags still stewing in them. They let her live, so clearly they felt she wouldn't be able to identify them; yet they didn't speak at all, so they felt there was some possibility that she might. So did they know her, or didn't they? What got me was why they would have tied her to a chair and left her there, forced to look at her dead husband? If they were ruthless enough to blow a man's head off, why didn't they just kill her? Some form of conscience? I doubted it, and what they did damn near killed her anyway. Why didn't they just hog — tie her and leave her in the kitchen where she'd been assaulted? It would have been far easier.

The other thing that troubled me was why they bothered using rope. Jill had been gagged with wide electrical tape and tied with nylon rope, both of which the killers brought along with them. And, according to the techie guys, they'd bought new stuff for the occasion: they'd started a new roll of tape, and one of the rope ends was the sealed end. It was very much a planned attack. If it was me doing the home invasion thing I'd be bringing along as little as possible. I'd have used tape for the whole lot. A lot simpler and less chance of buggering it up.

My foot slipped on a wet section of moss and I teetered a bit before regaining my balance.

Jill's legs had been tied individually to the chair legs so she couldn't try and shuffle herself anywhere. God I hoped she'd given them a good kick where it hurt while they were doing it. Her hands had been tied together around the chair back so she was pretty much immobilised. With her mouth taped shut it was really quite Holly-wood, the stereotypical damsel in distress tied to the chair. I wondered if the perpetrators had a thing for old movies, a flair for the dramatic. But why did they want her to look at what they had done? What message were they sending?

I came to a halt, figuratively and literally, standing in the middle of the path, panting, sucking in great mouthfuls of air. Where was my mind going with this?

It swirled and circled but kept coming back to one image. Jill.

Had we been looking at this from the wrong angle? Thinking that John Henderson had been killed because of something he'd done. What if it was his wife who the killers were really targeting? What if they were sending her a message? A particularly nasty message.

Jill had been an utter mess since John's murder, which was perfectly understandable, given the circumstances. But time was supposed to heal and she seemed to be getting worse, not better. Was this because she was scared? Was she being blackmailed, or threatened? Or worse, was someone else she loved being threatened? Declan?

It was time for us to have a serious chat.

66

The Chinese Scholar's Garden was an odd little oasis in the city. When they built it the whole thing seemed completely out of place and superfluous to me, an extravagance on the part of the few. But despite that, it was a place I visited often; I had even bought an annual pass. Maybe it was a hark back to youthful martial arts days, or the result of too many wet winter afternoons watching old David Carradine *Kung Fu* programmes on TV. Whatever the reason, it appealed on some profound level, every part of it. From the hand-pieced Chinese buildings to the fish undulating in the water, to the trees and plants, to the mountain of rocks, I felt oddly earthed here.

Today I was strolling along the zigzag bridge towards the little pavilion in the middle of the lake. Ahead of me were the stooped shoulders of Jill Henderson. We sat down on the seats and shared a few moments of silence.

'Thanks for meeting me here,' I said, at last. If there was any basis to my suspicions and someone was keeping an eye on her, then I didn't think they'd be concerned by her taking a leisurely stroll around a garden with a friend. In an attempt at a disguise I'd worn a hat and brought along Maggie's camera, to take a few snaps of the exquisite latticed-wood buildings. It was about as close to deep cover as I got. Considering my recent brush with the media, I hoped it would work.

'That's okay. It's nice to get some fresh air.'

It seemed to have put some colour into her face, but she still looked haggard and tired. The way her clothes now hung was a testament to the kilos she'd lost since this all happened. I got the feeling eating hadn't been a priority.

How was I going to pitch this one? With my usual subtlety?

'Jill, has someone been threatening you?'

To say she looked surprised would be to understate it. She had a worse poker face than I did, which was quite an achievement.

'What do you mean?' Her voice was a hoarse whisper.

'I need to know if someone has been threatening you.'

'Why would you think that?' Why indeed.

I struggled with the words. 'You know we are working hard to find John's killers, but some things are just not making sense.'

'But I thought you had found John's killers, that it was those men, the ones who died. You told me you had warrants out for them, that they were the men you were looking for, that they were the ones who attacked us . . . that they killed John.'

God, she made me feel guilty for even suggesting there had been a different story behind that night.

'Yes, well, that's what we thought. All the evidence pointed to those men, but we are starting to have our doubts.' That wasn't entirely accurate. I was having my doubts. My colleagues had no such misgivings, but at this stage I wanted to instil confidence in Jill, not mistrust, so I'd resorted to using the royal 'we'.

'But how could that be?'

'We are beginning to wonder if it was an elaborate setup, that someone wanted us to think it was Gideon Powell and Jacob Sandhurst who killed John. They were men who had a lot of enemies.'

'But who, then?'

'If we could answer that, we'd have this all solved. It's not that straightforward. Whoever they were, they went to a lot of trouble to hide themselves, and they may have even gone on to kill Powell. We don't know for sure. But they must have had some close connection with the men they set up, or else why would they bother going to so much trouble? And we still think they must have had something to do with John, because, as you know, John was involved in some pretty serious things.'

She nodded slowly. 'Yes.'

'But what has troubled me most is the way they treated you.' She looked at me, a fresh frown barely discernible among the new creases that now seemed permanently etched on her forehead. 'The way they tied you up and left you like that, to look at John, it's as if they were sending someone a message.' I let it hang in the air for a moment. 'And I think that message was directed at you.'

She looked away, but not before I noticed the wide-eyed look of shock on her face. 'What are you trying to tell me?'

'What I'm asking is: do you know of any reason why someone would have killed John to get at you?' I could think of a few classic reasons. Spurned jealous lover, her own illegal enterprises, or an opportunistic blackmailer. Stranger things had happened.

She swung her head back then, and she looked up at the rafters above, hurt and confusion on her face. 'You think his death might have been my fault? Because of something I might have done?' She clapped her hand across her mouth and started to sob.

'Of course not.' This wasn't going the way I had planned, my questions kept coming out all wrong, and I seemed to be making things worse, not better. 'I'm sorry that this is causing you more pain. I only ask because the case is making less and less sense and I have to look at every possibility, no matter how strange. Jill, believe me when I say I'm only wanting to do what's best for you and Declan here. You know that, don't you?'

'Yes, I know,' she said, 'you're only trying to help.'

'So honestly, has anyone been blackmailing you, making demands for money or personal threats? Or has anyone threatened Declan?'

'No, there's been nothing.' The way she said it, haunted almost, made me almost believe her. I wasn't entirely convinced, though. Perhaps it was yet to come? Perhaps they were waiting until the dust had settled and the police had lost interest. There was still the alternative question.

'And there's nothing you have been involved

with? Something you haven't told me about? You don't need to be afraid of repercussions if there's anything you've gotten yourself into that isn't quite legal. We're interested in the big picture here.'

I didn't know how to read the look on her face. Was she about to admit to something?

'I'm overdue on paying a parking ticket,' she said, with an attempt at a smile. It gave me a glimpse of the beautiful woman she had been before all of this took its toll. I laughed, glad for the break in intensity.

'Last I heard, Dunedin City Council don't send out the hit squad for late fines.' If they did, my recidivist late-library-book habit would have made me toast.

She lapsed back into her serious demeanour. 'I was always very careful to keep out of John's extra business things. I was brought up very straight and narrow, very black and white. I still am. I was always afraid that something he did would hurt us somehow, and when it happened it would be like all my worst fears had come true. I thought it was all to do with John; it never occurred to me it could have been otherwise. Honestly, I can't think of anything I could have done that would have caused this.'

67

'We got the iPhone, Sam.' Paul was looking as pleased as punch. 'Recovered it this morning.'

He paused like he was expecting me to ask the next logical question. He even did a little 'come on' hand gesture. I humoured him.

'Where?'

'I played a hunch. The perpetrators seem to have left a trail of objects around Seacliff and on their trip back to Dunedin: clothes in the wheelie bin, tape at the little train station, shotgun in the culvert, almost like an Easter egg hunt. I thought, okay, what if they discarded the phone on the way too? It was a needle in a haystack. I figured it would be in the vicinity of the road, but the regulars had already had a good search around there. We needed to improve the odds, so I got a sniffer dog unit on to it.'

'Since when could they sniff out electronics? And it's a bit long after the fact for a scent trail, don't you think?'

He beamed. 'You'd think that, wouldn't you? But that's where John's iPhone was unique. Remember the scene photos, the sofa arm with the nice atomised blood spray and the clean white patch.'

'You're a clever boy,' I said, twigging onto his line of thinking. 'The phone had John's blood on it. Something strong for the dogs to sniff.' Although the weather hadn't been that flash, and the phone would have been exposed to the elements somewhat. That dog must have had an amazing nose.

He looked extremely chuffed with himself. 'Found it up in a macrocarpa hedge, only a couple of hundred metres from where we found the shotgun. The hedge was as dense as hell, so you couldn't see it from the outside. They had to dig into it.' The density would have protected it from the weather, to some extent.

'So they offloaded everything quite close to the crime scene? That's a bit odd, don't you think?'

'Perhaps they were worried Jill might manage to work herself free and call the police, so they wanted to get rid of anything incriminating before they hit the highway.'

'Yeah, but there's plenty of road between Seacliff and the turnoff onto State Highway One,' I said. 'Unless they were concerned with Declan arriving home and calling for help. From their level of planning, they must have known he existed, and seeing he wasn't there when they committed the hit, perhaps they made the reasonable assumption that he might turn up sometime soon.'

'Who knows what goes through the heads of people like that?'

'Greed, money, power, death, destruction, mayhem, to name a few.'

'Good point,' he said.

'So what has the iPhone revealed?'

'The SOCOs have got it as we speak. We're also hoping for prints. If they discarded their gloves earlier up the track, they might not have thought to put on fresh ones. They might have got sloppy. We could get lucky.' God only knew a bit of luck would be handy right now.

68

Monday morning's squad meeting was sparking with energy. It had been a bad weekend for crime as far as Dunedin was concerned, but as far as I was concerned it couldn't be better. As the saying goes, nature abhors a vacuum, and we were starting to see the effects of one of Dunedin's largest crime organisations having a sudden vacancy at the top. The Armed Offenders Squad had been called out to two separate incidents involving rival gang members, and there had been several other brawls reported that required a police presence. It was amazing who was coming out of the woodwork. It was the result of one of these brawls that had led us to the whereabouts of Mikey Chadwick. He was currently nursing a fractured skull in Dunedin Public Hospital. He wasn't going anywhere in a hurry, so a deputisation could wait until after the meeting.

The buzz was diminished somewhat with Paul's report on the recovery of John Henderson's iPhone.

'The only fingerprints found on the device were those of John Henderson and Jill Henderson. Mrs Henderson confirmed she had used the device on the night of the killing to make a call to her father. The perpetrators did not leave a trace, other than smearing the blood on the front plate, which did not reveal a print.' I noted that Paul had gone from naming Powell and Sandhurst when referring to the case, and had moved to the more generic 'perpetrators'. It made me smile.

'And what of the contents, Detective ?' DI Johns asked.

'We found little of interest. The telephone, text and email logs had been cleared. We have recovered most of these from his service providers, but at this point none seem to be of significance, and there was the usual string of unidentified prepay numbers. They're still being examined. It would seem there was something of interest recorded on the phone that the perpetrators thought may incriminate them. We'll find the connection.'

That was mighty optimistic of him. I hoped he did.

'Thank you, Detective Frost.'

DI Johns resumed his front-and-centre position, then looked around the room before his eyes settled on me. The way he looked gave me a portent of impending doom.

'Detective Shephard, do you have anything you would care to share with the group at this point with your . . . ' he paused, ' . . . alternative course of investigation?'

Bugger him, bugger him, bugger him to hell. I felt the familiar flush crawl up my face as every set of eyes in the room turned to look. Some looked most expectant — probably people waiting with relish to see if I would have another go at The Boss. Some looked smug — the ones who knew damn well I had been put on the spot and were delighted by it. And DI Johns knew bloody well I had nothing concrete I could give them right now, not even crumbs I was prepared to throw to the birds. I hadn't received the computer report from Toddy and I knew better than to talk about anything I couldn't back up with evidence. I'd just be shot down in flames.

'No, sir, not at this moment,' I said.

'Pardon, Detective, I didn't quite hear that. Can you repeat yourself?' I could hear the snigger go around the room.

'No, sir, I don't have anything to report.'

He stood there looking triumphant. The bastard had eviscerated me in public yet again.

69

I was sure Dickhead Johns was doing it as a punishment. Not content with making me look like a prize idiot in front of my peers, he had now lumbered me with Smithy, who was just as thrilled as I was at the privilege. I'd wanted Paul to come along for this conversation, but that manoeuvring bastard had made sure he had some other urgent task that required Paul's instant attention.

'So why are we going to see this moron? Why isn't the drug squad on this one?' he asked, as we walked into the Dunedin Public Hospital foyer. The fact we had been sent on a wild goose chase to ask Jimmy Clarke about this clown well over a week ago wasn't lost on him.

'Mikey Chadwick was the third in command in Powell's organisation. As far as I'm concerned, he had the most to gain from Powell and Sandhurst's exit from the scene. Word from drug squad is that this guy is as cunning as a weasel and he has done a very good job at not only keeping out of the clutches of the law, but keeping us in the dark as to who he was actually involved with. It's only the information we got from Sheila Sandhurst that confirmed he was even a part of Powell's crew, and a high-up part.'

'And you believe a word that bitch says?' he said. His tone told of his opinion on the matter.

We were walking past the café. I saw a young

guy with a stethoscope around his neck look at Smithy with a spark of recognition and come over. He looked all of about eighteen. I was sure they were breeding the doctors around here younger and younger. I wasn't even sure if this one had to shave yet.

'How's that cut coming along? Have you had the stitches out yet?' he asked.

'Not yet. Must get onto that,' Smithy mumbled.

'You should, they will need to be removed.' He headed off in the direction of the emergency department.

'What the hell did you do to yourself this time?' I asked.

Smithy's tendency towards the Kiwi can-do attitude had led him to the A&E department relatively frequently in the past, although this had slowed down somewhat since his accident. Not that being shot up by Powell's thugs could have been called an accident.

'You don't want to know,' he said. 'Lift's here. I'm not taking the stairs. Keep prattling.'

I didn't think I prattled. I was merely stating the facts as I saw them.

'I think Mikey Chadwick is a likely candidate for the murder of John Henderson and Jacob Sandhurst.'

'You're not still clutching on to that idea are you?'

'Well, I've got DI Johns' blessing to investigate it.'

Smithy gave me a look that made it quite clear my use of the word 'blessing' had been a vast exaggeration. The serene yet annoying elevator voice informed us we had reached our floor.

'By all accounts he's smart; he'd have the nous to plan the whole setup; he was high in the organisation, probably involved in the manufacturing, so would have had access to things like the discarded gloves, hair samples, all of that stuff.'

The constable on door duty nodded as we walked into the room. Mikey Chadwick was lying in the bed, his head swathed in a bandage, his left eye black and swollen, ECG monitor stickies on his chest and a variety of other cables wiring him for sound. He wasn't looking a particularly healthy specimen right at this moment.

'And he's a bloody big unit,' I whispered to Smithy.

Smithy just stood and nodded.

Mikey Chadwick was a big boy — tall and big, and not just lardy big, but muscular big as well. He was positively Powellesque.

70

Smithy was particularly quiet on our walk back to the station. In fact, in my opinion he was pulling an almighty sulk. When confronted by the physical similarities shared by Gideon Powell and Mikey Chadwick, even Smithy had to concede that there might be some merit in the they-were-framed theory. I could see why he would be disappointed. He wanted Powell to be done for this murder, for him to finally get a conviction on the kind of scale that would satisfy our need for justice for the murder of Detective Reihana. But it looked like Teflon man was going to get away scotfree again. Even if he was dead, he went to his grave without the irrevocable label of murderer. That galled. I left him to his lumbering silence.

As we got closer to the station I could see a familiar form in the distance. She spotted me and as we approached I could see the anxiety that was boiling beneath her skin. Even closer and I could see her pallor and the look of fear upon her face.

'Jill, what is it? What's happened?'

She didn't say a word. Instead she handed me an envelope.

71

I was standing outside DI Johns' office, taking a Zen moment to breathe and calm myself before entering the lion's den. There was a swirling hollowness to my stomach that could have been due to a number of reasons. My hand was poised to knock when the printer behind me in the corridor whirred to life, making me fair jump through the roof. After I scraped myself off the ceiling, I laughed at my own stupidity. What was I worried about? I held two articles in my hands to support what I was about to suggest. He could like it or lump it.

I knocked.

'Enter.' So formal. So typical.

He saw who it was and frowned. I think it was an automatic response, kind of like Pavlov's dog salivating to a whistle.

'Detective Shephard.'

'Sir.' We hadn't talked one-on-one since that moment in the hallway, and, judging by the plummet in room temperature, time hadn't made his heart grow fonder, as it were.

'What do you want?'

There was nothing for it but to plough in and simply present the facts. I stepped forward and placed the two objects on the table. One was a wad of paper. The other an envelope in an evidence bag. He looked down at them, and then back at me. His cold, reptilian eyes bored into me, adding to the chill.

'I take it you're going to explain the significance of these.'

I pointed first to the wad of paper, the report from Craig Todd.

'This is a report of the computer use of Gideon Powell on the night that John Henderson was killed. It shows that from eight o'clock at night, at regular intervals he was looking at internet websites and at the Free Market internet trading site. He continued to use the computer until eleven o'clock.'

'This was on his personal computer? This wasn't in the report from the techs when we examined it with the initial warrant.'

'That's because this wasn't on his computer, it was on Angela Powell's laptop. Her computer and his children's computers weren't covered in that warrant. No one looked at them.'

'So, that just means Angela Powell was surfing the internet while her husband was off murdering people, Detective. You'll need to be more convincing than that. What else have you got to show me.'

I'd expected this response. I flicked open the file to a copy of an email. 'Angela has signed an affidavit to say Gideon was at home that night, and using her computer. We have taken prints from the computer that belong to both Angela and Gideon.'

'Still not enough. He could have picked it up at any time. And who would believe a word the wife of a major criminal says, anyway?'

Ignoring his protestations, I continued. 'From

eight-thirty to just after nine-thirty, Gideon Powell was bidding on a listing on Free Market. He was bidding on a limited-edition City of Coventry Princess Coronation Class Model Train, 00 gauge, in red. He placed four bids on the train, including his final bid, which won the auction at 9.28 p.m. Seven hundred and eighty dollars.' I couldn't believe someone would spend that much money on a toy. I could have bought my entire winter wardrobe for that, or had a weekend away in Melbourne, or four weeks' worth of groceries.

'This could still have been Angela Powell, Detective,' he said. His voice told of how unconvinced he was. But I still had the trump card to play.

'Yes, but at 9.35, the time when John Henderson was already dead, and his killers were tying up his wife and doing everything they did out at Seacliff, Gideon Powell was sending an email. This email.' I pointed to the copy in front of him. It read like a very excited boy having just purchased his new toy: 'I'm delighted to have won your auction, I have been wanting this train for ages, please send bank account details and I will pay immediately, here are my postal details,' etc., etc., and, most importantly, typed at the bottom, 'Cheers, Gideon Powell.' In a way, when I first saw this, I felt quite emotional. I didn't know whether this was relief that I'd been right, or if it was just the hormones. But it had humanised Gideon Powell for me. There had to be some redeemable features in a man if he could find such pleasure from something so fanciful, so whimsical.

There was a moment of silence.

'This still doesn't mean it was him.'

'No, it's not absolute proof, but, it does raise doubt. And this raises more doubt.' I pushed the evidence bag in front of him. The envelope inside bore the name Jill Henderson, handwritten in a scrawly italic style. You could just see the top half of the Russell Road, Seacliff address line before it was obliterated by a large, bright yellow 'redirected by New Zealand Post' sticker that had her Moray Place apartment address on it.

'And this is?'

'This arrived for Jill Henderson in today's mail. It's a demand.'

I handed over one more piece of paper I had inside my jacket pocket. A copy of a letter. It was typewritten on an A4 piece of 80gsm printer paper, not handwritten like the envelope. I unfolded the creases in it and flattened it out for the DI to see. The message was simple, its meaning clear.

```
$100,000.00 cash.
You have three days.
Await instruction.
Don't go to the police or we kill
the boy too.
Fail to deliver?
The boy dies.
```

72

Jill and Declan Henderson had been placed into protective custody. They were in one of our safe houses, biding their time, playing Scrabble while their lives were turned upside down once again. Declan had been pulled out of school and hadn't been too thrilled. I thought it had been brave of Jill to come forward with the letter. But then, what choice did she have? Her son had been threatened. And where would she have been able to dredge up a hundred thousand in cash? Most people didn't have that kind of dosh sitting around in their wallets. She'd also probably realised that even if she did pay up, there was nothing to stop them coming back for more. People that ruthless and greedy weren't likely to stop at one milking of the cash cow.

The letter didn't give much in the way of information. It had been postmarked with the number for the Dunedin Postal Centre — sent locally, no surprise. The paper was negative for prints, but the envelope provided several. No doubt two sets would belong to Jill Henderson and the mailman, but we hoped there would be some extras. The likely contenders were in the process of being eliminated. Some poor New Zealand Post employee would be having their fingers ink-stained about now. Mine were absent because the moment I'd looked at the envelope when she proffered it, I'd frog-marched her straight into the station to get it properly put into evidence for processing. I didn't need the embarrassment of my fingerprints contaminating it.

The letter had been printed on a laser printer. Considering there were thousands, no, tens of thousands of them in Dunedin, this fact didn't help much, but the techs hoped to narrow the range down more. The forensic handwriting folk would be working their magic on the envelope.

The tide had turned. People were starting to believe me now, starting to realise that this was in fact one hell of a setup. I felt delighted and vindicated on behalf of Angela Powell and Sheila Sandhurst. I even felt the unusual sensation of being glad for the sake of two of the men I despised most in this world.

The troops were out visiting all known associates of Powell, Sandhurst and Mikey Chadwick, specifically looking for any that might happen to be of similar build to Jacob Sandhurst. I was on my way to a little rendezvous with Angela Powell, to bring her and Sheila up-to-date with what was happening on the case.

The only rain on our parade was the fact that Mikey Chadwick was still under sedation and was in no position to talk. I was very interested to hear what he had to say for himself.

I was about to ring Angela Powell to give her an update on events when my cellphone came to life in my hands. I saw the name on the display and smiled.

'Gidday.'

'Gidday yourself. So, what do you know?' he asked.

'That suddenly everyone is my friend; well, except The Boss, because he's an arsehole, and besides Smithy, because he's just damn grumpy.' I was sure Paul would have added a little 'and an arsehole' under his breath. 'What do you know?'

'I was hoping you were going to ask that. Our boffins at ESR have done their magic and isolated a blood sample from Gideon Powell's body that doesn't belong to Gideon Powell.'

'You've got my attention.'

'The sample came from the bottom of Powell's trousers. From the shape they think it was a flick from the knife as it was pulled out of his assailant.'

'So Powell definitely had a go at his killer.'

'Yup. So are you going to ask me who it was ?'

'They've got an ID?' They must have done a DNA profile on all the samples in an attempt to spot the odd one out. That would have been a hell of an expensive exercise. But hey, I wasn't paying, and it did the trick.

'No, but I can tell you who it wasn't.' The boy liked to drag it out.

'And?'

'It wasn't Jacob Sandhurst.' Yes. Again, that feeling of vindication.

'But we have a DNA profile?'

'I'm thinking a warrant for Mikey Chadwick's DNA will be in order,' Paul said.

There was only one potential fly in Paul's ointment. 'I've seen his medical report. Mikey Chadwick has no cut or stab marks on him. He's got injuries consistent with a beating, but there was no knife involved.'

'Bugger. Well, there's someone out there who had an almighty grudge against Gideon Powell and who'll be nursing their wounds right now.'

The moment he said it a shiver moved down my spine. I could think of someone who fit both of those criteria, someone very close to home.

73

What the hell was I going to do? My heart felt disgust and dread and pity all in one. Surely he wouldn't have taken matters into his own hands. Surely he wouldn't have put everything on the line for a piece of shit who was, at that stage, going to be put away for murder. But then I thought about the timing. Powell had been murdered on the Wednesday night, literally hours after he had walked out of the station, giving us the fingers because we didn't have the evidence to nail him at that time. He walked out a free man, and hours later he was dead.

'Oh, Jesus, Smithy, what have you done?' I whispered to myself.

And what was I going to do? This was one hell of an accusation to hurl against a fellow officer, and a friend. I tried to rub away the headache that was forming at my temples.

My agonising was interrupted by the sound of my phone.

'Shephard.'

'Sam, it's Sheryl.' My heart skipped a beat. 'I think you should come down here now. I think it might be getting close.'

74

My brain was phasing in and out. I had the attention span of a gnat today. Every time the phone rang my stomach tightened into a dyspeptic little knot. The particular phone call I was expecting was inevitable and the wait intolerable. I had gone back to staring at photographs again.

'Why are you here? You should be with them,' Paul had said earlier.

'I can't,' I had told him. 'I can't just sit and watch and wait for him to die.' It seemed, at the last, Dad's farming days were doing him a disservice. The man had been so fit and strong — he had the heart and strength of an ox. Now, despite his body fading away and realising it was time to call it quits, his heart just wouldn't let up. Even Sheryl, who by the nature of her profession had seen a multitude of deaths, commented on how protracted this was and how cruel it was to let him continue suffering. I'd abandoned the bedside vigil around midnight, incapable of staying awake any longer and unwilling to hover, like a vulture waiting for the death.

My colleagues were out on the job. Those who did wander in and out of the room had the sense to leave me to my own devices. In an attempt to look like I was doing something constructive I had spread the pictures on the desk in front of me. I'd turned the pictures of John, or what was left of John, face down. There was something a little too close about looking at those pictures. Poor Jill. We'd taken stills from some of the video Declan had shot. They were low resolution and therefore a bit grainy, but they were still useful. One was of her as he had found her, tied to the chair, tipped on its back, clearly showed her dislocated shoulder. I felt my stomach give a lurch at the sight of it. The last picture in the series was of Jill's hands tied behind the chair. Fortunately this picture was angled a bit better, so it avoided the gut-wrenching view of the shoulder.

She must have had a reasonable go at the ropes, because they didn't look that tight and the knot was a bit agricultural and halfhearted. If she hadn't tipped the chair over and landed on her back, she might have been able to work them off, given a bit of time. I placed my hands behind my back, wrist over wrist, and imagined what that would have felt like. My body gave a gratuitous shudder at the thought of it, and at the same time as my eyes fell on the photograph, a little cascade of dominoes tumbled and a stab of an idea pierced my brain.

75

'What the fuck is going on here?' DI Johns bellowed as he walked into the squadroom.

I just about gave myself whiplash as my head spun around to face him. My bowels developed a sudden urgency. I could see why he might be a little upset, considering he'd just walked into a room with three detectives, two constables and a receptionist tied to chairs, and a number of spectators.

I handed him a piece of rope. 'Would you like to have a go?'

'No, I bloody well would not. You'd better explain yourself, Detective, quick smart.'

My bright idea suddenly felt a little less vibrant, but I had to stand by my convictions.

'I had a theory and I asked the others here to test it out. Call it an experiment. They have all tied their own hands together behind their chair. No one was allowed to look and see how the others had done it. They had to figure out the best way for themselves.' I gave a little pause for effect. I'd learned that trick from him. 'Anyway, the results are the same. Every one of them has tied themselves up exactly the same way. Have a look for yourself.' He still looked at me like I was certifiable, but he took a cursory tour of the hands. 'Which happens to be the same way as this.' I handed him the still that had come from Declan's filming of his mother. How cruel that the impulsive decision he'd made to record the horror of the crime scene would have such damning implications.

'Jill Henderson tied herself up. She did it. She set the whole thing up. She murdered her husband.'

76

The seething anger had been building up all afternoon. How could I have been so gullible? There I had been, feeling sorry for the woman, for all she had been through. She had been so shocked, so traumatised and so apparently horrified by what had happened. And all along it had been a ruse. I'd trusted her. She had played me, played us all.

Despite my resentment I was still surprised when the door to the safe house opened and Jill Henderson stood before me. It was as if something had sucked away her vitality and she had diminished away to a fraction of her former size. She had made some effort with makeup but it did little to hide the shadows and lines that tracked across her face. She invited us in and guided us to sit at the dining table. There she curled in upon herself and proceeded to chew at the corners of what had once been perfectly manicured nails. I couldn't pull my eyes away from the gauntness of her face. All vestiges of her former beauty had disappeared, and all that was left was the shell of a woman clearly not coping with what she had done. She didn't have post-traumatic stress disorder. She was suffering from guilt.

'Declan, I need you to go out for a walk with the constable,' I said.

'Why, what's happened?' he asked. He hovered

protectively beside his mum.

'I need to have a chat with your mother alone. I'll talk to you afterwards.' He looked to Jill, who gave a little nod. Only then did he head towards the door.

I waited until it had closed behind him.

'You know why I'm here, don't you?'

She winced at the accusation in my voice and her eyes flicked to Paul seated beside me.

'What do you mean?' she asked. 'Has something happened? Has there been a breakthrough in the case?'

I laughed, surprised by how bitter I sounded. 'Yes, there has.'

I held up Declan's photograph of her bound hands and dropped it onto the table before her. Then I held up a photograph of Paul's hands bound behind his back and dropped it onto the veneer surface beside it.

'We did a little experiment, to see what would happen if you gave someone a piece of rope . . . ' I held up a photograph of Detective Van Rij's hands and dropped it on the pile; ' . . . and asked them to tie themselves up.'

Then Detective Constable Richardson's.

'And you know what we found?'

Then Constable Johnston's, then Constable Wilson's, and then Laurie the receptionist's.

'Everyone did it exactly the same way.'

I picked up her photo again and held it in front of her face.

'Exactly the same way as you.'

There was silence.

I wouldn't have thought it possible, but her

face became paler, her eyes wider. They stayed transfixed on the photograph. I banged it down onto the table and she looked at me with a start.

'You killed John. Oh, you had us so convinced with your clever little scene. I especially liked the teabags stewing in the mugs. That was a nice touch, made it look so homey, so much like a normal night in with Hubby in front of the telly, minding your own business, until the big bad guys knocked on the front door and then blew your husband away.'

Her face went one step further, from sallow to semi-translucent, the blue of her veins a spider-web beneath her skin. Large tears began to roll down her cheeks.

'Except there weren't any big bad guys, were there? There was just a very cunning and vicious little woman. A woman who wanted her husband dead, but didn't want to have to pay the price. Wanted to walk away from it, looking like the poor, unfortunate, pitied widow.'

She still didn't say a word.

'But, you know, I don't think it all went according to plan. I get how you would have worked up the courage to ram yourself into the kitchen counter, to make it look like a struggle — which must have hurt like hell — but I don't think you expected to do your shoulder in like that, did you? And I don't think you planned to almost suffocate to death, either. You didn't envisage that. What happened? What went wrong?' Despite trying not to show how bloody angry I was with her and how hurt I was, because goddamn it, I did feel hurt at being duped and taken for a fool, I couldn't hide the bitterness in my voice.

'Answer me!' I said with more force than intended as I banged the table. I felt Paul's hand carefully slide onto my leg under the table.

She jolted with shock, and for the first time looked me in the eye. 'It was Declan,' she whispered. 'He was . . . ' She looked away again. 'He was late.'

That only made it worse.

'So you're telling me you planned it so your son, your own son, would come home and find his father dead. That he would come home and have to see . . . ' I stumbled with my incomprehensibility of it all, my arms gesticulating wildly, trying to convey the horror of it; ' . . . to see that. Jesus Christ, Jill. His father's brains were splattered all over the fucking room. You wanted him to see that? You planned it? You made it so that the last memory that boy would have of his father was that? You fucking bitch.' I shouldn't have said it, but I couldn't help it. Even Paul gasped.

'I didn't think it would be so, so messy,' she said, still whispering. 'I had no idea it would be like that. I never intended for it to be like that.' She was shaking her head, the tears snaking down her face.

'You didn't think that sticking a shotgun point blank at someone's head and pulling the trigger would make a mess?'

'No, not like that. I never intended to do that to John.'

'Then why the hell did you shoot him?'

'I did it for Declan.'

Like hell she did. And what gall. Even now she was trying to palm off some of the responsibility, lay it at the feet of the poor boy.

'What do you mean, you did it for Declan?'

'It was to protect him. I was just trying to protect him. It was John's fault. He wanted Declan to get into the business, to be a part of it. Not the legitimate business — his other empire, that other bloody evil empire. He even introduced him to those . . . those monsters. Those scum.'

'So you were there? When Gideon Powell and Jacob Sandhurst came to the house?'

She nodded. 'They didn't see me, they wouldn't have known I was there. John didn't realise I was home, but I saw him; he let our son meet criminals like that. He wanted Declan to become one of them and I couldn't let that happen. I couldn't let our boy become a part of that. I just couldn't. I had to do something.'

'So you thought you'd take care of John and the monster scum at the same time? Planted the evidence, set the scene. Gave us a pretty good description of the men, but not too good, so there would be some doubt — couldn't make it too easy for us. No one would ever suspect the only eyewitness, the poor, injured eyewitness, was lying her arse off. I'm taking it they were sloppy and left bits of themselves behind at your house — the gloves, hair.'

'It was all in John's workshop, in the rubbish bin. They must have been looking at samples of the drugs. He had those drugs in our home. I couldn't believe he brought things like that, people like that, into our home. With our boy

316

there.' Her voice was a whisper.

'So you took their leftovers, their rubbish, planned this whole thing, set up the crooks to take the fall and then calmly blew your husband's head off. Jesus Christ, most people would have just asked for a divorce.'

She laughed, and a hint of the bitterness cut through her façade. The kind of bitterness that could bring a woman to do such a thing. 'It wasn't that simple. God, I wish it had been that simple. But I had to assure Declan's future, our future.'

Somehow it always seemed to come down to money. 'The insurance?'

She looked down at the floor and wouldn't meet my eyes.

'You do realise your little ploy resulted in the death of two more men. That you are responsible for the deaths of Gideon Powell and Jacob Sandhurst, men who were innocent of this crime. It's not just your husband's murder that should be on your conscience.'

Her shoulders started to shake and she appeared to be working hard to stop herself from breaking down completely.

'Christ, you must have really hated your husband to do that to him.'

She took a shuddering breath. 'But you don't understand. It was the hardest, most awful thing I've ever had to do. I loved John, he meant everything to me, but I had to protect Declan.' She was pleading now. 'You have to understand, I loved John.'

She had a damn strange way of showing it.

317

77

I'd just helped solve a complicated and nasty murder, uncovering a clever and brilliantly executed plot, but it felt such a hollow victory. Two men had died unnecessarily, I had grave suspicions about the actions of one of my colleagues, many lives had been turned upside down, and for what? A mother's misguided protection of her son? That was at one hell of a cost. And, ironically, Declan had lost both parents now. Jill had achieved nothing. Add to that the fact that he was now having a hard time grappling with the enormity of what his mother had done, and that his footage of the crime scene had provided the evidence against her. He felt guilty, and he had no reason to. His mother had done that to him — she had left him with that legacy.

My hands drifted down to rest on my still-flat belly, trying to connect to the secret life within. What would you do for love? Could love, no matter how misguided, cause you to break the greatest rule of humanity? Thou shalt not kill. In Jill's case, yes it did. My mind drifted to my suspicions about Smithy's involvement, something I wasn't sure how to address, even if I wanted to. My head said I should, but my heart couldn't cope with the thought right now. The whole affair had left me feeling disheartened and drained. I slouched back in my chair and stared out the window at the cars and people on the street below, and wallowed in an almighty attack of the blahs.

I was pulled out of my reverie by the ring of the phone. I pulled myself upright and picked up. 'Shephard.'

I heard a long shuddery intake of breath and felt my heart sink.

'Sam, it's Mum.'

78

My fingers drifted down along his cheekbone, traced the shape of his nose, up to between his brows where the frown had finally erased. His skin was papery beneath my fingertips. Already he felt cool, too firm to the touch. But he looked asleep, at rest, tucked into the bed, arms over the blanket at his sides. My other hand felt the bones of his, the sharp swell of knuckles beneath his skin, a stark reminder of how frail he had become.

I leaned over and kissed him on the forehead, then smiled as I wiped the spilt tears from his cheek.

'Bye, Dad.'

79

'Sam, can I have a word with you please?'

Alison Cowan, the medical director for the community hospice had nabbed me on my way back from the toilets, where I'd retired to have a quiet chuck. The jury was out on whether the persistent nausea I was experiencing was due to my fragile emotional state, or hormonal state, or both. The company in Dad's room was rather tense. Mum was there and being stoic. My brother Steve had just arrived up from the farm and wasn't. Sheryl was barely holding it together. Big brother Mike was silent and unreachable in his own thoughts. The only thing that made it tolerable was the presence of my favourite niece and nephew. Kids made it impossible to wallow in the negative. Still, I leapt at the opportunity to avoid going back in there, even if it was only a brief respite.

'Come down to my office.'

I followed her down the hallway, and then sat down in the chair she offered. She shut the door and sat down on the other side of her desk.

'I'm not entirely sure how to broach this with you,' she said. The concerned look on her face had me going uh-oh — she'd sprung me and figured out the reason for my impromptu trips to the ladies' room. 'But,' she took a deep breath, 'I'm not entirely happy with the circumstances of your father's death.'

That wasn't what I expected. I shook my head to see if I'd heard right. 'What do you mean?'

She leaned forward, elbows on the desktop, looking at me squarely. 'There is a problem with the amount of morphine he was given.'

My mind grappled with her words, trying to grasp what she was trying to tell me. We wouldn't have been having this conversation if he'd been given too little.

'Are you saying that he was accidentally given an overdose of morphine by one of your staff?' The stress of the day was showing and I heard my voice rising.

Again, the sigh. 'Not by one of our staff.'

My mind rolled that around a bit before coming to a conclusion. 'Are you sure? How else could he possibly have had an overdose?' No medical institution liked to admit their staff had made an error that resulted in the death of a patient, not even one who was clearly dying anyway. I felt a swell of anger rising up in my chest. They'd made a mistake and were denying it.

'His syringe driver has been tampered with. It wasn't a mistake.' She could see I was ready to explode, and talked in a very calm and even voice. 'Listen while I explain. The syringe driver is designed, as you know, to give a slow and steady dose of medicine to the patient over a twenty-four hour period. We chart exactly the amount of morphine in each syringe driver, and the exact time it starts, and the specific rate of administration on the machine. When Jock died, we stopped the machine, and removed it, but the amount of morphine left in the syringe was not what it should have been, not even close.'

My head was just beginning to realise what it was she was trying to tell me and I tried to brush aside the thought, because it was too horrific to consider. 'But, what if you set it up wrong? Set the driver on the wrong speed so it accidentally pumped more into him?'

'I checked the machine. The rate was still set correctly, and the volume of liquid missing didn't equate to what should have been there, even if the machine was set in error. We have set the machine running with a saline solution in it to make sure it wasn't the unit at fault, but so far it is performing perfectly. Sam, it was deliberately tampered with. Someone has drawn up a large dose of morphine from the syringe driver and injected it into your dad.'

'But who would have done that?' I uttered. I felt a cold chill spread from my neck and down my spine, work its way around to my guts and squeeze. There were only two people who had been with Dad more or less constantly in his last hours. Two. I felt the bile rising in my throat, clapped my hand over my mouth and bolted from the room.

80

I leaned against the washbasin, hands clutching
the sides, as if hanging on to its cold, impersonal
porcelain would stop the swirl of emotions that
had thrown me off balance. I stared at the ashen,
shocked reflection in the mirror, my eyes tracing
the features held in common with the beautiful
man lying lifeless, murdered, in the room down
the corridor. I had his eyes, now bloodshot, and
his mouth, now trembling, and recognising the
likeness seemed to make the loss all the more
unbearable.

My brain struggled with the medical director's
words, 'not one of our staff'. The implication was
clear: not them, one of us. There could only have
been two. Sheryl or Mum. But who? It had to
have been Sheryl — she was a nurse, she could
pull it off. She knew how all the gadgetry
worked, she'd know where to inject him, she was
that one step more removed, detached. He
wasn't her dad, her husband. Could she? Would
she? It had to have been, because the alternative
was impossible.

The tightness in my chest intensified as the
chill edges of shock were replaced with the
bubbling heat of anger. She had killed my father.
She had stolen those last moments from me, that
last chance for something, anything. My jaw
clenched, and I found myself storming out of the
toilet and down the corridor. Dr Cowan must

have been waiting outside. I registered the look on her face before my stride took her out of view, and I could hear her scampering to keep up.

'What are you doing?' I heard her ask.

What was I doing? I didn't know, but by God I was going to get some answers.

'Sam, don't do anything . . . '

I strode around the corner into the room. Six faces looked up startled.

'What the hell did you do?' I yelled at Sheryl, bitterness leaching into my voice.

The faces changed from startled to shocked. I heard the click of the door closing behind me, and a steadying hand on my shoulder.

'Sam? Don't.'

I shook off Alison Cowan's good intentions. 'What, you couldn't wait for him to die in his own time? You had to turn around and kill him, for God's sake.'

'Sam!' This time there was admonishment in the voice, but I was beyond listening to reason.

'That's murder, that's what it is, did you know that? You have murdered him.'

Sheryl had been gawping like a goldfish. She finally found her voice. 'What are you talking about? What's wrong with you?'

'What's wrong with me? The question should be what's wrong with you? Dad's morphine pump was tampered with. He was deliberately given an overdose, to kill him. It was you. You murdered him. You murdered my father, and by God you'll pay for it, you bitch.'

Steve thrust himself to his feet, and before I knew it he was across the room and had slapped me hard across the face. The sharp sting made me gasp, and my eyes watered furiously. 'Don't you dare talk to my wife like that. You can't come in here and make all these ludicrous accusations. You take that back.'

I pulled my hand back, ready to give as hard as I got, but felt it caught and restrained, my head whipping around to see Dr Cowan, face contorted with the effort, holding me back.

'Don't be so bloody stupid,' Sheryl yelled back. 'What on earth do you mean?'

'I mean you killed my father, you murdering cow.' I saw a flash of movement and felt another sting across my cheek.

'Stop it, stop it, all of you.' I heard Mum's voice rising above the chorus of people all talking and yelling and crying at once. Then, that one voice, with pain and clarity, said five words that ripped through the mêlée and silenced the room.

'Stop it. It was me.'

Everyone turned towards the voice, movements suspended in mid-action like someone had hit the pause button.

'What do you mean, it was you?' I said, my voice a whisper.

She looked at me then, her eyes steady. I looked at the face in the corner of the room, a face that at once held grief and pain, and was it even defiance?

When she spoke her voice was anything but steady. 'He was in pain, Sam. He was in so much pain. He was, even when he . . .' As she struggled to find the words I could feel the anger and disgust that had been choking me moments

326

ago loosen their grip. Mum took a deep breath and visibly steadied herself against the chair. When she spoke, her voice had lost its quiver. 'He was suffering. I couldn't let that go on. Even when he was unconscious he was in pain. It was cruel, and it wasn't right. I did what I had to do.'

'But he was your husband, my dad. How could you just kill him like that?'

'I didn't kill him, I freed him. It's what he would have wanted. He'd have done the same for me if it was the other way around, or for you, or for the dog for that matter. There was no point in dragging it out any longer. It was hurting everyone.'

'But he might have come around again.' I felt the warm flow of tears running down my cheeks. 'We could have had more time with him.' Even as I said the words I could see Mum shaking her head, with the same look on her face she used to have when trying to make a petulant seven-year-old see sense. I felt the steadying hand back on my shoulder. I let it stay this time. The petulant child resorted to the age-old fall-back of repetition, with that other age-old standby, sobbing.

'But you killed him!'

★　★　★

Mum came over and gently cradled my face in her hands.

'I had to, Sam. I loved him.'

81

Once again I stood in the hallway, outside The Boss's office, but this time my heart wasn't racing, it was thudding, a jarring, hollowed ache, as if weighted by dread. My body felt like it swayed with each exaggerated beat. I knocked.

'Enter.'

DI Johns' eyes narrowed when he saw it was me, but the hostility on his face quickly changed to puzzlement, and then realisation. I may have even glimpsed pity.

'Sit down, Detective,' he said. 'I'm sorry to hear about your father.'

'Thank you, sir.'

He sat too, hands on his desk, lightly drumming his fingertips together. 'If you need to take leave, that's fine. Take as much time as you need.'

'I may need a while,' I said, trying to choose the right words. 'There has been a bit of a complication.'

'What do you mean?'

'I wanted to come to you first, before you heard it formally, but . . . ' I took a shuddery breath, my fortitude abandoning me. 'My mother has confessed to having overdosed my father with morphine.'

The finger-drumming stopped. I waited for the explosion.

'Let me check I'm hearing you correctly,' he

said, his voice carefully even. 'Your father was in the last days of his life at the hospice, and your mother gave him an overdose to hasten his death?'

I could only nod. I was so determined I was going to do this, and show my strength in front of this man, but it crumbled away, and the tears came despite my best intentions.

'She admitted this just to you?'

I shook my head.

'To the hospice staff?'

'Yes.'

He gave a large sigh and pressed at the sides of his temples as if this was another headache that wouldn't go away.

'Have the hospice indicated whether they are going to make an official complaint?'

'Yes, they said they have no choice.' And they didn't. Even if the person only had hours, minutes, to live, the law was black and white.

The thought of my mother having to face a murder trial was devastating. After the initial shock of what she'd done, and the realisation Dad was actually gone, I'd had to admit I felt relieved he was dead, that it was over, and that — and this was the hardest to grapple with — I was glad she did what she did. I hated her for it, but I loved her for it, too.

'Jesus Christ, Detective Shephard. You do take all.' He said it like a man who saw me as his penance in life, his cross to bear.

This had been a mistake. I'd been foolish to think he'd give me any quarter, any kudos for fronting up and baring all. I felt a surge of anger and was about to bite back when he continued. 'This is one hell of a mess, and it will have to take its legal course, you realise that?'

I nodded.

'And it will have to especially because you are a detective, and the police can't be seen as favouring their own.' He sighed again, and I caught a glimpse of something else in his demeanour, a look of something unexpected that left me feeling confused. 'But I'll see what we can do to make it as gentle as possible.'

82

I really wanted to avoid bumping into anyone, so took the stairs and the rear exit to the building. My plan was going well until I walked around the corner of the carpark to find, concealed in the corner, Smithy having a fag. Since when had he smoked? I could guess why he'd suddenly found the need to start.

'Sam,' he said, by way of greeting.

'Gidday,' I said as I hurriedly walked past.

I'd got ten feet before my steps slowed and I came to a halt. I couldn't do this. I couldn't not say anything about my suspicions, because if I didn't, what would that make me? Besides being morally wrong, and spineless, if they did prove correct it could make me an accessory. And considering the legal ramifications that were going to be hitting my family sometime soon, I didn't need that on my plate as well. In a strange kind of a way I didn't even feel nervous about the thought of confronting him. I just felt numb, dead inside.

I turned around and wandered back.

'I'm sorry about your dad, Sam.'

'Thanks. At least it's over now,' I said. I paused for a bit. 'How's your cut? Have you got those stitches out yet?'

He looked at me, a hint of caution flitting over the shadows of his face. He dropped the cigarette butt to the ground and crushed it under his shoe, blowing the last bit of fetid smoke from his lungs.

'It's fine. It wasn't that bad.'

'At least knife wounds are clean and heal well.'

With that he looked positively startled. 'What do you mean?'

I looked up at him, and wondered at how this colleague, mentor and friend had come to feel like a stranger.

'Now that we've got blood evidence on his clothes that suggest he got one in on his killer, we'll be checking with the hospital and medical centres for anyone who may have come in with what looked like a stab wound after the night Gideon Powell was murdered.'

'I don't know what you're talking about.' He'd stood up straight, and I felt acutely aware of the fact he was literally twice my size.

'And even though the fact that you were conveniently one of the officers present at the crime scene could go some way to explain away your DNA being there, it's a bit harder to explain away blood.'

He didn't say a word, just stood there rigidly, his tension tangible, almost audible.

'And although police officers' DNA isn't recorded on a database like our fingerprints are, the day will come when it's mandatory. But even before then, it might be requested if your name suddenly turns up on a list of people who had little mishaps with sharp objects recently.'

'What are you saying, Sam?'

'I'm saying that it seems a bit more than coincidence that you seem to have acquired a recent injury.'

'Jesus, Sam. God and everyone knows I had a

beef with Gideon Powell. But I'm not stupid enough to take matters into my own hands. So before you start with wild and fanciful accusations, I cut myself while trying to chop some wood. You can go read the ACC form if you like. I know you've had a bit of a shit time lately, and you're upset, but that is no reason to start pointing fingers and mouthing off ideas that could ruin a career. What sort of a man do you think I am?'

I looked up at him, with his tortured eyes, dishevelled, unloved look, sheen of sweat, and whiff of cigarette smoke and thought, I no longer had any idea.

I turned and walked away.

Epilogue

The warmth of the sun on my back felt delicious, and I leaned my head back, closing my eyes to enjoy it. I could hear a bellbird singing its glorious song in the distance, and the low breeze playing with the leaves in the nearby trees. I opened my eyes again and marvelled at the incongruity of a place so beautiful and tranquil being a place of such sadness. But, I supposed, if you were going to be somewhere for eternity, it may as well be picturesque. In a weird kind of a way the physicality of the cemetery seemed an antidote to the confused mess that had been the last few weeks — coming to the realisation that Jill Henderson had killed her husband, Smithy had likely killed his nemesis, and my mother had — well, killed wasn't the right word — but she had helped Dad to die. It was all too much to take in, but somehow being here helped to ground me, put it all into perspective. Then there was the other issue to deal with. The big arm around my shoulder squeezed me tight.

'How are you going?' he asked.

'Pretty well, considering.'

Paul and I had stopped off for one last visit to Dad's grave on the way back to Dunedin. The weather had been kind and the flowers around the freshly filled mound were still at their best.

'Do you think Jock would like it here?' he asked.

'Yes, but I think he would have preferred to have been planted down the back of the veggie garden at home, composting in the garden. But they don't allow that kind of thing. And anyway, Mum said if we did, he would probably ruin the carrots.'

The last few days hadn't been so bad. The turnout at the funeral had been immense, and, as was the nature of farming communities, the after-match function at the village hall had been a food-laden, beer-flowing, noisy and happily reminiscing kind of affair.

I closed my eyes again, concentrating, seeking, trying to sense the new life within me as I stood before the remains of the old. And there it was, a gem, radiating a solidity and warmth.

'What are you smiling about?'

'Was I smiling?'

'Yes.'

The last remnants of trepidation had fallen away in our time down here. I don't know whether it was seeing Paul so easily fit in with all my family and their friends and the locals, or the way he had unobtrusively been there as a buffer and a backstop, quietly organising, but not being pushy, but I'd come to realise he was my rock, and, actually, that that was okay. But despite this dawning, I could still feel my heart start beating harder in my chest, and a touch of light-headedness as I finally found the words.

'That's because there's something you really need to know.'

Other titles published by Ulverscroft:

CONTAINMENT

Vanda Symon

Anarchy hits Dunedin when a cargo ship runs aground on Aramoana Beach amid a crowd of onlookers. One of them discovers a skull in the sand while desperate scavengers fight each other for the best of the bounty. Waking up to the chaos and hurrying outside to give the police a hand, Detective Constable Sam Shephard cops a wallop before her attacker is himself beaten senseless. Returning to work, she is sent to help recover a body submerged in the water, the autopsy revealing that this was no accidental drowning but a lethal assault. The undercurrents from one morning's madness turn out to be far-reaching as Sam begins to tie events together. Who else will be caught in the backwash, with a killer on the loose? Can Sam stem the tide?

THE RINGMASTER

Vanda Symon

DC Sam Shephard is stationed in Dunedin CIB, a newbie at the bottom of the pecking order. When a university student is found battered to death and floating in the Leith, she is pushed to one side by her boss and given grunt work. Despite this, it is Sam who discovers that there has been a string of unsolved murders on the South Island, and that each has occurred while a travelling circus was in town — the same circus that is presently in Dunedin. Angry at being marginalised, Sam decides to work alone, ignoring the attempts of her friends to help her, and keeping her lines of enquiries secret. But her headstrong attitude, and the fact that she is human and makes mistakes, put her and those she loves in very real danger . . .

OVERKILL

Vanda Symon

When the body of a young mother is found washed up on the banks of the Mataura River, a small rural community is rocked by her tragic suicide. But all is not what it seems. Sam Shephard, sole-charge police constable in Mataura, learns the death was no suicide and has to face the realisation that there is a killer in town. To complicate the situation, the murdered woman was the wife of her former lover — and when word gets out, she discovers that small communities can have a mean streak with bigger, nasty nails than a Bengal tiger. When Sam finds herself on the list of suspects and suspended from duty, she must cast aside her personal feelings and take matters into her own hands. To find the murderer . . . and clear her name.

DEAD AND GONE

Sherryl Clark

Judi Westerholme has been through it. Brave and strong-willed, she's just about coping in her new role as foster parent to her orphaned niece, taking a job at the local pub to help make ends meet. Then the pub's landlord and Judi's friend, army veteran Pete 'Macca' Macclesfield, is murdered, and her world is suddenly turned upside down. Despite warnings from the city police to keep out of it, Judi can't help but get involved in the search for Macca's killer. But she soon becomes deeply entangled with some ruthlessly dangerous men. She must act fast and think smart to work out what they want — before anyone else gets hurt . . .